Other books written by Donna M. Bryan:

**TRUCK DRIVIN' MAN:
WARRIOR OF THE ROAD**

Jack is a Christian driver who has many exciting experiences as he travels across the United States helping others.

**THE MANSION
Discovering More Than Just An Inheritance!**

Ben discovers he is the sole recipient of his grandfather's will. He also discovers the beautiful lady JC is a policewoman. As he takes possession of the mansion, can he also take possession of her heart?

Spirit of the Mountain:
The Lion -
The Ranger -
The Journalist

Donna M. Bryan

Copyright © 2013 Donna M. Bryan

This is a book of fiction. Names, characters, and incidents are products of the author's imagination. Any resemblance to actual events, locales, or persons living or dead, is entirely coincidental.

All rights reserved.

ISBN-13: 978-1484088708
ISBN-10: 1484088700

Cover Image Credits:
flickr.com/alaskandude & flickr.com/clr_flickr

DEDICATION

I want to thank my children: Mark, Brenda, Bradley, Rebecca and David, for their support as I write. I have to add my sister Ellen, my captive audience, who has listened to the stories as we drive on our trips.

And also my friends from the writer's group who also feel like family, for their encouragement and many suggestions.

Claudia, Terri, Janet and Marlene, you have expanded my ideas and abilities.

Mary, Pat, Ken, Jean, Anita, what would Thursday mornings be without our input for each other.

Brenda, once again, you have made this all possible by getting it published.

Thank you all so very much!

Spirit of the Mountain:
The Lion -
The Ranger -
The Journalist

Donna M. Bryan

CAST OF CHARACTERS

Lacey McCann (Mrs. Shane Michaels)	Journalist/Photographer
Ken Dickinson	Mounted Forest Ranger
Winner	Ken's Horse
Missy	Young Filly
Gracie	Sam's Horse
One Ear	Lion
Dean	Photographer
Sam and Martha Swenson	Rancher/Friends
Gus	Ranch Foreman
Mr. Phil Conway	Magazine Owner
Jean Conway	Phil's Wife
Alice Wilson	Jean's Sister
Michael Donaby	Senator
Frank Collins	Captain of the Rangers
Charles Roberts	Judge
Bob Running Horse	Friend/Airplane Mechanic
Hank	Grocery Store Butcher
Gunner (Donald Werner)	Logger
Luke Pierson	Sheriff
Cal Berman	Pilot
Charlene Hartel	Blond Teenager
Richard Hartel	Charlene's Dad Reporter/Reno
Mona Hartel	Wife of Richard, Mom to Charlene
Dr. Martin	Local Physician
Betty	ICU Nurse
Miss Smith	ICU Nurse
Buster (Jackson)	Logger
Grizzly	Logger
Frank	Logger
Swede	Logger
Teach (Arnie)	Logger
Timothy Bartle	Lacey's Attorney
James Woodman	Ken's Attorney
Vernon Malone	Donaby's Attorney

CONTENTS

Chapter One: OLD LION	11
Chapter Two: THE LADY	13
Chapter Three: HE WATCHES	17
Chapter Four: SHADOWS IN THE NIGHT	23
Chapter Five: THE HOSPITAL	27
Chapter Six: HOSPITAL CONVERSATION	33
Chapter Seven: THE RANCH	39
Chapter Eight: MAKING THE ROUNDS	45
Chapter Nine: INFORMATION SHARING	53
Chapter Ten: THE RIDE	59
Chapter Eleven: THE MAIL ARRIVES	70
Chapter Twelve: WATCHING	78
Chapter Thirteen: NOISE ON THE MOUNTAIN	86
Chapter Fourteen: THE PHONE CALL	95
Chapter Fifteen: PLANS	106
Chapter Sixteen: THE TRUTH	112
Chapter Seventeen: WAITING	119
Chapter Eighteen: THE BUST	121
Chapter Nineteen: GUNNER	126
Chapter Twenty: THE JAIL	134
Chapter Twenty-One: THE HOSPITAL	142
Chapter Twenty-Two: QUIET	150
Chapter Twenty-Three: THE STRUGGLE	154
Chapter Twenty-Four: SOME POSITIVES	157
Chapter Twenty-Five: THE DARK NIGHT	161
Chapter Twenty-Six: FEAR OR STUPIDITY	165
Chapter Twenty-Seven: THE WATCHMEN	169
Chapter Twenty-Eight: THE MOUNTAIN	175
Chapter Twenty-Nine: NOW WHAT	181
Chapter Thirty: THE LONG HALLWAY	185
Chapter Thirty-One: INTENSIVE CARE	192
Chapter Thirty-Two: SHARING	198

Chapter Thirty-Three: GUNNER AND THE MEN	202
Chapter Thirty-Four: TODAY'S NEWS	206
Chapter Thirty-Five: THE SALE	212
Chapter Thirty-Six: HAPPY	216
Chapter Thirty-Seven: THE MEETING	221
Chapter Thirty-Eight: NEW PLANS	228
Chapter Thirty-Nine: HOSPITAL VISITS	236
Chapter Forty: THE SIGNING	244
Chapter Forty-One: ANOTHER CHALLENGE	246
Chapter Forty-Two: MOUNTAIN SOUNDS	254
Chapter Forty-Three: DONABY	259
Chapter Forty-Four: NEWS FLASH	265
Chapter Forty-Five: THE DAY BEFORE	271
Chapter Forty-Six: MORNING OF THE BIG DAY	276
Chapter Forty-Seven: THE WEDDING	279
Chapter Forty-Eight: THE RIDE	286
ABOUT THE AUTHOR	292

CHAPTER ONE

OLD LION

The old lion lay upon the rock warmed by the sun. As he watched the activity of the camp below him, his tail swished back and forth in an agitated motion.

As he licked his injured paw, his stomach growled. Slowly getting up, he hobbled down the rocky slope always cautious to stay out of sight of the man. He could smell the scent of the gun the two legged enemy carried and had shot him with.

At the edge of the fast running creek, he paused, sniffed the air, listened and turned looking for any danger. Slowly lowering his head, he drank his fill, and then put his hurting paw into the cold water, hoping to get some relief. He had learned cold water helped to numb the pain. Removing his throbbing paw, he licked it. Somehow that always made it feel better.

Noise from the camp area caused him to take cover in the low bushes by the creek. He crouched low, smelling food. His nose twitched and his stomach growled again. With his paw so sore, he couldn't put any weight on it to catch some prey.

Slowly he crawled closer careful of the injured paw and watched the hunter. The smoke blowing toward him made him nervous. Fire was bad.

The sun went down over the mountain and the air became cooler. Still old One Ear (that's what the ranchers called him, after part of his ear had been chewed off in a fight) lay still. Moving hurt.

Finally the fire was doused and the enemy went inside the canvas cave. Cautiously old One Ear waited.

When the moon came out, One Ear stiffly got to his feet. He could still smell food and he needed something to eat.

Holding his right front paw off the ground, he slowly hobbled his way along the creek bed to the quiet campsite. He stopped and sniffed the air. The food was just ahead and he painfully made his way toward it. Pushing against the box, he tried to find a way into it. He nudged it with his head. The top moved scaring him and he jumped back. He stood at alert. When nothing moved, he cautiously inched forward, leaned into the box and seized a piece of meat.

He kept his jaws clamped tight on his meal as he struggled up to the rock at the top of the hill. Although his paw was aching with the effort of the climb, he didn't rest, but bite down tearing off a chunk of the meat. He chewed quickly, swallowed and took another hunk. It wasn't long and he had consumed the whole piece.

The animals of the night were out foraging for a meal as he slowly made his way back to safety in the forest. Exhausted, he crawled into his small cave for protection from the cool night air; turning around to face the front he got as comfortable as he could.

CHAPTER TWO

THE LADY

In the early morning light, Lacey quickly hiked up the trail. She didn't need her compass; she had grown up in these mountains. Looking at the crushed grass, she wondered what type of camp Dean would have set up; he really wasn't what she would have called an Eagle Scout.

Part of her was angry that he didn't wait for her; the other part was surprised that he had enough guts to try it alone. But his one weekend of camping close to a busy city didn't teach survival in a wilderness like this.

Stopping, she took a deep breath and adjusted the frame of her large back pack. Sam the rancher had given her a ride as far as he could while it was still dark. As she headed for the trail, the sun had been slowly peeking over the mountain tops. If Dean had followed her map, she should only be about ten minutes away.

The magazine they worked for had received a hush-hush lead that a lumber company was trying to get permission from the government to log there. This company was known to over cut and this could cause erosion and loss of habitat for the animals. They were also known to bend the safety rules. She and Dean were given two weeks to photograph and comment on the condition of the forest.

One of Sam's hired hands had helped bring the camping equipment in on a pack mule along with some food. He would come back to the clearing in a week to renew their supplies.

As Lacey came upon the camp site she observed one of the food containers tipped over and empty. Evidently their four footed visitors of the forest had a banquet. The other container was latched tight. She shook her head, totally irritated with Dean.

"Hello the camp." She stood still not wanting to scare him or barge into the tent.

"Hi, just a minute. Glad you made it." The zipper on the tent slid down and Dean's head with his red tousled hair appeared. Oh, oh, one look at her face and he knew she wasn't happy about something.

Lacey slid the heavy pack off her shoulders. "It looks like you had visitors last night." She pointed at the empty cooler.

Dean groaned as he placed it upright. Everything in it was gone. He looked up at her, "I guess I didn't put that strap with the lock around it like you told me to always do. Sorry."

"Yeah, sorry it is, that was the meat for a few days. Look here, one recipient of your mistake was a mountain lion." She pointed out the various paw prints.

His face paled as he looked where she showed him.

"Um, the lion is injured; most of the tracks show he is favoring his right front leg. He could be dangerous if hurt and might be back looking for another free lunch. I'm glad I brought my gun." She patted her shoulder holster.

Speaking low, Dean told her, "I, I shot at something yesterday evening, before the light was totally gone. Maybe that was him."

"What! Are you some kind of freaking idiot! You don't shoot at anything you can't see. It could have been a hiker for crying out loud! Did you go check to see if you hit anything or what it was?" She glared at him with her hands on her hip.

"No. When I didn't hear anything, I assumed it ran away." Dean scuffed the dirt with his toe of his boot.

"If it was the lion that you shot at and injured, it will be back. Now, I will have to kill it, because it will be dangerous to us or to the domestic animals, if it can make it to one of the ranches. Also it will be in pain. Is your gun on safety now? I don't want to get shot by it going off somehow if I move just right. This never would have happened if you had waited for me like I told you."

"I'm sorry, Lacey. I just wanted to get things set up and ready to go. I'll never do anything stupid like this again. Do you really think the lion will be back?" His face registered fear.

Lacey shook her head in disgust at his ignorance of the woods. "Yeah, we are his supermarket if he can't hunt. If we don't see him, we can assume he is dead."

"Let's clean up and then we need to look over the area." She stepped into the tent noticing at least this was organized and their equipment was safe.

Once she was satisfied with their site, they had a protein bar and an apple for breakfast. Packing some jerky and a few apples, they slung a canteen of water over their shoulders. Lacey put on her holster with the hand gun and picked up her still camera and tape recorder to record what she was seeing.

Following suit, Dean picked up the video camera bag and note pad and they began their research of the condition of the forest.

CHAPTER THREE

HE WATCHES

His ears twitched as he listened to the noise below him. Careful not to step on his aching paw, he inched toward the flat boulder to check out the camp. He watched as the humans walked away. He slowly made his way down the rocky sloop, then tripped and rolled a couple of times before righting himself. Standing up, he slowly limped to the campsite and sniffed around looking for something to eat.

The cooler containing last night's feast was empty. Finding nothing else, he turned to the creek to drink and once again put his paw in the cold water to ease the pain. It was feeling a bit better. He looked up at the boulder when the sun would have it nice and warm, but decided against the climb. Instead he hobbled down the path to a sunny spot and let the rays warm his old body. He might just snare a rabbit if he remained still.

***

Lacey pointed at a tree, "They must be pretty sure they are going to get the rights to log up here. They are already marking some of the trees. Um, wonder if they have an in with a senator or congressman."

Dean took pictures of the marked tree and others in the area. They had been doing this in sections all day.

"Let's go up this way a little bit and see the size of the trees and if there are any more markings. Also make sure to note the ground condition." Lacey was already walking up the rocky hill. "I wish I would have brought a walking stick."

"Yeah, I'm really tired lugging this equipment up and down too." Looking around, Dean didn't move, "Lacey, it's starting to get dark, I think we better turn around."

"Yeah, I think you're right. I just get so engrossed in the search." As she turned, she stepped to one side, losing her footing, slipped, screaming as she fell, rolling down the steep hill landing on her leg with a snap sound as she came to a stop at the base of a large fir tree. She tried to move off her leg but the pain stopped her. She let out a cry at the attempt to do so. Lacey instantly knew what was wrong, a broken leg.

Not knowing what happened, Dean placed the camera equipment down, looked around and carefully made his way down to her.

Lacey moaned. "Ow, my leg. Oh my gosh, the pain, oh…" Her voice trailed off.

Kneeling down by her, he tried to gently roll her over. But she screamed out in pain, and then he could see why. *Oh no, her leg was broken, a bone was showing through the skin.* "Lacey, what should I do?" Dean was beside himself, nauseated and starting to get hysterical and hyperventilating.

Even in her extreme pain, Lacey knew Dean was her only way to get help. "Calm down, Dean. Look at me. Take a deep breath. Let it out. Now, do it again." Lacey instructed in a soft voice filled with pain. She took a deep breath when he did.

It helped and Dean simmered down.

What to do? Lacey looked at him. They were about the same size. Dean never worked out, he had a slim build. There was no way he could physically carry her out. The pain was getting to her. She breathed deep. She was feeling really weird.

"Dean, you have to go for help."

"I can't leave you here alone!" The sentence came out as a dismal cry almost a sob. Dean looked so helpless.

"You can and you have to. There's no way I can walk or crawl out of here. You must get to the ranch or at least outside the forest and see if your cell phone will work from there." She stopped talking and groaned. "First get some twigs, and small branches we can break up. Then clean the area around me from leaves and pick up rocks so we can build a fire. Oh yeah, and give me your heavy sweat shirt. It gets cold here." She moaned with a fresh wave of pain from the movement. Beads of sweat formed on her forehead. She felt stupid for being so careless.

He did what she said. Putting some leaves and dry grass with some twigs, she assisted him verbally to get a small fire going. He placed the extra pieces of wood next to her. Then stood up and wiped his hands on his jeans.

"I, I guess that should do it. Are you sure you will be okay?" He felt so inadequate.

"I have my gun. I'll be okay." Her quivering voice wasn't very convincing. "You take the flashlight and stop at the tent and leave a note just in case anyone by some weird coincidence would come by. Take your rifle with you and don't shoot at anything unless you know what it is. Remember the distress signal is three shots in rapid succession. Now, go and see if you can get a hold of Sam at the ranch."

"Maybe I should stay here with you Lacey. I can't leave you alone." Dean was torn, what if something happened while he was gone and to be truthful, he was afraid to go. "What if that injured cougar follows me or worse yet, is out there watching you?"

She leaned on her elbow, "Dean, the leg won't set itself by morning. There isn't any other way, you have to do this." Her voice was rising; she felt she was losing control. "I'll be okay. I have my gun, and the fire will keep animals away. Just don't hurry and fall and sprain your ankle or anything. Now go." She waved her hand at him, laid her head back down, trying to keep from screaming as the tears flowed freely down her face.

Reluctantly he turned around and retraced his steps down the path. He was scared for Lacey and he was frightened for himself. What if he got lost? What if that lion was out there? Why did he ever come out here? He could feel the panic coming back.

Keeping a tight hold on his flashlight, he carefully made his way back to the tent, mindful of every sound out there, wondering what it was. Inside the tent he wrote out a note and fastened it to the tent zipper. Picking up his rifle, he checked to make sure he had bullets in it and the safety was on. Putting on his warm jacket, he went down the path as quickly as possible, praying he would come to the clearing and his phone would have reception there.

***

Lacey kept the fire as small and low as possible without burning out. She needed the warmth and it would also keep any animals away if she passed out. The limited amount of wood wouldn't last all night. Taking a sip of water from her canteen, she tried to figure out how long it would take Dean to get to the clearing. How she wished he didn't screw up, she didn't know how much longer she could hold on.

Dean had left the camera equipment next to her. She took out the camera and took a picture of her twisted broken leg, the fire and of one of the trees with the painted mark that would show someone wanted it cut down. Afraid to move to be a little bit more comfortable on the rough, cold ground for fear the pain would intensify, Lacey willed herself to relax hoping the pain would lessen. Taking another deep breath, she sent up a prayer.

She could hear the sounds of the animals as they walked their forest home, out looking for food. She loosened the gun from its holster, just in case. She knew mountain lions usually attacked when they were five feet from their victim. Then she waited in the dark, looking up at the stars in the sky glad for the full moon and sent up another prayer that Dean would make it to the clearing soon, very soon.

***

Dean reached the end of the forest in a sweat and hit Sam's number on his cell phone. He held tight to it, willing someone to answer. Relief fell over him when Sam said hello on the third ring. Dean rapidly told him what happened.

"Son, just calm down. I'll call the Forest Ranger station and we'll get someone out there. I'll meet them in the meadow. You go back and stay at your tent. Start a small camp fire so we have your location on the trail." The phone went dead.

Sam made the call. Help was on the way. He got Gus, one of his men, and the Jeep. Putting some blankets, a five cell flash light, some flares and a thermos of hot coffee into the back of the Jeep, they didn't waste any time getting to the meadow.

Once there, they set off the first flare hoping to let the rescue team and helicopter know where they were. It wasn't long and the sound of a helicopter filled the air. At the same time, a mounted Ranger loped across the meadow.

"Glad you're here." Sam reached up and shook Ranger Ken Dickinson's hand.

"I wasn't far from here. Normally I would have been back at your place where I left my truck and trailer." The ranger stayed in the saddle.

"Follow that path and you will come to the campsite. Dean, the young man will be there. I told him to wait. He is a tenderfoot and we don't need two people in trouble. Hurry, Lacey is tough, but..." He handed him up a blanket, then blew his nose. Lacey was one special girl. He'd known her all of her life.

Tying the blanket to the back of the saddle, the Ranger turned on his lantern and made his way up the trail as fast as it was safe for him and his horse.

CHAPTER FOUR

SHADOWS IN THE NIGHT

Old One Ear approached the camp where he had got food last night and watched the human as he walked around it. He knew there would be no food there for him. His paw was feeling better, but as he padded his way quietly along the path, he put as little weight as possible on it. He followed the scent of the humans up the path and into the dark forest.

Again he could see and smell fire, but he could also smell blood. His senses were suddenly at high alert. Then he heard a moan, which meant something was hurt and could be an easy prey.

The old lion made a circle around the flame; he disliked fire. The moist night air masked the sound of his limp as he walked on the fallen leaves. Then he located the smell, supper.

***

Lacey had an odd feeling of being watched and raised her head to look when she saw the green eyes peering at her and willed herself to be calm when she actually wanted to scream. Animals can smell fear. She reached for one of the sticks that was glowing at the end and waved it around and yelled, "Get away from me!" She leaned back and watched as the shining eyes backed away and did another circle around her.

Pulling out her hand gun from the holster she aimed it at the lion circling the fire. This must be the mountain lion that Dean so stupidly shot. Dean, did he make contact with Sam? Another wave of pain came across her and she groaned. The gun shook in her hand, she felt nauseated with fear and pain.

That's when she heard the growl, but she couldn't see the lion. Twisting as much as possible, she tried to locate where it was. Then she saw his eyes.

The lion intent on his prey, and Lacey afraid, didn't hear anything else as they watched each other.

The ranger seeing the small fire and the cougar crouching, ready to spring on Lacey, removed his rifle from the scabbard; raised it up to his shoulder and just as he was ready to pull the trigger, his horse moved. He missed, but the sound of the gun and the scattered dirt from the shell scared the lion who leaped away into the forest.

Lacy screamed from the sharp retort of the rifle but felt relief as the lion disappeared into the night.

Dismounting, he approached her, his gun still ready, the ranger murmured in a low tone, "It's okay, he's gone."

Ken kept his eye on the area around them as he closed the last few steps.

Lacey began crying with relief. Someone was here and the threat of the lion was gone.

Ken knelt down by her and put his arm around her in a comforting manner. When the fear dissipated and the tears slowed down, he said quietly, "Help is on the way; I just need to let them know where we are."

Picking up her hand gun, he rapidly pulled the trigger three times. It wasn't long and they heard the sound of men coming up the trail.

They stabilized her leg and wrapped her in a blanket. Ken mounted his horse, and they lifted her up into his arms and he headed back down the trail to the helicopter.

The men made sure the fire was completely out.

Dean picked up all the camera equipment and everyone left the area. Dean went back to the ranch with the men. He didn't want to stay out in the forest alone.

***

Ranger Ken Dickinson cradled the young woman securely in his arms. His well trained horse, Winner, had a smooth gait but any movement still jarred the injured woman's leg. Ken recalled the young, excited man named Dean, had called her Lacey. *That was an unusual name. I wonder why they were out in the woods in the first place. He saw some markings on the tree close to her campfire. At first light, he was going to be doing some investigating.*

He passed the campsite and soon reached the meadow, greeted by the lights of the waiting helicopter. He stopped his horse far enough away from it so as not to frighten him by the noise.

The medics reached up for Lacey.

Lacey looked at Ken, her eyes glazed with pain, "Stay with me." She started to sob. For some reason she felt safe with him.

Sam came up and heard her. "Ken, I'll take care of your horse, matter of fact, I'll ride him to the ranch, put him up and you can get him later. Go with the gal; it will make her feel more secure."

Ken stepped down from his saddle and handed the reins to Sam. "Winner has a soft mouth and responds to hand and knee signals so be gentle with the bit. Also, keep an eye on my rifle. I'll call the ranch and keep you up to speed on what happens and when I'll be out." Then he climbed into the helicopter and it took off.

Sam turned around and saw Dean clearly dazed standing there with cameras hanging by their straps over his slim shoulders and holding his rifle. "Hop into the Jeep son. Gus will drop you off at the house. Make yourself comfortable. The wife is visiting her sister, so help yourself to some grub. The horse and I will be there in a while, and after I give him a rubdown and some feed, I'll be up to the house."

With that he turned, patting the horse on the neck, spoke softly to him. Putting his foot in the stirrup, Sam swung into the saddle with the ease and motion of a man use to riding. Switching on the lantern, he squeezed his knees signaling the horse into a gentle lope and followed after the Jeep. He sure wouldn't classify this as an ordinary day, or night.

CHAPTER FIVE

THE HOSPITAL

As Ken waited for Lacey to get out of surgery, he went over what he knew about the two reporters' reason for being in the forest. He also hoped Sam took care of Winner properly. Sam had a reputation of being an animal lover and he really shouldn't worry, but his horse was special to him.

He smiled as he thought about the day he got Winner. The mare had been severely wounded by a cougar to the point they had to put her down. He had bottle fed her frisky colt and raised him. Winner was easy to train, a smart horse. Ken felt bad that he had to geld him, but there was no way he could have a stallion in the mounted Ranger program.

As the doctor entered the waiting room, Ken quickly stood up.

"Sit down," the doctor waved his hand as he himself took a chair. "The leg was a compound fracture. We set it and she is in a cast. She is to stay off the foot and use crutches for six weeks, and then come back to have the cast removed unless she has any problems." The doctor rose from his chair.

"I'm not a member of her family. I came with her after the rescue because she asked me to and she was afraid. I don't know any more than that about her. I think her co-worker out at Sam Swenson's place would know more about her." Ken shrugged his shoulders.

"When the nurses were undressing her, she gave us the information we needed. Her parents are out of the country on vacation and unable to come to her at this time. Miss McCann asked for you as she came out of the realms of her medication. You can go and see her now." The doctor opened the door to the waiting room and motioned for Ken to follow him.

Ken hand combed his hair and ran his hand over his chin. He knew he needed a shave.

"Miss McCann, Ranger Dickinson is here." The doctor turned to Ken, "Don't stay too long, she needs her rest." The doctor nodded at Lacey and the nurse and left the room.

Lacey reached out her hand toward Ken.

Taking the few short steps to reach the bed, he took her soft hand in his rough one.

Looking intently at the stranger, "I want to thank you for saving my life. I froze and just held onto my gun, that's not like me; I've gone hunting with my dad many times. I have never been that frightened." She leaned her head back against the pillow, exhausted. "I'm glad the old cougar got away though, even if he did steal some of our food."

"I was just doing my job, Miss McCann, all part of being a ranger." He shifted his weight to the other foot. "The doc said you will be on crutches for a while, but the leg should heal fine. Well, I better let you get your rest now." He smiled down at her. *Man she was pretty.*

In a tired voice she softly asked, "Will you come back tomorrow? It would mean a lot."

"I'll stop by if I don't get tied up with my work. I never know where I will be needed in the county. We rangers don't work the nine to five jobs." Ken reached down and took her hand and gave it a light squeeze. "You rest now."

Lacey murmured, "I will, and thanks again." She closed her eyes, comforted for some reason that he would come back.

***

Ken got a ride from one of his friends to his five acre place. He waited while Ken took a shower and packed a change of clothes. Then he drove Ken out to Sam's ranch since that was where his GMC Sierra extended cab and horse trailer was.

Ken loved that new truck and felt safe leaving it with Sam. Ken had left them there while doing some routine checking on horseback. He had been coming back to Sam's when he got the call. Luckily he wasn't that far away from the trail where the campsite was.

As they drove up to the old ranch house, the door opened and Sam stepped out on the porch. "How is Lacey doing?"

Grabbing his overnight bag, Ken shut the door and with a wave, his friend drove off. "She came through the surgery just fine. The doc said she will be on crutches for about six weeks. Probably let her out in a day or so. She wants me to stop by tomorrow. I wonder where she will go since she doesn't live around here."

"Here. Her folks sold the ranch next to mine; she grew up there. My missus will be home tomorrow and we'll take good care of her."

They were interrupted by a whinny from the horse barn.

"I recon Winner knows you're here." Sam laughed as he stepped down from the porch and led the way toward the barn. "I brushed him down, fed him and he should be happy to be inside tonight."

Keeping in step with the older man, "I spend so much time with him; sometimes I think he knows what I'm thinking."

"Yep, I know what you mean." Sam opened the barn door, "I've only had a couple of horses like that. Never really had to train them, it was like they were born knowing what to do."

Nodding, Ken added, "I heard that Roy Rogers said the same thing about both Triggers, they knew what Roy wanted, seemed to sense it."

Ken could see Winner moving around in the box stall, waiting for Ken to come to him. Sliding the bolt to open the door, Ken walked in and patted his gelding on the neck and ran his hand along his back. "You did a great job of getting that little lady to the helicopter, Winner. I was pretty proud of you not getting upset with that lion or me shooting so close to you. Good boy." Ken continued to walk around his horse murmuring to him. Winner gently pushed his muzzle against Ken, and was rewarded when Ken pulled a carrot out of his pocket and fed it to him.

Sam was leaning over the stall watching the big horse enjoy his treat. "You didn't tell me that having a night time snack of a carrot was part of his care."

Ken gave his horse a final pat on the neck and left the stall. "He doesn't get them every night; he did a great job and deserved it. Thanks for taking good care of him."

The two men shut the barn door and headed for the house. "I

checked his hoofs for any rocks too. That path had quite a few small ones on it. You must have had him re shod recently."

"Yeah, I did, last week. Say you don't mind if I bunk down here tonight? I got my sleeping bag in the back of the Sierra. The bunk house or barn would be fine. In the morning I want to check out if there are any more markings."

They had reached the porch, "You can take one of the bedrooms in the house. What time you figure to be getting up?" Sam opened the door to the house.

"About five. I thought I'd put Winner in the trailer and drive up to the edge of the meadow where the trail starts."

"Do you want some company? I'm a little curious too. Been some activity lately at the old McCann place that just doesn't seem kosher to me, if you get my drift." He closed the door. "Some senator bought the place and isn't there very often and all of a sudden, a lot of strange faces around. Busy little beavers but not normal ranch life. Not a friendly bunch either. Tomorrow, Gus is going to drive the young man into town to see Lacey so that leaves me free. If they get back in time, they were going to take the pack mule in and disassemble the camp site."

"I'd appreciate your company. Just be aware, it could be dangerous if I find out who is messing around up there." Ken was serious.

"Well, I cleaned your rifle, and mine too, so I guess I'm ready. Coffee, and breakfast and we will be off. Can I get you anything else tonight?" Sam stopped at the bedroom Ken would be sleeping in.

"No thanks."

"Well, the bathroom is across the hall, towels and stuff in the cupboard, help yourself. Good night then." Sam ambled down the hall shutting off lights as he went to his own room.

Ken closed the door, sat down on the chair by the desk and removed his boots. Then taking off his shirt and jeans, slid between the sheets and was sound asleep the minute his head touched the pillow. It had been a long busy day.

CHAPTER SIX

HOSPITAL CONVERSATION

"Lacey, I'm going back to the city. The boss wants the pictures we took and he said for you to write something about it. I told him A. The rangers are keeping the equipment since they are now investigating and B. he can't publish anything while the investigation is going on or he could be in big pile of you know what with the government." Dean was pacing back and forth in her room, clearly agitated. "What am I to do? If we don't write up something I'll be fired, and if I do and he publishes it, I can be arrested!"

"Simmer down, Dean. The law is the law and Mr. Conway isn't going to fire you. He's not going to risk a law suit and you are too valuable of a photographer to let some other magazine snap you up. I have to tell you too, you were pretty brave heading down that dark path to get help for me. Thanks a lot. You saved my life." Lacey was sitting up in the bed, still a little pale but wide awake. The pain pill was taking the edge off the injured leg, but it still hurt like crazy.

"Really? You think I was brave? I was scared to death. I don't ever want to go up there again." Dean shook his head, "Matter of fact, I'm going to get my things from the motel and fly back home. Sam said you were going to stay at his place until you feel up to traveling. His wife Martha is coming home today and will see that you are mothered. I guess she was visiting her sister."

"Dean, you can't leave our tent and personal things up there, it's the national forest and the equipment and all is expensive."

"Cool down. That ranger fellow and Sam were up at the crack of dawn and said when Gus got back from bringing me into town, he and another hand would bring the stuff back to Sam's if they weren't back with all of it. Since you will be staying there, that should be okay. They said I could have my cameras but not the film chips. Well, at least I can work on some other job.

Oh, by the way, Gus is waiting in the parking lot for me. He said to say take care and he will visit when you're not hurting so much. Do you want me to pack up the rest of your stuff at the motel to take out to Sam's place? Sam offered to pick up your things, but I figured since Gus was here it would save everyone a trip, if it's okay with you. The magazine is paying for the rooms but if we aren't using them seems like a waste of money. I'm flying out as soon as I can get a ticket." Dean had quit pacing and was sitting on the chair.

Shaking her head, "Oh, Dean, you really are safer here than in the big city. But you're right, best to give up our rooms. Sam and Martha are like an aunt and uncle to me and would insist I stay there. There's not too much to do at the hotel. Thanks. Give me a hug." Lacey reached out her arms to her co-worker.

Dean gave her a big hug.

"Remember, Dean. You aren't to talk about what happened. If anyone at the office asks, just say I just broke my leg and I'm taking the time off while it heals. Tell everyone we didn't get a chance to do anything on the assignment. Mr. Conway was already called by the officials. And thanks again for going for help." Lacey leaned back, exhausted.

Dean stopped when he reached the doorway, "Give me a call or email me and let me know how you are progressing." With a wave, he was gone.

***

Ken made another notation in his notebook. "I'd like to take a mold of these footprints and then we can leave."

"You were smart to think of bringing that along with you. The sole of that boot sure has an odd pattern, not the normal work boot worn by loggers around here." Sam watched as Ken made up the mixture. "You actually think taking some of that paint scrapings will do any good?"

"Well, we'll see if it will match up with any cans we may find, that might tell us what batch it came from and we can find out where in this area it is sold. So far we've found too many trees marked." Ken shook his head in disgust, "this is government land for the people to use, not abuse."

The two men were standing at the place where Lacey had been injured. The image of Lacey so frightened that night by the fire with the lion crouching ready to spring came to his mind. If those men hadn't planned on doing illegal logging, and her boss sent her out here to investigate, she never would have been hurt. "You didn't hear it from me, but if, I mean when, I find the creeps responsible for her being out here"…he shook his head, "you didn't see the pain Lacey was in."

Sam put his hand on the young man's shoulder. "Vengeance is mine saith the Lord. We'll catch them and let the judge deal with them. Plus, I think this is bigger than we think. First of all, look how much land we have covered, someone is going to ruin this mountain if they start. It doesn't take long with those big machines to strip a hill. I can't shake the hunch that the ranch next to mine, that was Lacey's folks' place, has something to do with all of this."

"What makes you think that?" Ken began packing things away.

"There is a lot of commotion going on. The place is almost a mile away, less if you cut across that grove of trees and a couple of fields. At night, sound travels out here and some large equipment has come in but is nowhere to be seen. There are a lot of men around but they aren't running any cattle or horses." Sam checked the straps on the other side of the pack mule.

"How do you know all of that?" Ken looked over the mule at Sam.

"I had some beef cattle to take to market on that pasture by the old McCann place and with all the noise, I was afraid some of my cattle might go missing. There's big tarps over some things and I could see the sheds had a lot of activity going on. And out here, it's considered neighborly to stop in and see folks, but they have a no trespassing sign on their main gate and others placed on the line fences. No rancher does that around here."

"Hum. I think I need to get a court order to check the premises, just in case I need to go on the land. In the meantime, I think we need to get nosy from our side of the fence. I've got some really good binoculars in my GMC, how about you?" Ken gave him a grin, then turned serious, "You realize, I shouldn't be putting you in danger or sharing any info with you about this."

"Son, I'd be checking this out with or without you. No one hurts our Lacey; I'd call it attempted murder. Why, if you hadn't shown up when you did, she'd be dead. DEAD! That gives me every right in the world to assist you. Unless it's necessary, no one needs to know but you and me."

"Thanks. But remember, don't do anything on your own, we do it together. Now, let's get back and plan our next steps, plus I think Martha and Gus are bringing Lacey to your place today." Ken mounted Winner.

Sam handed him the lead rope of the mule then followed suit and settled himself on Gracie, his mare. "I think you should plan on staying at the ranch while you're doing this investigation. Having your vehicle coming and going would raise more attention than if it just stayed there. Besides, I have filly that needs some training and you are helping me if anyone asks. And if one of our horses or cattle happened to stray through an opening in the fence…you get my drift?"

Adjusting his leather western hat Ken questioned Sam, "What about the women and Gus? Living with them they aren't going to accept the 'I'm helping train the filly' bit. These ladies have seen you train too many horses."

"Me and Martha have been married a long time and we have never kept any secrets from each other. She will not say a word and she is a marvelous cook. And Lacey could be an asset to you since she grew up on that ranch and her folks only sold it to the senator around three years ago. She knows every nook, cranny, hill and dale over there. If someone is doing something illegal over there, she'd want to help, especially if they were responsible for her injury and loss of wages." Sam unscrewed the cap from his canteen and took a couple of long swallows. It didn't pay to get dehydrated in the mountains, only visitors or tenderfoots made that mistake.

The two men were approaching the Sierra and the horse trailer. The sun was going down and by the time they got back to the ranch it would be dark, covering up their movements, if they were being watched. One never knew.

CHAPTER SEVEN

THE RANCH

Gus, Lacey, Ken, Martha and Sam had finished their meal and were sitting at the round wooden kitchen table having coffee and homemade cookies.

Ken watched as Lacey deep in thought was tracing her finger around the edge of the mug, "I remember my parents telling me, Senator Donaby said he wanted to use the ranch as a retirement place, run a few beef cattle during the summer, and let his friends use it for vacations and hunting during season. He paid by a cashier's check except for the last 100,000 which he paid off during this past year. According to Dad, the check arrived every month like clockwork."

Martha got up and refilled their cups. "According to the papers, he isn't the most well liked Senator in Washington, but you can't go by that."

Gus added to the conversation in his quiet way, "From what I've seen as I've gone about my chores, there is one older man who stays there all the time." He took a gulp of his coffee.

"And?" Ken waited.

"Well," Gus continued as he looked over at Lacey, "The guy has a nice size fenced in garden to keep the deer out of it, and has kept flowers on the porch like your maw always did. In the winter he plows out the place."

Smiling to himself, Ken thought that was the most amount of words the man had ever said at one time. "Anything else you noticed over there, Gus?"

Taking a deep breath Gus continued, "That old timer gets downed wood from the forest to burn. The gas man came out but just once this year. Lately though, there has been a lot of traffic. You can see the dust from all the vehicles coming in billowing from the road over here."

Removing his small notebook from his shirt pocket, Ken flipped it open to a new page. "Since we are in agreement on watching the ranch and working toward finding the culprits, I'd like to assign some things that need done." He looked over at Lacey. "Since you're a journalist, could you get on the computer and check out anything newsworthy you can about the senator like work ethics, outside interests, that type of thing."

She nodded yes at him.

"Sam, could you nose around town about any large purchases of food, vehicle gas or any flights with people headed for the Donaby Ranch? If asked why, you could say something like; you're wondering if the Senator was planning any hunting parties because you want to keep your stock close to the sheds in case they do some target practicing."

He looked over at Gus, "You keep your eyes peeled for anything unusual." Ken handed Gus a pad similar to what he was using. "Write it down on this little notebook, but remember, we can't let anyone else know the real reason of what we are doing."

Gus nodded at him.

"Me, I'll be checking out paper work while in town tomorrow. I need to see about getting two court orders that lets me investigate the ranch if I need too. One will be for checking out anyone there for legal hunting license, which will be my excuse for being on the land; the other will be if I need it to find proof of sale of any cut logs if I find any on their property. In the meantime, if anyone asks, my cover for being here is that I'm training the filly since I may buy her."

"Boss, you ain't selling our little Missy are you?" Gus looked over at Sam with an unbelievable expression on his face like a child who just heard there isn't a Santa Claus.

"No, Gus, she's here to stay, but she does need more training since she is old enough to ride now. Well," Sam glanced around the table, "I don't know about all of you, but this ole man needs to hit the hay. Night all."

"Night Sam," came the chorus of voices.

Gus stood up, "He has the right idea. Good night." Taking his hat from the peg by the door, he left the house.

"Lacey, do you want some help getting ready for bed?" Martha asked as she placed the empty mugs on the wooden tray.

"No, I'm fine, but thank you. I'm getting the hang of this old heavy cast and the crutches."

"Okay. I'll just put these in the dishwasher, let Shadow out, lock the door, and join Sam. It's been a long day." She smiled at the young couple.

Lacey and Ken, sitting at the table, could hear Martha talking to the dog as she waited for Shadow to finish her nightly visit outside. When the dog came in, Martha patted her on the head, closed the door and locked it. Shadow turned around a couple of times and settled down on the braided rug by the door.

Yawning, Martha in a typical motherly way admonished them as she went down the hall, "Don't stay up to late, we all have a lot to do tomorrow."

"Night, Martha," They answered as one grinning at each other like a couple of teenagers.

Opening up his notebook, Ken perused his notes. "Lacey, what or who gave your boss, ah," he looked down, "Mr. Conway, the idea for this photo shoot on logging in this area?"

"I really don't know. We were all sitting around doing some brain storming, throwing out topics of interest from following one of the politicians or actors, you know like 'the week in the life of ... and what they are interested in'. All of a sudden, Mr. Conway stated he thought maybe an article on how our National Forests might be misused by those hunting and fishing or if logging was being done. He wondered how it affected the livelihood of people living in that area. The next thing I knew, Dean and I were assigned here and the other two got the 'go to Washington' gig."

Frowning Lacey asked, "Do you think that he knew something he didn't say. Doesn't it strike you odd that one of the senator's properties and a National Forest are so close?"

"Does Mr. Conway know that you were raised around here, actually on the ranch that Senator Donaby purchased?"

Lacey was silent for a moment, thinking, "I've only worked there for a year. I lived in California before I went to work for the magazine. My folks sold the ranch three years ago. I don't recall ever mentioning living here."

"Did you use anyone as a reference on your resume from around here? Sometimes they ask for someone you have known for five years along with your past working experience." Ken took a drink of his now cold coffee.

"No, I used my education and part-time jobs while at school and the free lance work I did. He was more concerned about samples of what I wrote although I did have many photo shots too."

Removing the old gold pocket watch from his shirt pocket, Ken checked the time. "I didn't think it was this late! We better quit for the night. I'm keeping you up and Martha will chew me out in the morning." He snapped the lid down on the watch. "I'll give you arm to lean on and walk you to your room."

Lacey reached for her crutches. "What time is it?"

Ken chuckled, "Fifteen minutes to twelve."

"I didn't realize it was getting so late. I don't know if I'll be able to fall asleep with all the thoughts racing through my mind right now. Perhaps something else will come to me."

Ken assisted her as they slowly made their way down the hallway to her room.

She looked up at him, "Thanks. What time are you heading out tomorrow?"

He thought she had the most beautiful shade of blue eyes. "I think we will work with the filly a bit, just in case for some odd reason anyone is observing us, then Sam and I will leave at different times."

"That makes sense. Well, good night." Giving him a warm smile, she stepped back and closed the door.

On the way to his room, Ken mentally made a note to talk privately with his boss, especially since he needed to get a court order to check out the property if necessary, and also to be free from his normal routine work as a ranger to concentrate on the information. This was a puzzle and he needed to find all the missing pieces to it.

CHAPTER EIGHT

MAKING THE ROUNDS

Old One Ear stretched his body and sniffed the cool mountain air. His paw had healed and for a ten-year-old mountain lion he felt pretty good. He had battle scars to prove he was strong. Yawning, he sniffed the air. It was time to patrol his thirty-mile hunting range. He marked his territory area by refreshing each small pile of leaves and urinating on it, his way of telling any other males that this was his area and stay out or be prepared to fight. He might tolerate a female if she infringed in some of his space, but not any males.

About five miles from his cave, he smelled the female scent. Normally males get the urge to mate from December to March, but females are willing at anytime. He quickened his step, his ears alert for any sound as he followed the scent he recognized. They had mated three years ago.

There she was, a sleek, tawny brown lion waiting cautiously, ready to race off if necessary, not sure of what reception she would get. She had nothing to fear. One Ear was more intent on being amorous than dangerous.

They frolicked and mated a few times; she purred and then left his company, she got what she came for, to mate. Her other litters sired by him had all been strong and lived with her until they were old enough to strike out on their own. Climbing up the hill, she turned back and trained her eyes on him. The mountains could be harsh. Would he be here next time she had the urge to mate? With a switch of her tail, she gracefully turned retracing her steps back to her area; she didn't need a male to take care of her or her litter when they were born.

One Ear watched her quietly leave until she was out of sight, then he too left to unceremoniously continue marking his territory.

***

Martha was talking on the phone with her sister as Lacey, on her crutches, went out to the porch. Carefully maneuvering the few steps, she proceeded slowly to the corral where Winner and Missy were enjoying the freedom of being out in the air. Not sure if the lion that had been shot would try for easy meals taken from the stock at the ranch, they had kept the horses locked in during the night.

Lacey propped her crutches against the wooden rails and leaned her arms on one to watch the animals. Soon they both came trotting over. Reaching out she petted Missy, talking softly to her. Winner, not wanting to be neglected, got closer to Lacey nudging her arm with his head.

"Ah, getting a little jealous there are you?" Chuckling, Lacey ran her hand along his neck, "I bet you both would like a little treat." Reaching into her pocket she pulled out a carrot she had cut in half before she came out and gave it to them. The two horses crunched it down quickly and looked for more.

Lacey laughed. "You two are like a couple of kids, always wanting more." She took the crutches, adjusted them under her arms and returned to the house. Her task this morning was to get on the computer and do the research she agreed on last night.

Martha was mixing up some bread dough when Lacey entered the kitchen.

Lacey paused by the counter and watched Martha. "I'm going to be on the computer for awhile unless you have anything you want me to do."

"You go do what you need to." Waving her hand with flour on it, Martha continued, "I've got a pot of stew started for supper. I don't expect the men back until then. Gus will be at the bunk house with the men when they return from checking the cattle, so I'm going to settle on the porch with a book my sister loaned me."

Sitting down at the desk, Lacey wrote down a list of ideas she wanted to research. She wondered if Ken would object to her talking with her boss, because he might save her a lot of time. She would ask him tonight, in the meantime she was going to look up whatever she could find about Senator Donaby.

Looking at her watch reminded her of the old pocket watch Ken had. Even the chain attached to it was old. She wondered if it might have been his dad's or even his grandfather's. Putting her elbows on the desk, she rested her chin on her hands and thought about the ranger. It was odd how she felt so attracted to him. After her husband was killed, she had no desire to love anyone again, it hurt too much. What was it about him that intrigued her? Was it because he saved her life and she was grateful?

She smiled thinking how he looked. He stood a little over six feet in his western boots. The brown uniform he wore fit his well-muscled body. Instead of the regulation Mountie type hat, he wore a western leather hat that when he removed it showed the white space on his head that wasn't tanned. His hands were strong and calloused, yet had been so tender when he held her in his arms on the painful ride down the mountain to the helicopter. When he smiled, his whole face smiled. Ken was a man's man, and oh, it wouldn't take much for him to be her man.

She giggled when she thought of how Ken carried a little bag of lemon drops in his pocket. Somehow, a man carrying lemon drops with him was funny. The good thing was he didn't smoke or chew that yucky tobacco.

Shaking her head, she looked at her list; she had some investigating to do via the computer. It was important she could show some info when they shared after dinner tonight.

***

Frank Collins, captain of the rangers, put his hands behind his head and leaned back into the chair. "Ken, I need something more concrete than your gut feeling to relieve you of your normal duties and let you go to the judge for a court order."

"I took these pictures of the marked trees." Ken placed those down on the desk along with the mold of the odd boot prints. Taking out his notebook, he began sharing what he had with the captain. "There is something going on at the old McCann ranch that the senator owns. I wonder how much Lacey's editor really knows. He must have gotten wind of something to send two people out to check the conditions of the national forest, especially in this locale. According to Lacy, he didn't know she was raised in this area."

Standing up, Ken went over to a large six-foot map on the wall, and with his finger, traced the areas that he and Sam had gone over and where the trees were marked. "All of this is National Forest. Have you had anyone come in for a permit? This isn't just some rancher coming up to clean out the dead wood to burn for heat. These are the large trees. Whoever wants these is not going to be reseeding. If they would take even a small amount of timber out that area," Ken turned back to the map and circled the area with his finger, "we would have mud slides and the animals would lose their territory."

Quickly stepping back to the desk, he leaned on it. "You know Sam isn't a man to spread gossip or exaggerate. When he says something unusual is going on at the McCann ranch, he is worried. None of the equipment under cover has to do with ranching, or raising beefs for the market. Too many men there and they aren't cowboys. There are 'no trespassing' signs along the fences and the main gate going onto the ranch. They aren't growing any hay or anything else in the fenced in acres. You know as well as I do, if they go in with that big equipment, that side of the mountain will be wiped out in no time. Then are you going to get a court order for them to desist after the damage is done? I'm just trying to prevent this. Also, I found some traps up there. Why, and who? They aren't being checked every twenty four hours either." Ken sat down watching his captain.

Frank leaned forward and reached for his phone sitting on the edge of the desk. "Okay, but I'm going with you to see the judge. I'll give him a call first and see if we can do it right away. He will give you the papers since he loves this land. You keep me informed on everything. Send me an email from the ranch or call me. I'll have the other men overlap on their patrols to pick up your area and give them a heads up on anything unusual. That's all they will know for now."

Dialing the court office, Frank spoke briefly with Judge Charles Roberts. Replacing the receiver, Frank smiled, "The judge said he'd have the papers ready by the time we get there." Taking his hat off the peg, "I'll take my own vehicle, save you a trip back. How's that new Sierra you got, handle pulling the horse trailer up and down the hills?"

"Great. I really like it. I'll see how it takes the winter out here." Ken closed the door of the office behind him. Pulling out his truck keys, he clicked to unlock the door, "I think I spent more time trying to keep that old one running than I did driving. Meet you at the judge's chambers."

***

Sam gently shut the door to his Jeep and swept the area with his eyes to see if he could find Bob Running Horse, the best airplane mechanic around. Bob also kept his nose out of others' business. Sam walked over to the closest hanger. There he found Bob busy working on an engine.

Wiping his greasy hands on a rag, Bob reached out to shake Sam's hand. When Bob was a teenager, Sam was thrown from a horse he was training and broke his arm and leg. Bob went out and took care of the chores. Grateful for the help, Sam and Martha paid his tuition for the mechanic school. They remained good friends.

"Got a minute, Bob?" Sam asked.

"Yeap. What do you need, trouble with the Jeep?" Bob looked over at the old vehicle he had worked on many times.

"No, just wondering if you've heard of any big hunting parties flying in to the Donaby Ranch. There seems to be a lot of activity over there. I just want to make sure I move my cattle and horses closer to the ranch building if there is. They aren't the friendliest people what with those No Trespassing signs all over the place." Sam looked Bob in the eye. He didn't have to say any more.

Looking around and seeing no one, Bob leaned close to Sam, "No one scheduled to fly in, but the other guys were talking and said there is a big crew out there. Guess they got a little rowdy in the bar a few times and they were asked to leave. They aren't the usual rich hunter friends of the senator, but dressed in rough work clothes, not ranch hands either. Want some of my relatives to patrol around your ranch?"

"No, but if you hear anything unusual, give me a call, and you're always welcomed out at the ranch you know. Martha just mentioned the other day you haven't been out in a long time. Say, we got Lacey McCann staying there; she slipped and broke her leg while hiking. I'm sure she'd love to see you too. Well, son, I got to get a move on." Sam took a hold of Bob's arm as he shook his hand. "Proud of you." Sam left the hanger.

Sam's next stop was the only grocery store in town. He went in the back door by the butcher. "Hi Hank, can I see you for a moment?" and Sam stepped back outside. He was joined shortly by Hank.

"What can I do for you Sam? A steer break a leg and you don't want to dress it out?" Hank laughed.

"Nah, just a bit of nose trouble. I was wondering if anyone from the old McCann ranch has ordered a lot of food from here. Seems like a lot of activity over there."

Hank leaned down with his head close to Sam. "Yah know

Sam, there's something weird about them out there. The driver that brings in our meat said when he picked up our order, he overheard that a separate refrigerated truck was delivering directly out there next week. Another truck with non-refrigerated items was going out there too. So much for our making any money on a sale. Must be going to be some humdinger of a party. I didn't see anything about a party in the local paper nor hear anyone say they were invited out. Must just be the senator's Washington group. Never see him, only what I read in the paper or hear on the news, but he sure isn't doing anything for our state. I didn't vote for him though either, too many questionable activities surrounding him."

"Thanks Hank. I was just wondering if there was going to be some hunting, 'cause I'd want to move my cattle and horses closer to the ranch. Some of those green horns shoot at anything that moves." Sam laughed. "Well, see you later; I think Martha said she wanted to shop tomorrow." He waved and headed for his Jeep. As he drove back to the ranch, he wondered how Ken turned out on his quest.

CHAPTER NINE

INFORMATION SHARING

The evening chores were done, the dishwasher loaded and the table cleared ready for them to share what they had learned in town.

Sam related what Bob Running Horse had told him and his conversation with Hank.

While the men talked, Martha made a pitcher of lemonade and placed it on the table with a bowl of pretzels.

Ken mentioned how his supervisor Frank went with him to see the judge and from his shirt pocket, pulled out the two signed court orders to investigate the ranch and buildings if they thought it was necessary. Finished with his news, he poured a glass of lemonade drinking half a glass.

While the men talked, Lacey toyed with her pencil and tapped the eraser end on her notes anxious to share with them. "Well, I had a call from the secretary where I work that they need to email me a form to fill out concerning my Workmen's Comp claim, and they wanted to know where they should send those checks since they knew I was staying here until my cast comes off." Excitement was in her voice.

"It wasn't long and Mr. Conway personally called me." She

looked around the table with a smile on her face. "You aren't going to believe this, he admitted he had heard some not so kosher dealing about the senator and knew he had a ranch close to the national forest. He thinks the senator is being blackmailed into pushing through this logging job. Then when he found out I was here, he got worried, but…typical newsman wants any scoop on what I find out."

"You didn't tell him anything concerning what we are investigating?" Ken wasn't smiling.

"Of course not!" Lacey replied with a scowl on her face. "Not only that, but when I was searching online, I found out that the senator goes to Reno a lot and has lost more than he has won. There was also a picture of him with a scantily dressed woman, who isn't his wife. That could be two reasons for being blackmailed, but I don't see where the owner of this logging thing comes to play or who he is, unless…maybe the senator is the owner and is using this to get the money to pay off those gambling debts. These hard woods make good money."

Ken finished making a note and looked over at Lacey with a warm smile, "Good job. Do you think you could check and see if there were any break-ins or police calls to the Senator's home? Sometimes the gambling mobs use that tactic to put a little fear in the loser to get their money faster."

Happy with Ken's 'good job' remark, Lacy answered, "Sure I can do that, I'll check the newspapers first and then the open records for the police reports. In the morning okay?"

Ken nodded at her. "That will be fine. Could you copy down anything that we might need as proof later, dates, times, addresses, things like that? Again, I want to commend you for doing such as excellent investigation on the computer."

Martha chuckled, "She always has been good on the computer. Why I remember when she got her first one and set up the records for all of their ranch stock and supplies. No more messy hand written notes in a notebook. Her mom and dad were so happy with it; we had her show us how to do it. It sure saves time and money and we can read our numbers later." Martha glanced over at her husband, "sometimes our handwriting wasn't always the best if you get my drift."

Closing up his notebook, Ken slipped a lemon drop in his mouth. "Frank should be calling me tomorrow with the results of the paint samples and who makes and sells boots with that type of sole. In the meantime, I'm going to take a ride on your property tomorrow. I wonder if they have put in any gates or started bulldozing roads back there to get the heavy equipment through."

Martha spoke up as she gathered the empty glasses, "I need to do some shopping tomorrow, do any of you need me to pick up anything while I'm in town?"

Ken reached for his billfold, "Let me give you some money for lemon drops, and," he looked at both Sam and Martha, "I'd like to give you a check for feeding me and my horse. I appreciate the marvelous meals you've prepared and for the great care given to Winner."

Sam put his arm over his wife's shoulders, "We won't hear of it, remember as far as anyone knows, we are paying you to train Missy. But I do agree, this lady of mine sure knows how set a good table."

Martha blushed.

Lacey turned to Ken, "Can I ride with you tomorrow?"

Ken looked down at her cast, "Lacey, I'm going on horseback.

"I have it all figured out. You bring that stirrup up higher toward Gracie's front shoulder to take the weight off my leg and of course, I might need a little help getting on. Gracie won't be upset; you can mount her from either side. Just get her close to the porch. I can slide my good leg over and you be ready to help with this darn cast, it's heavy. No problem." Lacey looked at them waiting for approval of her idea. She was sick of being inside.

Ken didn't want to be the one putting a damper on her idea which he didn't think much of. "Ah, I thought you were going to be busy on the computer."

"I'll do that first thing in the morning; you're waiting for a call from your supervisor, Martha is going to town, and Sam has to do some ranch things with the men. I'll be wonderful company and tell you how it was when mom and dad had the ranch, you know, the good ole days." She gave him a beaming smile.

With a twinkle in his eye Sam looked over at Ken, "I guess you got yourself a riding partner tomorrow." Then he turned to Lacey, "You remember that Gracie is trained to kneel down if you need to get off and stretch and get back on, but, if you can take an hour of riding, I think that is all you should do until that cast comes off."

Ken shook his head, "One hour, that's it. I still think you shouldn't do this, why, you can't even get your jeans on over that bulky cast."

Lacey pointed down the hallway, "There's a large size bib overalls in the closet that will do just fine. Don't worry. Now,

Mr. Ranger, what time do we ride in the morning?"

"How about ten? I'll work with Missy while you are on the computer. Is that okay with everyone?" He said it all in a dull tone; he thought this idea was crazy, too many unforeseen things could happen out there.

Sam covered a yawn with his hand, "Ken, don't wear your uniform, wear Levi's and a shirt and vest. Anyone watching the ranch will think you're training the horse and just having a nice ride. Well, I'm turning in, night all."

"I'll be right along, Honey. I need to let Shadow out." Martha told him.

Ken stood up, "No need to Martha. I'm going out to the barn and talk with Winner a bit. He is use to having me around more. I'll let Shadow back in."

"Okay. Thanks, night you two." Martha followed Sam down the hall to their room.

Looking up at Ken, Lacey quietly asked, "Want some company?" She wondered if he was irritated with her for being so pushy; she didn't want him to be.

He smiled at her, "I'd like that. It's a nice night, a bit cool, need a jacket?"

"No, I'll be fine." Lacey adjusted the crutches and headed toward the door, relieved that his tone of voice was friendly and relaxed again.

Ken opened the door and Shadow dashed through, racing around the yard and then followed them, sniffing here and there on the way to the barn.

The stars were shining making it look like diamonds in the velvet sky. The air was fresh with smells from around the ranch: the hoed garden, flowers around the house, the pine trees that lines the road, and the faint smell of manure removed from the barn.

As they slowly made their way to the barn Lacey commented, "I love this place. I felt bad when Mom and Dad decided to sell our ranch, but they are getting on in years and people don't know it but Dad has a bad heart. Journalism and photography were stronger for me than running the ranch. At least I can always come home so to speak with Sam and Martha. How about you, why are you in this place?"

Sliding the bolt on the door Ken quietly answered, "I'd rather not talk about it at this time." He opened the door to let her walk in.

The horses nickered as they entered the barn. They both gave the horses attention. Somehow animals always know when their humans need comforting and nuzzled them too. The animals were rewarded with a carrot.

After they returned to the house and each went to their own room Lacey got settled into bed. The last thing on her mind before she went to sleep was the question of why Ken didn't want to talk about why he was here.

CHAPTER TEN

THE RIDE

Leaning on her crutches, Lacey stood at the window watching as Ken did stretching exercises and lifted some hand weights he had taken from his truck. He was muscled and trim with no extra body fat. She remembered how secure she felt cradled in his arms on that painful ride down the trail. Lacey had the urge to rub her hands over his bare shoulders and then wrap her arms around his waist. She sighed.

When Ken finished with his workout routine, he put his shirt back on and headed for the barn to work with Missy.

Sam had quietly come up behind Lacey while she was observing Ken. "He keeps fit, it's important in his line of work to stay healthy."

Startled at being caught watching Ken, she turned toward Sam with a red face wondering how long he had been there, "Do you know where he came from and why he is here? Last night when I asked him, he said he didn't want to discuss it. I wondered why. It seemed a simple request, I didn't ask for his life history."

Sam waited while Lacey sat down.

"As you know, I'm on the city council and privy to some

things. When Frank came to us with the three applicants he approved of, he said his preference was Ken. I read over resumes and references of all three. Ken had excellent performance record and had worked as a police officer but wanted to be in the country, not the busy city. I understood why he should be picked and agreed. Ken had lived in Montana with his pregnant wife."

Lacey's head jerked up. *Pregnant wife? Ken didn't act like a married man.*

Sam paused for a minute, not sure if he should really divulge this information. "Ken was the arresting officer in a huge drug bust and was scheduled to testify at the court proceedings. About a week before the hearing, he received an envelope with a lot of money suggesting he get amnesia or better yet, not appear at court. Of course, being the ethical police officer he was, he turned the money in. Then a few days later, he received a note with the letters cut out of the newspaper saying he would be sorry if he testified. There were no finger prints on the paper." Sam ran his hand over his chin and shook his head.

In a quiet voice Lacey spoke, "Let me guess, he went to court and told the truth and the men went to prison."

Sam nodded, "Yeah. About a week later, his wife said her car was making a funny noise and she had a doctor's appointment, so Ken left his vehicle for her to use and took hers to drop off at the garage. He figured the timing was off, or something, and it was due for an oil change."

"And when she turned the key in my car it blew up. They wanted me. They took what was most precious to me, my wife and unborn baby."

Lacey and Sam both jumped, they hadn't heard Ken come in.

Ken kept talking in his monotone voice, "It took me six months of working the streets as an undercover cop but I found out who they were. I wanted to make them pay, and I wanted to be the one to do it." He paused and was quiet for a minute, keeping his emotions in check as the memory flooded over him, "But I couldn't, wouldn't, stoop to their level. I got the arrest warrants and gave it to the captain. Then I turned in my resignation, I couldn't live there anymore. Every street, the house, everything I looked at reminded me of my wife and unborn baby who died in my place."

He put his hand on Sam's shoulder, "I want to thank you for your vote to hire me. My coming here was a blessing. I've healed inside. The memories will always be there, but the hate is gone."

Tears welled up in her eyes as Lacey reached out her hand toward Ken, "I'm so very sorry. Last night when you were hesitant about talking about your past, my journalism nose of always wanting to know the 'what' and 'whys' got the best of me. Forgive me."

Martha came down the hall with her purse and a list of things in her hand. "Why so glum?"

Sam gave the two a quick look and stood up, "We just checked the cookie jar and it's empty. Better put some fixings on that list, I'm hungry for those chocolate chip cookies with lots of pecans in them. Now if you're ready to go to town, I changed my mind and I'll drive you in. Gus has things under control." He went and opened the door and waited until his wife went by, "You two be sure and take the canteens with water now."

He gave them a salute and followed his wife. When Ken retold of his loss, it reinforced how precious Martha was to him.

Ken looked at Lacey, "If you're ready to ride, I have the horses saddled and waiting out front."

"Are, are you sure you still want me to tag along?" Her voice was very quiet.

Crouching down by her chair so they were eye-to-eye level, Ken spoke quietly, "This was probably a good thing to happen, to talk about it. You are the first woman that I have given a second thought to since Jolene died. That night I held you in my arms as we rode down the path to the helicopter my emotions came alive, I didn't feel dead inside anymore, like nothing mattered. You were so strong and when you asked me to stay with you, I wanted to give you some support." He slowly stood up thinking *she probably thinks I'm some kind of nut.*

Reaching out for his hand, Lacey began to talk, "I guess I should confess too. I was frightened and hurting like I've never hurt before. You saved me from being killed by that mountain lion. A *second* later and he would have attacked me. Just one short *second* and I could have been marred for life if I even survived. Then as you held me close and murmured I was safe and you talked softly to Winner keeping him calm... I, I, oh, I can't explain it but I knew if you were with me I'd be okay. I didn't want to be alone on that helicopter." Her eyes were tearing up again.

He gave her hand a slight squeeze, "I'm glad I could give you some peace."

Standing up he said gently, "Hey Lady, time's a wasting, let's ride. I'll fill the canteens, you need anything else?"

She shook her head no and used her crutches to walk out to the porch and the waiting horses. Putting on her hat and gloves, she waited for Ken. He was right; it was a good day to ride and forget bad memories.

Ken led Gracie as close to the side of the porch as possible. Lacey took a hold of the saddle horn and swung her good leg over the saddle. Ken slid the injured leg into the sling he had fashioned so it wouldn't hang straight down.

He pushed back his hat and looked up at her, "Comfy?"

"Almost as comfortable as sitting in that rocking chair up on the porch." Lacey rolled her eyes and they both broke out laughing.

Handing her a canteen, Ken placed his in the saddlebag. He proceeded to buckle on his shoulder holster and put on his vest. Then he slid the rifle into its place and, adjusting his leather hat, swung into the saddle. "Ready?"

"Yes, but where's my rifle, I'm really a good shot you know. I only freeze up when a mountain lion is staring at me ready to bounce."

"I think you will have enough to do with the riding, even a short way. And we walk the horses. Cast or no cast, we have to let the leg heal. I'm not sure the doc would have given you the okay to ride today." Ken frowned at her.

Lacey squared her shoulders. "Well, lots of people have broken legs, stuck two sticks on each side, wrapped something around it, got on their horses and returned to their cabin…I'm from that stock."

Grinning Ken shook his head. *Women.*

"Did you want to head over by the fence dividing the properties? I could point out some places of interest."

"Okay with me," Ken adjusted his hat, "It sure is a beautiful day for riding."

Ken kept roving the terrain with his eyes. *Gus hadn't said anything about unusual activity nor did any of the hands, but things could change.* "What was it like growing up out here especially in the winter when the roads would be six feet deep or more with snow?" Ken asked.

Lacey smiled remembering back, "Oh we got snowed in a lot. We always kept a huge supply of cut up wood next to the house for the stoves and fireplace and dad would have a rope strung along posts that went to the barn, chicken house, and the outhouse. We didn't have indoor plumbing. I thought it was a great time. Mom would bring out books and we'd read and draw. Of course, we baked and would do some knitting. Dad would fix ranch equipment in the shed off the barn, oil the harnesses; go over feed bills and things like that. Once the snow quit, it was time to make some paths. We didn't always get plowed out like we do now. Even today, some of the ranchers that live way off the county roads have to get themselves out, only the main road gets plowed. A lot of them actually use snow mobiles to get to the county road since they may live a mile or so back from it." Reaching her hand down, she gently massaged the upper part of her leg.

Ken observed her action, "Do you want to get down and rest a bit or turn around and head back? I could go and get the truck if you like."

Shaking her head no, "It hurts anyway, even if I was back at the house, I just haven't been on a horse for awhile. But maybe we should go back." She wasn't about to confess how much it was aching.

Ken was in silent agreement but surprised she didn't put up a fuss. "Do you mind heading into this grove of trees, I'd like to take out my binoculars and look around. It will just take a couple of minutes."

"Fine. I haven't noticed anything suspicious though have you?" Lacey looked over at him.

"No, but then they could have a camouflaged telescope trained on us and no sun would reflect off it. I don't know why they would be watching us since we really don't know if they know I'm a ranger. I haven't had any contact with any of them when I've been in uniform. They don't seem to be worried about anything over there right now." He led the way into the grove of trees and stepped down. Removing his binoculars from the saddlebag he went over by the hill and looked around. He didn't see any activity.

Returning to Lacey, he slid the binoculars back into their case, then took a deep drink of water. He patted Winner on the neck.

"Ready to go back now?" Ken pulled the brim of his hat down a little.

"Yeah, let's go back this other way, there is an old cabin still standing that Sam's grandpa lived in when he first moved on this ranch." She smiled at him. "I use to play over there with my friends and Sam's son."

Ken looked over at her as he tightened the chinch on his saddle. "Sam never said anything about having children. But then the subject never came up."

"His name was Lyle James. He got thrown from his horse when it stepped in a gopher hole and his head landed on a rock. He died instantly. They never had any more children of their own. They did take in a two brothers when their parents died so they didn't get sent to an orphanage. Don't know what the parents died from, I was too young to remember. I think the boys were in their early teens at the time. They joined the military after high school and made it their careers traveling all over as they have been stationed out of the country. They fly in every so often to see Sam and Martha. They're both married with families. Martha has a photograph book of pictures."

She paused with a puzzled look on her face, "I don't remember when Bob Running Horse came to the ranch. To me back then, it was a just ordinary thing, people were always helping people and for all I knew, he was just being a hired hand to Sam. The next thing I knew he was off to some school. Now look, he is an excellent airplane mechanic."

Ken went around Winner to check how Lacey's leg was. "Do you need me to adjust the sling we have your leg in? The stirrup looks okay with your foot though, not too much of a slant."

"Nah, it's okay, awkward as can be." She grinned at him, "You just wait until this cast gets off and I'll do some racing with you. Let's make it tough race and go bareback."

They were interrupted by the loud sound of four wheelers following the line fence of the McCann ranch. Ken took a hold of the reins of both horses and pulled them back farther into the bushes out of sight and watched.

The first one went by faster than was safe for the terrain, followed close by the second four wheeler. Both men were dressed in rough logging clothes had rifles slung over their shoulders and were drinking. The last driver threw his empty beer bottle hitting a post where it shattered into many pieces.

"What an idiot! Drinking, driving and smashing bottles so animals can get cut. We need to go pick up the broken glass." Lacey was irate.

"We can't today, it would be too obvious and you did see the guns didn't you? I need to get you back safely and we'll have Gus and the boys take care of it later. I'll have him come by the other way so it will just look like he took this way back and discovers it by accident. We don't want any trouble right now." The last thing Ken needed was a fight and she couldn't race away with that leg. Those type of men would have no trouble knocking down the fence and coming after them. He had to make sure she was safe.

Lacey wasn't happy, "You have your gun too, aren't you a good shot?"

Ken figured she thought he was a coward, he groaned inwardly, "Lacey if we start a fight out here now, we won't get to resolve the logging problem and who is in charge, plus I can't have you as a target or our horses."

She looked at him, "You're right, I can't ride fast I'd fall off right now even hanging onto the saddle horn. It just makes me furious that's all. The needless bad behavior and possible damage to the cattle or horses and the small game around the ranches…" she shook her head and touched Gracie lightly with her foot.

Ken swung into the saddle, looked behind him and then followed her. They were going straight back to the ranch buildings, better safe than sorry was his motto.

When they returned to the ranch, they rode the horses straight into the barn. Ken dismounted dropping Winner's reigns as most western horses were trained to stand when both reins were on the ground, then went to assist Lacey. He slid her leg from the sling and she brought her good leg over the saddle horn. Lacey placed her hands on his shoulders, Ken put his on her waist and she gently eased down to the floor.

She didn't let go and he didn't release her but wrapped both arms around her. They stood that way for a moment in a gentle embrace, neither one wanting to move away. The sound of Sam's Jeep driving into the yard got their attention.

"Unless you want me to help you to the house right now, why not sit down on the bench while I unsaddle the horses and brush them down." Ken looked at those beautiful blue eyes that intrigued him and wished Sam hadn't picked this time to return home.

"No, no, I'll keep you company here. I could brush Gracie." She didn't move.

"Ah, I think you shouldn't be standing without the crutches to take the weight off the leg, but thanks." He picked her up and sat her down on the bench. Then Ken began to taking care of the horses.

It wasn't long and Sam came into the barn carrying Lacey's crutches. "Saw the barn door open and figured you two were in here." Sam placed the crutches next to Lacey, "Supervising the curry combing of the horses?" He joined her on the bench, took off his hat and wiped his forehead with his arm.

"Ah hah, and he is doing to my specifications."

They all laughed

Sam looked over at Ken, "See anything unusual on your ride?"

Lacey stamped her good foot, "We sure did! Two men on four wheelers with guns slung over their shoulders were drinking and threw their empty beer bottles against the fence post as they went by. Of course they shattered! And the morons never stopped and picked them up the pieces! I wanted to, but Ken said we can have Gus check tomorrow when they move the cattle to the other pasture."

The men exchanged looks, "Well, I think that was good advice. One, if they men came back they would wonder why you were messing there, two, getting you off and back on the horse would have been very uncomfortable for you and three, you didn't have anything to put the broken glass in." Sam put his arm around her, "but you are safe and I think it is time to get back to the house. You ready?" He stood up, and held her crutches for her.

Ken finished taking care of both horses; let them out in the corral. Picking up the saddle bag, canteens and his rifle, he followed the couple up to the house. His stomach growled, he hoped Martha had something good to eat. He sure was getting spoiled with her cooking; it beat the jerky and apples he usually had when he was in the mountains.

CHAPTER ELEVEN

THE MAIL ARRIVES

Martha was busy putting away groceries when Ken entered the kitchen. The aroma of the stew in the crock-pot got his immediate attention and his stomach growled loudly.

Martha laughed. "As soon as the table is cleared off, we can eat. Oh Ken, your lemon drops are there by the mail."

"Thanks, Martha, I appreciate it. When Jolene knew she was pregnant, I got in the habit of taking one to replace a cigarette when I quit smoking. I knew it was healthier for all of us."

As Ken reached for the small bag, his hand knocked aside the pile of mail. There was a package addressed to Mrs. Shane Michaels. The other mail was for Lacey, Sam and Martha.

"Sam, I think they put someone else's mail in with yours. There is one here for a Mrs. Shane Michaels."

There was a sharp intake of breath from Lacey. "That's mine."

"Yours?" Ken looked at her with a raised eyebrow.

"Yes." Lacey sat down at the table and slowly pulled the package toward her. The return address was from Tom Nelson, one of the men that had been in the military with Shane. She

THE MAIL ARRIVES

stared at it, her face white and void of emotion as the memories flooded over her.

Martha had stopped what she was doing and had turned around to observe. Sam stood still next to her, waiting, always protective.

Ken looked at the couple with a quizzical look on his face. *What the heck was going on? Who was Mrs. Michaels? It was illegal to open someone else's mail. Why did she say 'mine'?*

Lacey picked at the tape on the brown wrapping paper. It didn't give.

Removing his pocketknife Ken pulled out the small blade and offered it to her.

She shook her head. "You do it."

He slid the blade under the tape opening one end. He then ran the knife along the side to release the rest of the paper. Closing the knife, he returned it to his pocket. He wasn't sure if he should leave her alone or stay.

Reaching slowly Lacey removed the lid from the box. On the top was a letter and a picture of a group of men…the men that shipped out with Shane. She ran her finger over his picture, he looked so proud in his uniform.

Picking up the letter, she silently read it.

"Dear Mrs. Michaels,

Once again I wish to express my condolences for your loss of Shane. I also know how hard it is when you don't have his body to bury. He was a good soldier. I don't know why this wasn't with his other things when they sent them to you. I've been holding on to it and now that I'm state side wanted to send it to you, but I didn't have an address.

I saw a photo shoot you did with your picture and professional name credited to it. When I called and inquired, they gave me this address.

Once again let me tell you Shane was a hero, he saved us by his actions.

Yours truly,

Dan Hanson"

Inside the box were letters from her to Shane, a couple articles of clothes and some pictures of the two of them.

"You okay honey?" Martha put her arms around Lacey and rested her chin on Lacey's head.

"So many memories came back." Lacey put both of her hands on Martha's.

"Do you want to talk about it or be left alone for a while?" Ken spoke softly, but he was curious. He hoped she would explain what this was all about.

She looked over at him. "Sit down. You told me about your life before coming here; I guess it is my turn."

Martha gave Lacey a hug then went back to putting groceries away.

Sam hit the button on the coffee maker and leaned against the counter. He knew the story.

Lacey looked over at Ken, "My last year in college was the same year mom and dad sold the ranch. It was in January that I met Shane. Well, I actually tripped when someone pushed their chair back. Falling against him caused him to drop his food tray and made a mess in the cafeteria. I was so embarrassed. Everyone was laughing and he had food all over. My tray was on the floor..." she looked at everyone with a smile on her face, "And you know what he did? He looked down at the mess and up at me and said, "Hi Graceful, I think we need to go through the line again."

She smiled as she reminisced, "We did. Then we sat down at a table, ate our food and talked and talked and talked. We missed our afternoon classes. After graduation he would be joining the Army. He was already signed up through the ROTC and with his degree, would be an officer and reimbursed for his college tuition.

The folks sold the ranch and came out for our graduation and small wedding, and then they began their travels that they always wanted to do once they were retired.

Shane and I had six months together before he got shipped out. I was doing some free-lance work and had kept my maiden name for that. Then came the dreadful day the two officers came to my door with that terrible news." Lacey stopped talking, her face showing the pain as she relived that moment.

She swallowed and took a deep breath. "The worst part was the memorial service when they gave the gun salute. My heart was breaking. I never thought one could love someone so much in that short time that I had loved him and..." She reached into her pocket for a tissue and blew her nose. When she spoke her voice was very quiet. "All I have to show for the short time we were married is our marriage certificate, my wedding band, his death certificate and this." She pointed at the box. "Sometimes it almost feels like it never happened.

As Lacey slowly placed everything back in the box and placed the cover on it she gave a huge sigh. "That was the yesterday of my life and this is now. I can't live in the past."

Placing the rest of her mail on top of the closed box, one thick letter fell off. "Wait a minute, here is a letter from Mr. Conway." Lacey gave them all a questioning look.

Quickly running her finger under the flap she pulled out the papers. One was a check; the other had some articles and a letter to her. The pictures were of the senator with different men in the same rough working clothes that loggers wear.

The articles and pictures were of the senator at parties and having a great time. Lacey placed them on the table so they all could look at them. His body guards were seen as glorified baby sitters making sure he got home.

Lacey was the first to speak. "Evidently the bodyguards couldn't prevent pictures of the 'ladies of the evening' with the senator and none of them were his wife." She put up one finger. "So he has a wife threatening divorce, and two, he was being pressured with past due bills. Look here, another picture shows him after he had been roughed up by unknown assailants." She looked at everyone around the table. "According to the time factor, that's when he was photographed next to the men in logging clothing. Now, what do you think about that?"

Sam chuckled, "Perhaps he didn't meet the payroll for them."

Lacey quickly went through the rest of the letter and then

shared with them. "The letter basically said to be careful but he was waiting for anything he could legally use. Typical boss man, wanting to be the first one out with the news, ratings you know." Lacey shook her head.

Ken pointed at the papers on the table. "Can I have those articles and pictures available? I really want to look at the men. They might be the ones up here. Perhaps we can make some copies so Gus could be on the lookout too." Ken's face was serious and so was his hungry stomach as once more it growled loudly.

Martha laughed. "Move that mail to the desk. Time to eat."

Ken wasted no time getting the table cleared.

***

Lacey lay in bed. Something just wasn't adding up with Mr. Conway's wanting more material on the senator. It kept nagging at her but she couldn't put a finger on. Why was he so insistent on this saving the national forest from the loggers, especially now since the rangers were investigating.

She got out of bed, hobbled over to the desk and turned on her computer. She didn't have time earlier to check out the other newspaper articles or the police records like Ken had suggested. She put the senator's name in the search and then clicked on 'campaign'. Scrolling through the different areas, she stopped when she saw the name of Jean Conway under volunteers. Was this her boss's wife? Mr. Conway had a picture of his wife on the desk, but she had never looked at it closely.

Searching some more, she found another picture of her. Yes, it was Jean, and Senator Donaby had his arm around her waist and smiling at her. There were other people in the room so this could have been congratulation for working on his campaign, or…Lacey leaned back in the chair, trying to remember if Mr. Conway had ever said anything about his wife volunteering or being away from home. They only discussed business, not family.

She back spaced to see if it showed where the picture was taken. Looking carefully she could barely make out the hotel's logo on the wall. Well, it wasn't unusual to have large fund raisers at fancy places in Las Vegas.

Going back to the other people working for the re-election and the meeting dates, she found pictures of the two of them very close, heads together and smiling, until she looked back at the dates, six months ago. Jean was no longer smiling but seemed strained and stiff and the senator was keeping his hands off her. By the pictures it looked as if he had traded her in for a couple of the 'working' girls at the casino.

Six month ago, her folks got the balance due on the ranch of a hundred thousand dollars in a check. Lacey wondered if there was a connection between the two. Did Jean and the senator have an affair and the senator blackmailed her boss so he could make the last payment to her folks? Lacey shook her head; you would think it was the other way around. Or, maybe Jean was working undercover for her husband and did start to fall for the senator who discovered that bit of information. Was there any way she could find out about a large amount of money removed from Mr. Conway's account, maybe put under donation to the campaign?

Tired, her head full of questions, Lacey reached over to shut off the lamp and close down the computer. She needed to run this by Ken tomorrow.

After getting settled back in bed, Lacey lay there going over the package that held things from Shane and thought how it had affected her. One year from the time they met until he was killed. She had thrown herself into working hard not to think about it all. She had even dated a couple of times, with nice conversation, but no connection.

Ken. She felt attracted to Ken quickly like she had with Shane. She knew he had feelings for her too. Was this a bad omen to be fond of someone so quickly?

CHAPTER TWELVE

WATCHING

One Ear lay quietly along the limb of the tree watching through the leaves as the two-legged creatures messing around on the ground scared away his meals. His tail moved in agitated motion. All they did was make a lot of noise and brought smells he didn't like that stained the ground and didn't go away with the rain, along with those noisy creatures that didn't have fur and were hard like rocks.

After they left last night, he had approached the metal intruders and scratching up some leaves urinated on them, his way of telling them that this was his area. Evidently, they were ignoring him, since they were back again disturbing his space.

Shifting his weight he continued to watch, maybe he could get one of those unwelcomed animals and attack it like he does those young male lions who try to trespass on his territory. That would tell them to stay away.

He reared back and snarled in fright as one of those monsters came to life and the two-legged animals got in and left, leaving the forest quiet. Then he noticed one stayed behind and began poking into the smaller monster. One Ear jumped down.

***

Ken was busy working with Missy when his cell phone went off. "Hello?"

"Hi, Ken, Frank here. I just got some information you will be happy to hear. They traced the paint samples and boot print. It seems that the I LOG COMPANY uses that paint regularly and has their men order their boots through a company that makes a special boot for loggers. Guess who is the silent figure head of this company? None other than our very own, Senator Donaby. This company is so ruthless that some states have barred them from operating in them. For the record, I didn't find any code violations against them in our state."

Ken rubbed Missy's neck as he talked. "Okay! I didn't expect the results back that fast. The fact remains there isn't a permit for them here and they are slowly moving their equipment up to the east side of the mountain. From the looks of things, they will start bulldozing a rough road tomorrow or in the next few days."

Picking up the brush, Ken ran it over Missy's back. "I got word a plane is coming in with more people and large quantities of food are being delivered. Do you want me to take the warrant over there and investigate or wait until they start moving dirt? You, the boys and I think the sheriff and his men should be there at the time or I might be fodder for some earth worms."

"No," Frank responded, "Don't do anything right now; we will wait until they remove the first tree. We could get them when they began making a dirt road, but we don't want them getting out on any technicality. You're right; we need some strong support when we go in. How many men do you think they have over there?"

"Hard to tell," Ken paused, "I haven't got a clean count but I think the numbers will be around thirty by the time the plane lands. I'm assuming working men are on the plane but it could just be party time too. This isn't a small operation. I think they plan on coming in and doing their thing and be out before anyone can get an injunction to stop or arrest them." Ken began walking to the barn and Missy followed him like a dog.

Frank standing with the phone cradled between his neck and shoulder was looking at the large map on the wall as he traced with his finger the route the loggers would take. "How far up can they bulldoze before they would have to dynamite for a road? It's been awhile since I've been over in that section. I want them stopped before that; I don't want any dynamite going off."

Ken's voice had disgust in it as he responded. "When I rode over there today and looked, I'd say they will probably start cutting trees then snag them out as much as possible, and then the bulldozers will get into action to make a road. They have the trailers there ready to load the logs on. From checking out the markings they've made on the trees, I can see they will be wasting a lot of wood knocking down the smaller ones to get to the big ones. It won't be a good harvest; they will just be destroying the mountain, not thinning it out."

Frank wrote on a pad as he talked. "Okay, this is our plan then. One, let everyone get onto the national forest and start cutting trees. Two, take close-up pictures of it that show the date and time. Does Lacey still have a good camera out there?"

Ken bristled at the thought of Lacey being in danger. "She does, but I'm not letting her get in the danger zone, she has a broken leg for crying out loud. Add to that those cameras are expensive with a capital E and they are so sophisticated, we don't know how to use them." Ken kicked at the dirt out of frustration.

Calmly Frank spoke, "Ken, that camera also has long range capabilities. Three, we will have all the teams out there for the arrests. Now, keep me posted on things and I will let you know when I get anything more."

Ken heard the click of the receiver. It was getting dark out but he needed to work off some steam. He saddled up Winner and they galloped down the lane leaving the ranch. He could tell Winner was enjoying stretching out in a run too. Slowing down, he looked around for anything unusual. Not ready to go back he got a gut feeling to go around the backside of the ranch area.

After he was satisfied things looked normal, Ken was ready to return when the sound of a speeding four-wheeler was swiftly approaching him. It was unnerving considering it was dark and he had no light to show he was there. He turned Winner so they were facing the sound, so he knew which way he could escape.

The beam of the light was on him when the four-wheeler started making choking sounds as if it wasn't getting enough fuel, when it died about twenty feet from Ken and his horse.

The driver was a big brute of a man but oddly in a state of fear. He scrambled off the seat and hurried over to Ken, grabbing at his leg.

"You gotta help me. Something is after me." He looked behind him, "I don't know what it was, but just as the engine took hold, and it jumped at me. The noise scared it and it took off." Sweat was pouring off him. His eyes registered his fear.

"Relax man. Let go of my leg. Where were you?" Ken stepped down from Winner.

The agitated man kept moving around as he answered. "By the McCann trail to the mountain, I need to get back to the house." Glancing over his shoulder, then back at Ken. "Give me your horse! I need to get out of here!"

Ken kept his voice low. "I don't think so. I know your upset, but no one takes my horse. You aren't too far from the house; I'll walk along with you."

The heavyset man suddenly lunged at Ken, causing him to fall. "I said I want the horse!"

Winner reared up in the air, whinnied and stood pawing the ground between Ken and the stranger who quickly backed away his hands high in a waving motion.

Ken stood up and touched his horse. "It's okay, boy, it's okay."

Looking over at the confused and frightened man, "Simmer down, mister and I suggest you stay away from my horse. Now, as I said before, I'll go with you to the fence by the house."

The man shook his fist at Winner, "That horse is dangerous, you better put him down. I'm going to talk to the authorities about him!"

"Yeah, and when you doing that, don't forget to tell them why he acted that way. By the way, I'm Ranger Dickinson and I could arrest you for assault of an officer. Start walking and tell me what happened to you, where did you say you were?"

"Ranger? Ah, well, I was just at the edge of the property." The man was clearly nervous.

"Well, you were lucky to make it away. Because the Indians say there is a spirit that watches over the mountain for anyone that tries to harm it. Sometimes it takes the image of a person, sometimes an animal. There have been some that we have never found their remains." Ken talked in a quiet voice as they walked in the dark of the night.

"Do, do, does it show up during the day too?" The man was scared and constantly looking behind him.

Ken had all he could not to laugh and was glad it was dark outside to conceal his mirth. "According to the Indians, yes, but usually you won't see it until it's too late. You weren't trying to hurt the mountain were you?"

"No, no, just take some of the big trees. Are we almost there?"

Ken couldn't believe that in his fear the man actually admitted why he was there. "Yeah, I think if you go over to the fence there by the broken beer bottle, you can cross over that field and you should be at the house in no time at all." Ken mounted Winner.

"Ah, maybe you could just take me to the house." The man had turned around and was walking backward as he watched behind him. "You said you were a ranger."

"But you have no trespassing signs up and I sure wouldn't want to trespass." Ken was really enjoying this.

"I'll vouch for you. There is a gate right up here."

"Okay. Just to the gate. They won't shoot at us will they?" Ken wasn't trying to be funny now. "That could get everyone arrested, shooting at a ranger."

"No. No. They will either be eating or in the bunkhouse. Should be a small party tonight 'cause the senator suppose to arrive tomorrow and that is when we have the big blast." Being closer to the main gate, the man was slowly getting over his scare.

Winner's hoofs made a soft sound on the ground as the slowly made their way.

Ken asked in a nonchalant voice. "What's your name? You work for the senator?"

"The call me Gunner."

Ken questioned, "That your real name?"

"No. I'm just the one who works on the equipment, the guys gave me that handle. What's it to you?"

"Because if I do need to make a report that you were visited by something on the mountain, especially if something happens to you or say for example you mysteriously disappear. Just doing my duty." Ken wondered if he would say his name.

"Donald. Donald Werner, that's my name."

Ken continued with the questions. "Where do you hail from, Donald."

"Oregon. Why all the questions?"

"Just in case I have to notify next of kin, that's the nasty part of my job. Have you worked long for; what did you say the name of the company was?" Ken popped a lemon drop in his mouth.

"The I LOG COMPANY. This is the second job I've been on for them. They pay good. Real good. Keep us supplied in booze too. And everything and anything to do with work, stays on the job, if you get my drift. Well, I guess I can go on the last bit by myself."

The lights of the ranch house were visible.

More composed, Gunner looked over at Ken. "Thanks ranger, and don't tell anyone you helped me, they wouldn't take kindly to it." The man quickly dissolved into the night.

Ken debated if he should snoop around and thought better of it. He didn't want to be caught over there; he wanted to catch them in the act.

Signaling to Winner with the reins to turn, Ken headed to the house, hoping there were some leftovers to eat and to share Frank's conversion and this last episode with the family. Family? When did that word come up?

CHAPTER THIRTEEN

NOISE ON THE MOUNTAIN

Lacy woke up to a rapping on the front door. She heard Sam holler from the living room, "Coming." She glanced at her clock, six am. Man, she over slept. She reached for her crutches as she heard conversation going on.

In the kitchen, she discovered Sam talking with Gus. Ken was sitting at the table going over the papers with their notes from last night. Martha joined them tying on her apron. So she was the only one that was late.

The phone rang. Martha answered and handed it to Sam.

He listened and hung up the phone. "Bob Running Horse said Senator Donaby's plane is arriving today with about twelve people on it. He didn't have any names." Sam took a drink of his coffee. "Then Gus just told me one of the big trucks moved slowly down the lane leading to the pasture land that adjoins the area to the mountain."

The phone rang again. "My goodness seems like grand central station around here this morning." Martha picked up the phone, "Morning, Swenson residence." Once again she handed the receiver to Sam.

He listened. "Thanks a lot Hank. The next beer is on me."

Sam looked at the questioning look on their faces. "Hank said the two trucks that have food coming in for the senator's ranch just passed the store. I'd say there was going to be some action going on pretty soon."

Conversation stopped as Martha ground the coffee beans.

"I'd like to share something I found when I was on the computer last night." Lacey related what she discovered about Jean, the senator's wife. "I wonder if there is any connection of the payment to my folks and Mr. Conway's desire to find info on logging in the national forest."

"Good job, Lacey. Can you dig into that a little more today? I think they need to list all donations from businesses. I'm going to take the truck and drive up to the trail and nose around, right after a dish of those eggs and hash browns Martha has cooking." They all laughed as Ken gathered up his notes and put them in a folder.

"Should I follow the truck that left or go with you?" Sam put the coffee mugs on the table and reached for the coffee carafe.

"I'm not exactly the door post here." Gus stepped forward. "I can check out the large truck and see for sure where it's headed."

They all looked at Ken for approval. "I can't ask any of you to put yourself in harm's way."

"Seems to me you ain't a askin' us to do anything so we're a tellin' you, Gus and a couple of men will take a different route to check things over. I'm going with you after you contact Frank. You shouldn't be alone on this. I don't think they will start anything until the plane lands, just starting to get their equipment to the location. I wonder who will be on the plane.

So far no one has seen or heard any lumber cutting business names." Sam slid one of the full mugs toward Ken.

Martha turned to Gus. "You joining us for breakfast?"

"No ma'am, I ate with the boys. Thank you, your coffee sure smells good though." Gus took off his hat and hung it on the peg.

"Yours might taste better if someone washed that coffee pot out once in a while." Martha chuckled and set the cookie jar next to Gus.

Looking at Ken, Lacey asked, "Why not take one of your official papers and check out things over there?"

"Because I need more evidence for this and it would only cause a problem right now. We have to pick our battles, and win them. By the time I return today, and everyone is there, I may do that. It all depends on what Gus finds on his little excursion.

Everyone filled their plate and took a seat around the table. Gus dunked a cookie into his coffee.

Lacey reached for the saltshaker and gave it a few sprinkles over her food. "I still think I should go with you because I know how to adjust the camera for the best shots, especially when you want clear pictures of the faces."

"Lacey, we are going on horseback and staying under cover. That means we may be crawling around or climbing a tree to get those pictures. I can't have you in that situation with your leg. Plus, we need your investigation of campaign money, remember." Ken's voice was firm but he smiled at her.

The men all glanced at each other and nodded. They agreed with Ken.

Picking up the coffee pot, Martha spoke up. "I totally disagree. First, Lacey showed me some of those sites she was on yesterday. I may not be as computer savvy as Lacey, but I can look that up and press copy. Second, Lacey on the other hand, knows how to ride, shoot, and operate that fancy expensive camera of hers to get the shots you need. Knowing you men, you'd probably forget to take the cover off the lens." She began to refill the coffee mugs.

She had their undivided attention.

Martha let her eyes slowly go from man to man, "Now, the way I see it, Lacey wears the overalls again and some tennis shoes. Forget that sling thing. Gracie is the horse for her since she can kneel down if Lacey needs to get on by herself. Lacey will take a couple of Tylenol before you all leave. Put both horses in the trailer as usual. Sam will drive the truck just in case, plus you need that on our side of the land out of sight."

Once more the men all exchanged glances.

Sam spoke quietly, "Well, Martha, dear, you can't assume Ken wants me driving his new truck."

"And maybe if some men I know come home hungry and supper is peanut butter and jelly sandwiches…" Martha's voice trailed off.

Gus leaned close to Ken and whispered, "I think you better do as she says."

Lacey pushed her chair back. "Martha's right. I will even sign an affidavit not holding the rangers or the state responsible if something would happen. I'm a pro, I've taken chances on jobs before and I will have the first hand scoop to all of this when you make the arrest. Ah, I can see a bonus check with lots of zeros when Mr. Conway sees the article. Give me a minute to dress and I'll be ready to go. Nice breakfast, Martha. Sometime you will have to teach me to cook."

As Lacey made her way down the hall to her room she heard Ken say, "What just happened here?"

***

Lacey lay on a knoll concealed by small bushes on Sam's land having a perfect view of everything as she used two different cameras to get her pictures. She had her notebook, water canteen and plenty of film. Unbeknown to Ken, she had also slipped her hand gun into her bag.

So far the activity at the base of the forest was getting the equipment in place and marking where they would start digging out the road when they had removed the trees that were in the path. It was noisy and some of the biggest machines Lacey had never seen before.

She kept looking around and behind her. She was still a little leery about that mountain lion. They moved so silently and could jump twenty feet although they usually liked to attack at five feet and behind the prey. She didn't want to be prey. For all her huff and puff, she wished Sam or Ken would return.

Snapping long and short-range pictures of the equipment and the activity, she concentrated on getting good shots of the men. It was hard to get the face since most of them were wearing hard hats and a lot had beards; the others just had caps on. Lacey wondered if that was a violation of rules, not wearing hard hats anytime they were working. She wished she was closer and could hear the conversation.

None of the men were working hard, merely doing the basic. They were joking and leaning against the big equipment. According to that man Ken had talked with, it sounded like they would be partying tonight. She smiled. Working with a hangover some of them would need a day off, not putting up with the whine of saws and diesel motors sounds.

She moved to ease her leg a bit and changed the chip in her camera. Um, that one big burly man kept glancing over his shoulder all the time. She wondered if that was the man Ken told there were spirits on the mountain.

Lacey believed in that legend. When Bob Running Horse came out to the ranch, she would have him tell Ken about the Indian beliefs concerning the mountain.

The hairs on the back of her neck brought her senses to alert. She slowly turned her head and breathed a sigh of relief; there was Bob.

He got on his stomach and looked over the hill.

"I'm glad to see you. How did you know where I was?" Lacey smiled at her friend.

"Lacey, Lacey, you should know by now, the spirits told me." Bob smiled at her. "And Frank when I stopped by the ranger office to let him know what I overheard when the senator got off the plane. He told me Ken was up here."

Lacey gave him a poke in the arm. "I'm glad to see you. Did you find Ken?"

He nodded. "He was watching them notch some trees and said you were here. He said to tell you he got some pictures too, with the cap off the lens."

They both laughed.

"What did you have to tell Frank?"

"It appears that there is going to be some humdinger of a party going on tonight. The senator has two vans with "ahem" ladies driving in. That ought to cause some fighting. As it is when some of the men come into town, they drink too much, want to start fights. Add that to some half dressed women...I really doubt they will be in the condition to work tomorrow."

They were interrupted by the roaring of the big machines as the loggers put them though their motions to make sure they were tuned up and ready to go. The noise shattered the peacefulness of the mountain.

***

Old One Ear thought so too as he backed further away into the forest. He was confused with all this invasion of his domain. He didn't know how to fight these odd animals. He was afraid. The only thing he ever feared was a pack of wolves or those two-legged animals with their hunting dogs. But he could still fight those. He didn't know how to fight these. He snarled, retracted his claws and crept back to the safety of his cave.

***

Lacey glanced at her watch. The logging crew was getting ready to leave. She was glad; she ached all over and was hungry. That peanut butter sandwich she shared with Bob for lunch had been eaten a long time ago.

Ken and Sam stayed at their watch place since they knew Bob was with her.

They waited until all the men were gone; they had counted twelve, before Bob went to get Gracie and his own horse. The terrain was too uneven to bring the truck and trailer up this far and they didn't want it to be seen or leave tire prints, just in case.

Bob had Gracie kneel down. Lacey put her leg over the saddle and said, "Up Gracie." Bob handed Lacey her bag that held the two cameras, a case for the clips, her notebook and gun.

They reached the truck just as Ken and Sam came out of the woods. Good timing.

Ken assisted Lacey as she got off the horse. Sam led both Winner and Gracie to the trailer.

"Thanks for staying with Lacey, Bob. Are you going to join us at the ranch house for supper?" Ken didn't remove his arm supporting Lacey.

"Oh yes, I wouldn't miss that. Have you had some of Martha's biscuits yet? Um, they are so light they just about float out of your hand." Bob had raised his arm up in the air. "I would like to know what Frank is going to do tomorrow and maybe the next day. I have a feeling that most of these men are going to have some big hangovers tomorrow. Twenty of my people will be here tomorrow and the next day to assist. We know this mountain. The Spirit of the mountain doesn't want these men to take her bounty. They have not prayed and asked for it. They do not take it to stay warm or build their home. The Spirit is not happy."

Ken didn't know what to say about them being involved or the spirit. He has been trying to scare that man last night; this was the first he heard someone talk about it that really believed it. "Well, I agree, we will talk with Frank. Sorry there isn't room in the trailer for your horse."

"We will be there by the time you are back and have taken care of your horses." With that Bob waved and lightly touched his horse into a lope. They were soon over the hill out of sight.

CHAPTER FOURTEEN

THE PHONE CALL

Excited, Lacey came down the hall waving papers in her hand. "I found where my boss and his wife each contributed fifty thousand to the senator's campaign fund about the same time as my folks were paid their final payment. And on the public police report there was a harassment charge against my boss by the senator. Um, now what do you think that was all about? Mr. Conway may be the normal nosy reporter, but he doesn't go around bugging senators. And it was also about this time that there were no more pictures of Jean or her name anywhere associated with the senator."

A light tapping on the door interrupted them and Bob Running Horse entered the kitchen. "Hi, all. A few of us were sorta watching the senator's place and if I could borrow your camera, I think you may have some interesting pictures for discussion, if you know what I mean." He had a half smile on his face. "I wonder if having the ambulance on standby might be a good idea."

Ken wasn't smiling. "Bob, they have NO TRESPASSING signs all along the fences. There is a hefty fine for being on their property without being invited or having legal authority and a reason to be there."

"Well, they left the gate open and we just happened to be

crouched behind the large rock at the entrance, and when that passenger van slowed down to go through for the cattle barrier... we just hopped unseen onto the back of the van. So, technically we weren't trespassing since the van had the okay to go there. When they slowed down, we jumped off and watched for a while. There is going to be some x-rated action going on."

"And you want to take pictures of it? That's sick Bob." Lacey had a shocked look on her face, "You aren't like that."

Bob threw up his hands, he was no longer smiling "No, no, no! They have drugs there and lots of booze. There are going to be fights with that combination. Those men fight all the time in town, nasty dirty fights. Some white men are like that. I tell yah, there are going to be problems. Add to the fact that these women who came in aren't dressed like St. Theresa. If someone gets hurt or killed, you will have pictures." He looked around at them, "And people in jail can't damage the mountain." He lowered his voice. "To bad that ranch wasn't leasing reservation land, then we would have tribal rules."

"It's still against the law." Ken stood firm.

Lacey joined in, "What about those sting operations we always see on TV shows? You do have a warrant for over there. You could call Frank and get an okay to check things out."

Ken stood with his hands on his hips, "We need to wait and close them down when they began logging down the trees. They don't have a permit and they won't get one for that section. We have to follow the law. How would you feel if we were having a small party here and they busted in or snooped around? The word is privacy with a capital P. Unless we are called on for assistance we are trespassing plain and simple."

No one said a word, but all eyes were on Ken.

He could feel their desire for action as he continued, "We have two different situations here. One, the illegal logging of trees off the mountain; two, a private party on posted land. Do you want me to break the law or uphold the law as I've sworn to do? I have no reason to go on their land at this time. I didn't see any drugs or anyone using them and we won't because we weren't invited."

"Call Frank." Lacey said quietly. "Let him make the call either way."

In a somber tone Bob added, "When the senator and his male chums got off his private plane and were waiting for their luggage, they were talking about all the drugs they had and how nice it was not to have to go through TSA check in. Later, when I was talking with the pilot while he waited for a ride to the motel, he commented on the fact that most of them were higher than the plane was and he was glad for the door separating him from the so-called important men from Washington. He said this was his last time flying for the senator. It wasn't safe."

"I wonder." Lacey looked around the group, "I wonder if Jean Conway saw any of this drug usage when she was working for the senator? I'm going to give Mr. Conway a call."

"Why, Lacey? I am supposed to be dealing with timber, not a drug bust." Ken was getting exasperated. "Do you honestly think he would tell you that?"

"Yes. Remember how they contributed all that money to the senator? That wasn't chicken feed and they aren't the type to give that much for politics. They are more for helping out the veterans and soup kitchens. That might have been blackmail money." Lacey's eyes were getting excited. "Think about it, in those pictures, at first, Jean was happy and smiling, and then on the later ones she had a strained look on her face. Why, the senator was re-elected, that was the goal, so why wasn't she joyful too? We might be getting him for illegal logging and drugs! I'm going to call Mr. Conway."

Ken was thoughtful. "Wait, let me call Frank and relate all of this and see what he says, then call Mr. Conway if you want. But, remember, we need to be legal."

Lacey shook her head. "You call Frank. I'll call Mr. Conway. Be back in a minute." She grabbed her crutches, went to her room, and closed the door.

***

"Mr. Conway, I wonder if you would share with me why you really sent us out to this national forest. Wasn't the real reason you were interested in Senator Donaby activities? You knew he had a ranch out here and owned a logging company? What about his gambling addiction, were you aware of that too?"

There was a pause before Mr. Conway spoke. "What are you getting at Lacey? I'm just concerned about our national forest, that's all."

Lacey on one hand was frustrated that he wouldn't readily share with her and on the other, if what she was thinking of about Jean and the senator was true, she could understand his reluctance in sharing.

"There is an investigation going on here that I can't legally divulge to you, but if you can be open and honest with me, I

THE PHONE CALL

can certainly make sure you have an exclusive report with pictures that will increase your magazine circulation and put your senator in a very tight vise." Lacey waited silently for him to respond.

When the connection remained silent, she asked, "Where is Jean, Mr. Conway?"

"What? Why would you be asking about my wife?" He asked nervously.

"Because I know she was working for Donaby's re-election. I have pictures of them together smiling, his arm around her waist and then a non-smiling Jean, an unhappy Jean. The next thing, each of you donates fifty thousand dollars to his campaign and there are no more pictures of her on his team. Why?"

Silence.

"Mr. Conway, are you still there? Mr. Conway?" Lacey wondered if he was okay.

"Just, just a moment."

Lacey heard the receiver placed on the desk, then the sound of his office door being closed.

"Lacey?" His voice was one of a very exhausted man.

"Yes, I'm here."

"I don't see why the where a bouts of my wife has any bearing on this tangent you've gotten involved in while your leg is healing."

Lacey could hear his fingers drumming on the desk. Why was he so agitated? He was usually pretty laid back for an editor.

"Because I think the senator may have gambling debts he needs to pay off. There was a police report of him being roughed up in Reno where he was reported to be doing some heavy gambling. We also know he owns a lumber company. And," she paused, "I think he black mailed you for some reason to get that money that you two donated. That's more money than you would normally contribute and most of your donations are to charities and the veterans. My parents just happened to receive the last check due on their sale of the ranch from Donaby at that time. Did you know the senator had purchased my folk's place?"

"No Lacey I didn't. I will admit I knew he had a logging operation and he was ruthless in his business dealings. Since he got closed down in that other state, I figured he might try sneaking into the nearest National Forest. That logging equipment isn't cheap and he couldn't afford to let it sit idle. It was just my newsman's hunch, nothing more. But, if he got into some serious hot trouble…well…"

Lacey heard the long sigh emanate from him.

"Payback time, eh? So what is it he's holding over your head? I want to help if I can and I have some resources here you don't know about." Lacey didn't want to push him; she could hear the unspoken struggle he was going through, yet she felt he knew more.

"Mr. Conway, I know for a fact that there is going to be a huge wild party at his ranch. He has a passenger van of women there, food, liquor and drugs. If your wife could reveal any of his actions or activities at parties that aren't acceptable, we might be able to get a warrant to check it out. We could see if the women were of legal age, and if they are call girls and check on the availability of illegal drugs."

Lacey waited for him to respond.

She heard him blow his nose and when he answered his voice was choked up. "I don't know how to say this or how much. Whatever you do, I don't want Jean's name in the news. She couldn't take that added stress. I don't know what she might do. If you could see her now…" A sob followed the last word.

He took a deep breath to compose himself. "What I'm going to tell you is confidential. My wife is staying with her sister and under the care of a doctor. She is being treated for mental stress." There was a pause. "The only reason I'm telling you is because you said there would be women there and I worry about their treatment. I don't know if this would be of any value with your investigation."

Lacey didn't comment. She knew he would either tell all or totally clam up. He was waging a silent war within himself. His wife's mental health balanced on one side of the scales and his quest to see the senator's downfall on the other.

"My heart aches for my wife. Because of what happened, she won't come home. She says she isn't good enough for me: she's soiled. I'm afraid she might attempt to take her life. She has a nurse twenty-four-seven at her sister's home and is under a doctor's care." There was a long pause.

His voice changed into low growl. "I never thought I could hate, but Lacey, you have no idea how I despise that despicable man!"

She jumped when she heard his fist hit the top of his desk.

"Jean was asked to come and help with the campaign, see that the ballrooms were organized for the fund raisers, the media notified and things like that. There was always a money crunch. One night, one of the other women, Karen, said the senator wanted them up to his suite to discuss the next day's meeting. Jean didn't think anything of it because this had happened before and the senator would be cating a late meal away from the throng of people.

When they arrived, Donaby was sitting at the table and asked Karen to pour them all a glass of wine. What Jean didn't know was Karen had been told to put some of that date rape drug in it or else. Evidently ole Donaby had something on her and she followed his order."

The controlled hardness in Mr. Conway's voice was that of a man who was terribly angry.

"When my wonderful wife passed out, they undressed her and she was sexually assaulted by that sleaze ball and his two body guards. They took many, many pictures. When she woke up, in pain, sick and frightened, they callously informed her if she went to the police, these photos would be spread all over the internet and news media, anonymously of course. Then, when they took her to her room, he told her that if we donated $100,000 dollars to the campaign we would get those pictures, but not the chip that held the originals." He was silent for a minute.

"She called me crying. I said we were going to the police. She pleaded with me not to, just pay them, if I saw the pictures, I would pay them. She couldn't go through the public humiliation. She was afraid our business would be ruined by the scandal. I told her I didn't care about the business, only her. She cried so hard. I called her doctor and he met us at the hospital. After they treated her, he called in a psychiatrist since she refused to talk to the police about the sexual assault. You will never know how I felt when she wouldn't let me touch her, hug her and refused to come home with me, but went to her sister's because she said she was used goods. My God! We have been married for thirty years! I love her with all my heart!"

The heart-wrenching sob that came out of him brought tears to Lacey as she felt his grief and anger. She didn't say a thing, just waited. What do you say to a man who just revealed all of this damage to his family, the evil done to his wife?

After a minute, he composed himself and continued, "I did as I was instructed on getting the money and took it there. That turd took the envelope with the two checks and made an obscene comment about her physical attributes. I had all I could do not to knock him down! But he had his henchmen around and I knew I'd end up in jail. He still registered a complaint with the police as a warning of what he could and would do." He took a deep breath.

When he spoke it was the tone of a spent, exhausted man. "I have the pictures. Her face and naked body are fully shown, but not the faces of the men, only their naked bodies, in various positions as they abused my wife. I wish those animals were all dead. Tell me, what can I do and still keep my wife's sanity?"

Shocked by what he had revealed, tears filled Lacey's eyes at the pain these two people were still going through. She wasn't sure what to say. "I'm so very, very sorry for you both to have been put through this horrible tragedy. Have you talked with an attorney, the police? We can't let him and those thugs get away this."

"No, I haven't talked with the attorney. I don't mind losing the business, I just care about Jean. Don't you understand what the publicity would do to her? Her face plastered on the newspapers, that swine laughing and lying about it?" His voice pleaded.

"Would Jean swear to the fact that there are drugs at his parties? If you could get her to do that, we have a judge here who would work with us. We could get an undercover man dressed in logging clothes get in the party and take pictures. They are going to be too drunk and high to know if he is a regular or a new one that just came in. If the women are being used as prostitutes, we can nail him without your wife being brought into this or pictures being shown. But," Lacey hesitated, "But, I will have to share the drug info with the ranger and the judge who is working with us on this case."

Lacey held her breath, hoping he wouldn't say no. She could feel the tension over the phone. This could be the final reason for the judge to okay investigating the ranch.

Lacey jumped when Mr. Conway began shouting. After mauling over the hell he and his wife had gone through, he was ready to get even. They weren't going to be pigeons anymore waiting for the order of more money.

"Let's get em, damn it! They can't do any more harm to us! We won't be victims any longer! I'll wait here for you to contact that ranger and judge. You have my cell phone number. I can fly there if need be. Anything, I'll do anything."

Gone was the fearful man, her old boss was back and he was ready to fight.

"Thanks, oh thanks so much, Mr. Conway. I'll get the wheels

rolling on my end here. Together we will put him and those other creeps behind bars! I'll be in touch. Bye."

Lacey quickly headed for the kitchen. Ken would be making more calls when she shared what she had just heard. It was going to be a long night.

CHAPTER FIFTEEN

PLANS

"Come on, Gunner, there's no such thing as a mountain spirit that turns into a body of an animal or a person." Pete, one of the new hires twisted the lid off a cold bottle of beer, guzzled about half of it and let out a huge belch.

Gunner leaned closer, "I'm telling yah, I've been in this business a long time and I ain't never felt the hairs on the back of my neck stand up. I swear I felt a hot breath on my neck and I saw a shadow, something."

"Ah, you've had too much to drink and just think you saw something." Pete was young, cocky and getting drunk. He turned around in his chair and watched the scanty dressed women dancing with the guys. "Forget it, Gunner. Let's have some fun. I ain't never worked for a boss that threw parties with willing gals, steaks and all the booze you can drink."

Gunner was irritated by the young upstart's remark, "I wasn't drinking that day. You think you're so brave, a big hot shot. I bet you wouldn't go out there at night either. I was there, alone and I know what I seen and felt." Gunner shuddered. "It's weird in the mountains, one minute the sun is shining and the next, night seems to fall."

He stopped talking as they were interrupted by a tall, very thin young woman who wrapped her arms around Pete's shoulders. "You look a little lonesome over here, Buddy Boy. You're not laughing. The boss likes his people to be *happy*. We got a little *happy* powder over there, or we could dance or..." she twisted around landing in his lap, pulled his head towards her. Any thoughts of going out to the lower mountain hills went right out of Pete's mind as he kissed her hard, picked her up and danced over to the end of the bar where the *happy* powder was.

Picking up the whiskey bottle, Gunner poured another shot and slammed it down in one big swallow. Wiping his mouth with the back of his hand, he knew there was no way he or anyone else would be working tomorrow.

His thought was distracted when he saw the senator coming out of the bedroom tucking his shirt back into his slacks. A gal young enough to be his daughter came out behind him, her clothes disheveled and her hair messy.

He watched the senator who pointed at the bar and the woman was staggering toward it when a logger grabbed her and danced around with her. They went twice around the floor when the man picked up the girl that was having a hard time standing up and disappeared into a room.

Gunnar debated if he should have another drink or go to the bunkhouse; he thought he could make it that far on his own. He looked over the ladies of the evening and knew there was no way he was going to make a connection with any of them tonight. He poured another drink, put his feet up on one of the other chairs and watched the activity around him as he sipped from his glass.

***

Judge Roberts pulled a note pad closer, "Are you sure both Bob Running Horse and the pilot will swear to the fact that there were drugs on the plane? Did they see them? If so, we can get them for transporting illegal drugs across state lines. We need to move fast. I can call the sheriff to stop at the motel and have him talk with the pilot. Can you have Bob sign an affidavit saying he overheard them talking about having drugs. He didn't actually see them exchange any drugs. Correct? We can also check for possible prostitution. Now you realize, they can post bail and be out within twenty-four hours unless we find a mess out there. I don't want the county sued for false arrest either." Judge Roberts looked over at the clock, 8:30 PM.

Ken voice was serious, "I'm aware of that sir. I'm positive the pilot will be able to shed more light on the actions of the senator. He has been flying the private plane for quite awhile." Ken paused, "And, I, well, I do have some confidential information about the senator's escapades with other women which I can't divulge my source at this time. I seriously think we will find all the evidence we need without it. I should also tell you we have about twenty tribesmen here too. They came originally to watch over the forest because the spirit told them to protect it."

Judge Roberts leaned back against his chair, "Okay, I'll have the papers ready; have Frank confer with the sheriff after Luke talks with the pilot. Then he can send the men out. Oh, and never underestimate the Indians when their spirit talks to them. You all be careful and someone keep me up on what is transpiring. There is no way I can go to sleep now." The judge hung up the phone.

Ken immediately punched in Frank's number and related what the judge said.

"Okay, I'll call Sheriff Pierson. You have Bob and the men by the gate so Pierson can deputize them when he gets there. In the mean time no one do anything crazy." Both men hung up.

Frank sure hoped this wasn't a big mistake and they broke up a fund raising party for the senator. He personally didn't like the man and would see him pay the consequences for damaging the mountain, but there wasn't a law about having a good time on your own property.

Ken turned around and related the two conversations.

Bob wasn't very happy when he was informed they were to stay by the gate. "But, if Luke and Frank come barreling down the road with the deputies and other rangers, they are going to find a bunch of drunks and drugged out men and women. Now, if we were to quietly look into windows and take pictures, there is the proof before it could be flushed down the toilets or dispose of in some way"

Lacey slid one crutch under her arm to lean on and walked over to Ken, "He's right you know. A picture is worth a thousand words. The party will be loud. Bob and someone with him, wearing moccasins and with my camera can get pictures. If he takes my bigger one, he can actually take a video with sound. Come on, that's evidence." Her eyes pleaded with him to say yes.

Ken was torn with her logic and the fact that Frank said to stay put by the gate. He glanced at his watch, 8:45 PM. He thought of the little bit of information Lacey had felt she could share with the group about Jane. He remembered his wife being killed by the drug dealers. He straightened up.

"Lacey, get me your cameras. Give us a quick lesson on how

to use them. Bob, I'm going with you, we'll take our horses, it will be faster and quieter. Sam, keep the women inside and lock the doors. Gus, have your men know that we will be doing a raid on the ranch when the sheriff and Frank gets here. I expect if anything we may have some physical action, but I don't expect any shooting. I'm taking my gun just in case, I'm not sure about the body guards and what they will do especially if they are all drunk."

Lacey grabbed Ken's arm. "Let me go, I'm a pro with the cameras and I'm a journalist, I can describe the details."

"No!" Ken's voice was firm. "You can either get your cameras or I'll grab mine from the truck and we'll use that, but lady, there is no way I am letting you get in harm's way for a picture."

Lacey backed away. The look in his eyes and the tone of his voice let her know she wasn't leaving the house this time.

"Okay, I'll get the cameras." Lacey said softly as she went to her room, sad in one way not being able assist in what she was good at and at the same time feeling protected because she knew he cared about her and not just because it could prove to be a dangerous. The look in his eyes told her.

Bob was anxious to get moving, "I'll bring our horses up, saddles or bareback?"

"Saddles, we'll leave them away from the house so no one would hear the leather. I don't think they would anyway."

Gus and Bob left together. Ken went to his room for his revolver. Sam and Martha pulled the shades.

Lacey returned to the kitchen with the two cameras in cases.

Ken quickly came down the hallway buckling on his holster. He had also switched into a pair of moccasins.

Lacey handed him the camera he had used in the mountain for pictures.

Quietly Bob entered the house. Lacey showed him which button was for pictures only and where it would be video. He nodded and looked at Ken, he was ready to go.

As the men turned to leave, Lacey softly said his name, "Ken."

"Yes?"

She stepped closer to him and put her free arm around him. He put both of his around her and they hugged. "Be careful," she whispered.

Bob sighed and rolled his eyes, "I'll make sure he is careful if you could let go of him so we can leave," and went out the door.

Ken gave her a quick squeeze and followed Bob.

CHAPTER SIXTEEN

THE TRUTH

Sheriff Pierson and Deputy Smith stood outside the motel room Cal Berman was in. They didn't hear anything. "Ready?" The sheriff said quietly.

Deputy Smith nodded and knocked on the door.

Knowing everyone associated with the senator was at the ranch, Cal was surprised to hear someone at the door. Looking through the peephole, he saw a police officer standing there. Opening the door, "Yes, can I help you?"

"I'm Sheriff Luke Pierson, this is Deputy Smith. Are you Cal Berman, pilot for Senator Donaby?"

"Yes, is there a problem?"

Sheriff Pierson spoke, "May we come in? I have a few questions and a couple of things I would like to discuss with you."

Stepping to one side, Cal waved them in. "Would you like to sit down?"

"Over there by the table where we can all sit would be fine." The sheriff looked toward the bathroom, "Is anyone else here?"

"No."

Officer Smith went over and pushed the door open and confirmed the room was empty.

"What is this all about, has the senator or any of my family been injured?" Cal was feeling apprehensive with the unexpected visit from the local police.

"No." The sheriff removed a small recorder from his pocket and placed it on the table. "I'm going to tape our conversation for legal reasons. You are not under arrest but anything you say or reveal can be used as evidence if needed in the court of law." He then proceeded to read Cal his Miranda Rights.

Sheriff Pierson noticed the perplexed look on Cal's face.

"Miranda Rights! What's this all about? I haven't done anything illegal I can assure you. Do I need an attorney?" Cal looked at the sheriff and his deputy but their faces showed no expression.

"Sorry, I didn't mean to upset you if you want one that can be arranged. You can refuse to answer any of my questions if you wish; we are not trying to do anything to incriminate you." He reached into a pocket removing a small note book and flipped to a blank page. "We have reason to believe that Senator Donaby and others with him may have illegal controlled substances. Since you spend a lot of time with him, could you confirm this? Have you personally seen him use any type of drugs or those with him and are you aware if he or any of the others brought some with today on the plane?"

There was a long pause, "I only fly the plane, I don't check the luggage or do a personal search of those getting onto the plane. I don't want to be held responsible for the actions of the senator or his guests."

The sheriff nodded. "So noted. You do realize though transporting any drugs across state lines makes you an accomplice. But any information you can give us concerning the senator's actions will be taken in consideration."

"What? I can be an accomplice for knowing what I do, not being one of them! That's crazy!" Cal sat very still as he weighed his unwitting role in this.

"That's the law. Some kingpins don't use it and their minions sell it so they think their hands are clean, but they reap the rewards."

Leaning forward Cal put his arms on the table. "First of all, I don't want to be held accountable for anything the senator and his henchmen and friends do and I want a copy of what goes on that recorder."

The sheriff and deputy remained silent.

Cal continued, "It's ironic that you are here. As a matter of fact, I told that young mechanic at the airport that this was my last trip. I'm tired of the drugs and other activities I've seen or overheard. It's not safe even though I can close the cockpit door."

The sheriff was taking some notes even though the recorder was running. "How long have you been flying the plane for Donaby and are you the only pilot he has?"

Cal looked at both of them, feeling wary yet he didn't know why. Maybe he should wait and get an attorney "You need to know, I don't do drugs." He paused a second, then answered the sheriff. "It depends. If the senator is going on a long trip or making many stops, there are two of us. Fred, the other pilot, well his wife just had a baby and since this was a straight short flight, it was safe to pilot alone. I'm sure he would also comment on the situations that have happened while the plane was in the air."

He cleared his throat, "I've been with the senator for a year now. I retired from the military and wanted to continue flying part time. I thought this would be the ideal job, some extra money and a lot of free time because of the senator being in session. Boy, was I wrong, he has a lot of irons in the fire, all over." Cal shook his head.

The sheriff looked him straight in the eyes, "Time is of an essence, will you state with truthfulness that you personally saw people on the plane taking drugs and be willing to sign an affidavit stating that?"

Hesitating for a moment, Cal knew he was about to put himself in a difficult situation. "Telling you what I know puts me and my family in a dangerous position. One doesn't indulge anything to anybody about the senator and his life. The senator is ruthless. He has his ways. I know I shouldn't bite the hand that feeds me, but enough is enough. They were smoking so much weed that the air was terrible. They were popping pills and I know they were injecting something because they leave syringes behind at times and none of them are diabetic."

He took a deep breath and continued, "At least this time they sent the women ahead in a van, some of their activities are immoral and I bet illegal. As I said before, we usually kept the door closed. But yes, they had to bring drugs with them.

Again, I didn't actually see them carry it visibly out in the open as they got onto the plane." Cal looked with sincerity at them, "And I will sign that I have seen them using, they don't make any attempt to hide the fact they are doing drugs."

"Thanks." The sheriff clicked off the recorder and put it back into his pocket. "You've been most helpful, Mr. Berman. Don't leave town or contact anyone at the ranch. If for any reason they call you or you feel threatened, call this number." The sheriff handed him a card. "I'll be in touch with you tomorrow." He shook Cal's hand and the two officers left the room.

Back in the four-wheel drive SUV, Luke punched in Judge Robert's phone number on his cell phone. "Charles, we have the information we need to make the arrest. Drugs came across the state line. Mr. Cal Berman also has some other interesting things we may be able to use. I'll swing by and pick up that warrant. Then we are on our way to the senator's ranch."

"Okay, I'll have it ready when you get here. I want to hear what you recorded too." The judge hung up.

Then Luke called Frank to put out the call for everyone to assemble by the entrance to the lane of the old McCann ranch. They were told to leave only their parking lights on so they wouldn't be visible to anyone at the ranch. He glanced at his watch. 9:00 PM. They should all be there by 9:30 PM.

***

Ken felt his phone vibrate in his pocket. *Oh Great.* He ducked down from the window and moved away out of sight. With all the noise going on inside, it was doubtful Frank would be able to hear him. "Ken here."

"We are ready to drive in, lights will be off. You get any pics?"

"Yeah, got a real nice almost porno movie here, drinking, drugs and some moves I guess they would call dancing. The senator is in the main house with his two bodyguards and six of his cronies. The others are at the bunkhouse. If you leave the vehicles by the barn, you can have some of the men around each of the buildings and we all can go in at the same time. We will have them on drugs and prostitution. A few of the girls are being used pretty badly. I don't know if they put up with it because they are dependent on the drugs, or money. We'll find out later with the questioning, but I think they may need medical attention. And we have a lot of it on tape. You did bring the EMT's with?"

Frank came back with, "Of course, and who is we?"

"Bob Running Horse is with me. He has the videos, I've got the stills. I think that young man just got an education on the nasty side of life."

"Okay, we are coming in." The phone went dead.

Ken bent low and went back to Bob and signaled for him to follow, leading the way to the meeting area by the barn.

Luke and Frank divided all the men so the deputies, rangers, and the Indians were well balanced. The he assigned the groups to the different buildings.

"Men, my main concern is that we get the senator and his buddies, I think only the body guards will be packing, but we don't know if they are all high, drunk or what. After we read them their rights, we need to check to make sure no one is going to OD or need any other medical attention before putting them into the vans to take to jail."

Frank continued, "I'm not too concerned about the loggers, but again, we need to check for any over dose or alcohol poisoning, since they sure can drink a lot when they are in town. Now they might be ready for fist fighting. If they are combative and won't listen to reason, don't hesitate to tazer them if need be and cuff them. Once a few get subdued, the rest will quiet down. Remember before entering the building or room if that door is closed, to knock on the door and call out, 'Deputies, coming in, we have a warrant.' Let's synchronize our watches: I have five minutes to ten. At ten sharp, we go in. Now no one be a hero, just do our job. God bless and be careful."

The men quietly went to their designated areas. They waited as the minutes slowly ticked off and then, it was action time.

CHAPTER SEVENTEEN

WAITING

Sam and the two women sat around the table, cell phones in front of them and their guns close by.

Tapping her fingers on the table in an agitated drumming motion, "I don't know about you two but I am very frustrated. It has been hours since Ken and Bob left and we haven't heard one word from Ken." Lacey frowned, "And I personally think he was going a little bit overboard with his security bit with us."

Martha put her hand over Lacey's, "I think, my dear, that Ken was so afraid that something might happen to you, I should say us, that he wanted to make sure we were safe. Now, Sam has locked the door, we have our gun nearby and Shadow in the house for security. She will growl if something is amiss outside."

Sam nodded in agreement with his wife. "It wouldn't take long to have someone trying to flee arrest to hot foot it across the field to steal a horse or vehicle. And if they were desperate enough, they could be dangerous." He smiled showing a relaxed state of mind, "I sure hope they don't try getting into the barn for any of the horses. Gus has the men scattered through both of them and the garages are locked tight. I'm sure we will hear something soon. And remember, there is a chance that they won't have a warrant to go on the property."

Lacey shook her head, "I don't agree. If they didn't have enough information for Judge Roberts to issue a warrant, they would be back here by now."

Laughing Sam replied, "Oh maybe Ken and Bob joined the party."

"That's not funny, Sam. Maybe they got caught and are being knocked around. You know the caliber of person the senator and his so called associates are." Lacey was twisting and untwisting the napkin in her hand.

Looking at her watch, Martha and got up from the table, "Well, I've had enough of this sitting around discussing what if, so I'm going to make up a batch of cookies and some soup. Sam will you put veggies on the table and get Lacey a knife to cut them up? Oh yes, and a pan to put them in. I think there is some left over ham with the bone in, add that. I'll start the cookies. When the men come back, they are going to be ready to talk and eat." She took her apron off the hook, pulled her mixer closer and assembled the ingredients for the cookies. She was worried too; but it was better to keep them all busy than to sit around thinking the worse.

CHAPTER EIGHTEEN

THE BUST

At precisely ten, the deputies following their instructions from Sheriff Pierson, knocked on the doors. "Deputies, coming in, we have a warrant to enter," was heard at the bunkhouse, barns, the two guesthouses and the main house.

The men in the bunkhouse, mainly loggers, were either asleep or close to it and didn't cause any problems as they pulled on their pants and followed the officers.

The two guesthouses were occupied by the friends of the senator in the rooms, some being entertained with the 'ladies of the evening'. With the announcement of the deputies coming in, there were screams and obscenities shouted as people hustled to put on a robe or wrap a sheet around their naked bodies.

After calming them down and everyone was covered, they were read their rights before being questioned. The officers were verbally attacked at but only one offered any physical resistance.

It was at the main house where the troublemakers were at. The few rough and tumble loggers who liked to drink and fight and also the two mean body guards. They were having the time of their life having been relieved of their duties while at the ranch and no one to tell them to back off. They were busy dipping into the available drugs on the counter and manhandling the women.

As the officers announced coming in, one of the bodyguards, who had been a football player charged at the officers and was stopped by a muscled deputy with a shoulder to the midsection. They both went down with a thud, wrestling to be the one on top. The bodyguard threw a few punches at the officer. Getting the best of the man, the deputy stood up breathing heavy, pointed his finger at man on the floor, cautioned, "Stay put. You try charging again and you'll go down with the strength of the Tazer. Do you understand?"

The drunk rose up on his elbows, nodded his head, and, surrendering lay down. He wasn't use to being on this end of a fight, especially an even matched fight.

The few loggers still parting stayed where they were sitting or leaning against the bar, even as inebriated as they were, they weren't stupid. Fighting with men was one thing, but these men wore uniforms with badges and guns.

Looking around at those in the main house, Ken leaned toward Bob and whispered, "I don't see that young blond who was with the senator, the one young enough to be his daughter. She was pretty wiped out when she came out that door and then went back with one of the loggers. I wonder where she is and if she is okay: she looked like a teenager."

Searching, they found her in the back bedroom lying naked on the floor, totally unconscious. Pulling the sheet off the bed to cover her, Ken got on one knee and took her pulse. He looked over at Bob, "Go get one of the EMT's. We need the ambulance and help, her pulse is so weak I could barely get it."

As Bob went out the door, he informed the Sheriff where Ken was and his need for help. Once out on the porch, he cupped his hands and yelled, "I need a medic at the house, now!"

Ken shook his head. For all the years he had worked as a police officer in the big city and also as an undercover cop, he never got over the ruthless way humans treated one another. He had seen this type of beatings before. He could never understand why some men couldn't get aroused without cruelty. It was very obvious she had been violated.

He felt helpless but Ken didn't want to move the girl for fear of causing her more discomfort while he waited for medical help. From the looks of this young lady, she may not make it and they would have a murder charge. They not only raped her, someone had knocked her around and she was beaten to the point Ken wondered if she wouldn't need surgery if she survived. No telling how the rest of her body was affected by the blows that wasn't visible. He clinched his hands forming fists. The anger going through him made him want to go out there and give those excuse of men a taste of their own treatment. Ken took a deep breath to calm down. He wasn't the judge or the jury. Looking at her battered face feeling sick to his stomach, oh why did some men have to be cruel to enjoy sex. Unsteady as she had been the last time he saw her during surveillance, there was no way she could have defended herself.

He better find evidence to ascertain who did this terrible thing. Ken photographed where the body was and everything strewn all over the room. Putting on a pair of gloves, he pulled plastic bags from his pocket putting items in each one as evidence marking what and where it was had been located. There were needles and other drug paraphernalia. He found a few used condoms on the floor. They went into other plastic bags. The medical team came with a gurney just as he was about to put beer and wine glasses into individual bags. There had to be enough DNA on these to get the scumbags that had mistreated this young girl in such despicable manner.

As the EMT'S stabilized her, Ken looked for a purse or something to identify the Jane Doe. He could hear murmured comments from them as they got an IV in her arm and gave her oxygen.

Under the bed, he found a backpack with a billfold in it. Checking it for an ID, he saw she was only sixteen. Not good. The name on the driver's license was Charlene Hartel. Hartel. Why did that name seem familiar?

Following the medics out of the room, he took in what was going on in the main room. People were lined up or sitting on chairs depending on how drunk or high they were and being questioned. He saw other deputies or rangers collecting different items for evidence in that room too.

Sheriff Pierson joined Ken at the bedroom door. "I just saw them take the girl out. Her face was battered pretty bad! We need to find out which monster did that."

"Luke, I've got evidence here in bags and I took pictures first of her position and every article I picked up. I think we will have more than one man on rape charge and according to her driver's license she is only sixteen. Her last name is Hartel, I've heard before, but can't place it. Familiar with you?"

"I think there is a news reporter down in Reno with that name." Luke replied as he jotted a few things in a notebook.

"That's it." Ken made the connection, "Lacey has an article where the senator was roughed up, and that name was on there. I can get it from her. I wonder if this is his daughter, why is she here, you think payback time? I have a gut feeling she isn't here by choice." He shook his head, "But a minor, that is jail time."

"I don't think the senator expected to get caught." Luke sighed rubbing his eyes, "Let's take all the women to town, we want to talk with them separately after they have had time to sober up or come down from whatever they took." Then he smiled, "Guess we better have the nurse bring in a few more urine specimen bottles too. We are going to keep the lab busy."

As the people were assembled and being put into vans for the trip into town, be it the hospital or jail, Ken looked over the faces. He didn't locate the one logger he met before, the one afraid of the mountain spirit. He shook his head; maybe he was in the first vehicle that left.

CHAPTER NINETEEN

GUNNER

The noise was getting to him. Gunner let his feet flop down from the chair. If he was lucky, he could find a place to sleep that didn't have snores so loud it sounded like a buck saw or someone puking up a storm from the booze or drugs. He walked unsteady with his hand on the wall as he made his way to the door. In the corner was an old milk can holding some walking sticks. He grabbed one.

Once outside on the porch he looked with bleary eyes where to go. Then he remembered there was a cot in the tack room by the empty horse stalls. Weaving his way over the rough ground, he was almost there when he heard the sound of motors. Leaning against the side of the barn, he peered into the night and made out vehicles. Knowing everyone was at the party, whoever was coming up the lane with their lights out wasn't good.

He looked back at the house, should he warn the senator? Nah, there was no way he could navigate his way back to the house before whoever was out there got to the yard. Plus, he had no idea where the senator was.

No more had he closed the tack room door then he heard some talking outside. He backed tight against the wall hoping if anyone opened the door, they wouldn't look behind it.

"Deputies coming in!"

The door opened but not enough to hit him. He held his breath as a flashlight beamed around the dark room.

"No one here, let's join the rest of the men, they sound pretty busy at the main house."

The door closed and Gunner let out the huge breath he had been holding. *Should he stay put or try to leave? Where to go? That ranch across the field? If he could get there, they had horses.* He didn't like horses, but he could take one and make it to where the rigs were by the edge of the forest. They, whoever they were wouldn't look for him over there.

Opening the door a crack, he carefully looked out. Vehicles had pulled up into the yard. An ambulance, vans, plus sheriff vehicles were parked in the yard and surrounding field. No one should be by the four wheelers. He knew he left a rifle on one of them. No way was he going to be out there in the dark without a gun. Slipping out the door, he carefully made his way behind the building and retrieved the weapon. Putting the strap over his shoulder to keep his hand free, he used the walking stick to steady himself. *Would he even be able to make it that far? My head is throbbing, man, I could use a drink and I really need to lie down.* He looked around, he feared the police more than whatever might be out there in the dark. No way did he want to be arrested; he was still on parole and shouldn't be drinking. He stumbled, caught himself and started walking.

What should have been a fifteen-minute walk took him almost forty-five minutes. He kept stumbling and trying to walk in a straight path. The sweat was pouring off him even though the night air was cool. He kept looking behind him; he didn't see anyone or feel anything. *Did that spirit come this far from the mountain?*

Stopping to catch his breath, licking his dry lips, he crawled between the bars on the wooden fence. He looked around the Swenson buildings. Something wasn't right. No lights were on, all the doors were closed on the out buildings. No matter, he could hot-wire that red truck over there. He patted his pocket; yeah his jack knife was there.

Inside the house, Shadow stood next to the door and whined, then let out a low growl.

Sam walked over to the dog and patted her on the head, "Good girl. Someone out there?" Shadow wagged her tail.

"Turn off that small light and I'll raise that shade a bit and take a look." Sam made his rounds peering through the windows. He couldn't see anything. He had resisted putting in those big motion sensor yard lights when everyone else did, maybe it was time. He debated if he should risk calling the bunkhouse for Gus, but was afraid in the still night that the sound might reach whoever was out there. He'd wait until someone tried to break in.

***

Ken walked up to the sheriff as the last of the people were put into the vans. "Luke, Bob and I need to take our horses back to the Swenson Ranch. I'll get my truck and we can come in and help with the questioning."

"No need to, Ken. You write up the report detailing what you heard and saw. We have the samples you collected. It's going to be some time to sort out everything and get their signed statements. Come in tomorrow sometime. Check with Frank, he is working with us tonight. And, I want to commend you two for your work. As for those pictures, I need a copy of everything. Night." He shook the men's hands and left for his vehicle. It was going to be a long night.

"Let's get our horses, I don't know about you but I'm hungry too." Ken began walking back where they left them. "So, Bob, do want to trade in your airplane mechanic license for a deputy badge?"

"No man. It made me sick to see how those men treated the women." He shook his head causing his braids to swing, "Animals don't treat their kind like that. At least when I work on a motor, I may get greasy, but I can wash that off. Those men and women can't wash away their dirt." He swung up onto his horse in one easy motion.

Patting Winner on the muzzle, Ken also got on his horse. "Why not ride over to Sam's with me. You can stay overnight or I can put your horse in the trailer and drive you over to your place. I don't want you riding out there at night."

"Yeah, I think staying at Sam's is a good thing. Besides, I think we should go over what's on the cameras. I don't think Lacey should be looking at that low life. She's a lady. I have to be at the airport tomorrow, so maybe Sam can let me take his Jeep into town. The sheriff said he'd call me there if he needs me for anything."

Each in their own thought, the men rode in silence the sound of the horse's hoofs muffled by the sod. About three blocks away from Sam's, they heard a shot ring out. Touching heels to the horses they raced toward the buildings.

Ken's heart was racing as fast as his horse was galloping. If anything happened to Lacey…

The porch light went on as did the one on the bunkhouse. The men reined in their horses by Ken's truck where Gus had a gun trained on the man who called himself Gunner. The man was lying very still on the ground. Shadow, growling, had her teeth in the man' pant leg. Sam was coming down the steps with his rifle in his hands. Martha stood in the doorway with the shotgun. Lacey was peering over her shoulder.

Stepping down from Winner, Ken asked, "What do we have here?"

"Make the dog let go of me. I don't like dogs." Gunner pleaded, his words still slurred from his over imbibing.

"Come, Shadow," Sam held out his hand and the dog released her hold and wagging her tail went to Sam who knelt down and petted her. "Good girl."

"Well," Gus spoke up in his usual lone tone of voice, "I decided to sit by the window and keep a watch on your truck. Everything else is locked up and we'd hear if someone was breaking in. I figured since we were the closest ranch, if anyone got away, they would head here." Gus paused and pointed at the man, "I could barely make out this dude in the dark, but I called Sam and told him to let Shadow outside. If someone was there, we'd sure know it when she barked and we could put on the lights."

Spitting on the ground, Gus's voice was hard, "He shot at Shadow, good thing he missed."

Ken pulled out his phone and called Luke. "I've got Gunner, one of the loggers here at Sam's place. He was trying to get my new truck started. I sure hope he didn't scratch it. So, where do you want me to take him?"

"What kind of shape is he in?"

"From the smell, he's put away a lot of booze." Ken replied.

Luke sighed, "Well, handcuff him if you need to and bring him in to the jail, he doesn't need any medical help does he?"

"No, don't think so, maybe a couple of aspirin in the morning."

"Okay, then see if Martha has a small clean jar and have our runaway pee in it. Time and date it. We are checking for drugs too. Don't feed him anything so we can test his breath. See you when you get here and thanks again." The phone went silent.

Ken looked down at the man, "Well, Gunner, the sheriff wants a urine sample and then we take you into town."

"I got money, man. Just forget I was here, I'll make it worth your while." Gunner was sweating in the cool night air.

"No way, plus, if I say anything to the sheriff, you could be charged with attempting to bribe a ranger." Ken turned his head toward Sam, "Can you get me a clean jar and lid? I need to take the urine specimen in with Gunner."

"Can do." Sam cradling his rifle walked with Shadow to the house and returned shortly with the jar, shutting the door to the women as he left.

Gunner gave his sample.

Bob leaned over to Ken, "I can ride in with you and spend the night at a cousin's home, that way I'll be there in time for work too. I'll get my horse later."

Nodding his head Ken replied, "Thanks, Bob, I appreciate that. Gus, would you put up Winner and Apache for us? Thanks for your aid in apprehending Gunner. Good job. I'll let the sheriff know it was you. Would you stay here with him, I need to go to the house for a minute."

"Yep, no problem. He lays still, I don't shoot."

Ken hurried to the house where Lacey was waiting in the doorway. She raised up her arms to greet him with a hug. He lowered his head kissing her warmly.

"I was so worried about you, are you okay?" Lacey stayed in his arms.

"Yes. We need to make copies of the pictures for the sheriff. Could I just take the cameras in with me and do it there. I really don't want you to see the ugliness of we humans." He hugged her.

"Okay. Are you hungry, we made some soup and cookies?" She still didn't move from his arms.

"I'll eat when I get back, don't wait up though; I don't know how long all of this will take." He kissed her on the nose. Waving bye to Sam and Martha, he went back to the men.

After unhitching the horse trailer from the Sierra, Ken put handcuffs on Gunner and settled him into the back seat of the truck. He locked the handcuffs into the holder that was installed for that reason. He never thought in a hundred years, he would need to use it.

As Ken was buckling his own seatbelt, Martha came quickly down the steps with a thermos in one hand and a small sack in the other. She reached up to Bob's window, "Here my boy, a little soup and some cookies. Ken said he'd eat when he returned, but I can't let you go away hungry." She blew him a kiss.

"Thank you, Martha."

Ken put the truck into gear, the clock on the dash said 1:00 AM.

CHAPTER TWENTY

THE JAIL

After leaving Bob at his cousin's home, Ken drove the few blocks to the jail. Once inside he took Gunner to the processing area. There Gunner had a breathalyzer done and Ken handed over the jar with the urine sample.

Leaving Gunner with the deputy, Ken figured he might as well make out his report now since he was here and get it over with while everything was fresh in his mind. He received permission to use one of the empty offices.

After filling out his report, he made a copy for himself and then printed off the pictures from the camera. He felt angry looking at them and to think those misfits thought they were having fun. Not sure how to download the video, he would have someone else do that.

Rubbing his eyes he leaned his head back against the chair.

"Trying to catch twenty winks?" Luke laughed as he entered the room. "I'd say it's time you went home."

Ken glanced at his watch. It was 4:00 AM. "Sounds good to me, I didn't realize it was this late." He tapped the folder on the desk. "That's my report and the pictures we took before you got there and the ones I took in the room Charlene was in.

The video camera here," he pointed with his finger, "I don't know how to unload and make copies."

"No problem. I'll have the morning shift do it and then Lacey can have her camera back. Tell her I'll take good care of it." Luke yawned, "We made our arrests with no one getting hurt tonight. I still have a few things to do, but you better go home and get some sleep." Luke shook Ken's hand and left the room with the camera and folder.

Picking up his jacket, Ken shut off the lights, went down the hall and signed out. Ken thought it was time to call it a night. Looking at his watch maybe he should call it morning.

***

In the crowded holding cell, no one noticed as Senator Donaby slowly sidled over next to Gunner. Leaning close he whispered, "You and most of the boys will be let out on bail, probably on a signature bond. I want you to take those men up to the forest and start cutting trees. Load them up at night and move them so they aren't seen to the place we discussed." Donaby cautiously looked around then continued, "I need the money from that sale to pay all of your wages and my bail money. Don't say anything about this until you see which guys go back to the ranch and are willing to work." He paused once more checking to make sure no one was eaves dropping, he spoke in a menacing growl. "Don't mess up, I won't be happy."

The senator moved away from Gunner hoping he wasn't so drunk he wouldn't remember exactly what he told him to do. He needed Gunner since he was the one who knew all the machines and how to keep them running.

Gunner let his head hang down. Now what? If the police do a check on him, not just let him go since he wasn't caught doing anything, they will know he is out on probation (thanks to the senator's actions) and he wasn't supposed to be drinking. Geeze, the law on one side and Donaby on the other. He feared Donaby more than the police. He knew what the senator was capable of doing. What if some of the guys decided to split and the others go along with the senator's orders? Would they get paid either way? He licked his lips. He could use a drink.

***

Shadow wagged her tail as Ken quietly entered the house. Ken was surprised Sam and Martha weren't up, they usually were at five in the morning.

Light from a lamp in the living room caused Ken to glance in and see Lacey asleep in the recliner covered up with a multicolored afghan. She looked so peaceful.

As he leaned down to shut off the lamp, he felt the warmth of her hand move up his arm.

"Are you okay? I waited up for you, but guess I fell asleep." Lacey yawned, "Hungry?"

Kneeling down by the side of her chair, he leaned over and kissed her. "Just tired. You should have gone to bed."

She smiled at him through still sleepy eyes, "You know me, I'm so nosy about what transpired last night and I was worried about you."

They both jumped when Sam spoke, "Yep, Martha and I would like to know what went on too."

Before Sam could say anymore he was interrupted by two raps on the door. "That would be Gus. Time for breakfast, then you can fill us all in on last night." Sam went to open the door as Martha took a clean apron out of the drawer and put it on.

Ken gave a huge yawn and knew it would be awhile before he would be getting any sleep. As he went down the hall to take a shower, he could hear Martha getting things ready to whip up a batch of cornbread and cooked some oatmeal with a handful of raisins in it.

The four were seated around the table with mugs of hot coffee when Ken entered the kitchen. His hair was still damp; he was wearing jeans, a tee shirt and moccasins and although he was clean, he was looking very tired. He sniffed the air.

"It sure smells good in here. I didn't realize how hungry I was." He took a seat next to Lacey who put her arm around his and briefly leaned her head against his shoulder.

The others exchanged knowing glances; those two were sweet on each other.

Sam filled a mug with coffee and slid it over to Ken as Martha placed a plate filled with slices of cornbread on the table and dished up bowls of the oatmeal.

Ken's stomach growled as he added brown sugar and milk on his oatmeal and stirred it around, then smothered a slice of the cornbread with butter and took a huge bite. "Um, um good! I'm so hungry. Thank you Martha."

She smiled at him. She liked cooking and nothing made her feel better than for people to enjoy it.

Lacey ate small bites of her breakfast but was having a hard time holding back with all of her questions about the arrest.

So far the discussion around the table had to do with ranching, the garden and the horses. They were giving Ken time to relax and eat.

After his second bowl of oatmeal and more cornbread with honey drizzled over it, Ken leaned back in the chair with a sigh of contentment. It had been a very long time since his last meal.

Lacey couldn't wait any longer. "Okay, what happened last night? What about that guy trying to hot wire your truck. Where's my cameras? Did Bob get to his cousins okay?" The sentences rapidly shot out of her.

Ken took a drink of his coffee and looked at her over the rim. "One, we arrested a lot of people. Two, Gunner's in jail. Three, your camera is in the truck, the sheriff has the video one, and he needs to make a copy." He looked around the table, "I don't know if any of you would be called in for jury duty so I'm not sure how much I can share with you."

Sam spoke up, "Considering we are such a small community and everyone knows everybody, I think this trial will go to the country seat. Plus since we were all instrumental in getting those arrests, I think it will be okay to talk about it." He peered over at Lacey with a kidding smile, "Unless you planned on writing up everything we say at this table for the newspaper or magazine."

Lacey shook her head no.

Ken nodded. He gave them what he knew without being graphic about Charlene's condition.

They were silent, digesting what he had told them.

"Lacey, do you remember a reporter by the name of Hartel? You know, that one that had the photo and article on the senator being roughed up in Reno?"

She nodded. "Yes, I think the reporter made some reference to the thugs being employed by the casino where it was standard practice to remind those that owed them some money they better get that bill paid, and quick. Why?"

Ken slowly shook his head and with a quiet voice, "I think it is his daughter that was beaten and raped to the point I don't know if she is going to make it. When I found her she was unconscious and barely breathing. I checked the suitcase under the bed and in the wallet was a driver's license with that name on it. My gosh, she is only sixteen. Just a kid and she is small for her age too. We don't know how or why she was there." He sighed deeply. "I don't remember the address on the license and I have no right to do anything about it. I'm going to call the department and see if the parents have been notified and who they are. I'm sure the sheriff and judge will be very interested. Also, that poor girl shouldn't be alone. She needs someone there with her. Even if she is unconscious, she will know someone cares about her."

They were startled when Ken hit his fist into his other hand. "You have NO idea what I'd like to do to that scumbag senator!"

His voice was so full of anger, even when he had told them how his wife and unborn child died; he didn't express himself in this explosive manner. Those in the room shared glances.

Martha immediately left her chair and with her motherly way

put her hands on his shoulders and began to lightly massage them. "Ken, you are exhausted, angry and need to do something. I understand totally. I think you will feel better if you call the jail and talk with someone there to see if the parents were called and who they are. Then call the hospital and get an update on the young lady. After that, I want you to walk out to the corral and give Winner a brushing. I think you might be able to rest after that. Get some needed sleep and then with a clear mind you will know what to do next." She squeezed his shoulders gently and went back to her chair.

Lacey's voice was also had a calming tone. "Martha's got the right idea. Call the Sheriff's office and the hospital. I think I'll go and have my leg checked and see about staying with Charlene for awhile until we find out when her parents can get here. I know how it felt to be alone." She smiled at Ken. "Thank goodness this town isn't so large we can't volunteer in cases like this."

"Yep," Sam stood up, "I agree with the ladies. "Make those calls, and then we can know what direction we take. Me or Gus can drive Lacey into town."

"Thanks." Ken went to the phone on the wall and entered the jail number. He stated his questions, listen, and thanked them. Turning to his waiting friends, "We were correct, that reporter is her dad and they are on their way. They are driving and it should be about twelve hours before they get here. Sheriff Luke has gone home for some needed sleep. Now to check with the hospital."

Looking up the number, he placed the call. A receptionist answered the phone. He explained who he was and his reason for calling. All the receptionist could tell him was the young lady was in intensive care.

Lacey glanced at the wall clock. 6:45 AM. "Guess it's time for you to talk with Winner then get some rest. I'm going to clean up and call the doctor to see if he can't put on a lighter cast that I can use a cane to walk with instead of these clumsy crutches and get permission to sit with the young lady for awhile."

Ken walked over and kissed her. "You're right." He left the house for the barn with Shadow tagging along next to him. Ken reached down and patted the collie on the head. Animals are such great comforters.

CHAPTER TWENTY-ONE

THE HOSPITAL

Dr. Martin watched as the nurse helped Lacey step on the new walking cast. "That cane needs lowered one more notch. If you use it at that height, you will injure your arm."

Lacey stood still as the nurse adjusted the cane. Handing it to her, Lacey took a few steps; she gave them both a smile. "You're absolutely right, it is much better this way. Such a relief for a lighter cast too."

"Now, Dr. Martin, if you would be so kind as to call ICU giving me permission to sit with Charlene, I can make my way up there." Lacey held her breath hoping he wouldn't change his mind and say no.

Rubbing his chin thoughtfully, Dr. Martin looked at Lacey. "She is in bad shape, you need to put your leg up, are you sure this isn't going to be too much for you to do?"

"Dr. Martin, I thank you for your concern for me, but I'm doing fine. This young lady isn't and she is alone. I remember how I felt when they were bringing me in and Ken came with me. Just knowing he was there in the waiting room, meant so much to me. And doctor, he was a stranger, but he gave me strength and calmed my fear. To Charlene, I will be a stranger, but one who cares and she won't be alone. When her parents get here, I will leave, I promise." Lacey put up three fingers, "Scouts honor."

Reaching for the phone, he turned, "But, you will let the nurse give you a ride in the wheel chair up there so you don't overdo it with this new cast on."

Lacey nodded.

Arriving at the Intensive Care Unit, Lacey was greeted by everyone working there. She knew them all from growing up in the area.

Betty, the nurse gave a small assessment as to Charlene's injuries. Then she had Lacey wash her hands and put on a gown and walked with her into Charlene's room.

Lacey's heart ached, as she looked at the young girl, so pale and unresponsive. There was a bandage over her nose, so Lacey assumed that had been broken too, her eyes were closed. Her swollen face was black and blue.

Thankfully, the teenager was heavily sedated. She had fractured ribs and surgery had been performed for a damaged spleen and on her torn female parts.

The nurse pulled the footstool from under the bed and slid it by the big chair that Lacey could sit in. "Don't stand to long, Lacey, you still need to stay off your feet for awhile."

Lacey nodded, lightly touching Charlene's hand began to talk softly to her, not knowing if in that deep drugged subconscious if she could hear or not. "Charlene, my name is Lacey. I grew up on a ranch not far from here. I just want you to know that you aren't alone. I'll stay here until your parents arrived later today." Gently with a light touch, Lacey rubbed

Charlene's hand.

Silently Lacey prayed for a swift healing for the girl, not only her body but also her mind. Lacey couldn't fathom how this young girl would process the assault on her body considering Jean Conway was struggling with what she went through and was older.

Pulling the chair closer so she could keep her hand touching Charlene, Lacey sat down and put her foot up. She knew Betty would be keeping an eye on both of them and report to Dr. Martin if she didn't stay off the foot.

Talking as though Charlene was listening, Lacey had all positive things to say. "I have a many friends especially some of my Indian ones who believe in imaging any injured body parts healing. I'm going to do that for you and you can do it too. You don't have to say anything out loud just visualize it."

Lacey would hum and talk about things in general. The nurses brought her in some water, tea and a sandwich. Once more, the nurses also checked the machines, put up another bottle of fluids and one of blood. They gently moved her and made other adjustments. Charlene never uttered a sound, not even a groan.

Lacey waited until the nurses were done assessing Charlene. "I want to thank you again for the sandwich and tea, I really appreciated it. Would there happen to be any books out there I could read to Charlene?"

"I'm sure there are some in the waiting room I can get you. Anything in particular?" The nurse inquired.

Lacey smiled, "Something a sixteen year old would like, something light, but please, none of those vampire books that are out now." She rolled her eyes.

It wasn't long and the nurse returned with a couple of books and a few magazines.

Lacey picked up the book *Horse Whisper* and began to read it aloud. She would stop after every chapter, get up, and move around the bed, talking to Charlene and telling her she was getting better.

This also was good for Lacey's leg, since it also was healing much faster that Dr. Martin thought it would.

This was how Mona and Richard Hartel first saw their injured daughter. A strange lady with a cast on her own leg, talking quietly as she gently touched their daughter's arm, telling her that every moment she was getting better.

The couple hand and hand slowly approached the bed, wanting to see their daughter yet afraid of what they would find. They both shook their heads in disbelief.

Lacey stepped away from the bed as the couple came closer.

Tears flowed down Mona's face as she gently touched her daughter's shoulder, "Charlene, Mom and Dad are here now. Everything is going to be okay. I love you." She leaned over and lightly kissed her daughter on the bruised cheek.

There was no response from her daughter, just the sound of the machines as they beeped and lights showed as they preformed their scheduled duty.

Lacey spoke quietly, "I'm Lacey McCann. I'm glad you are here.

Both parents nodded, "Thank you."

Richard's jaw was clenched tight as he looked down at his bandaged daughter. She looked so small and fragile lying there. "We're here, so rest, Sweet Pea, every things going to be okay." He looked over at his wife and walked out the door and down the hall devastated at the condition those swine put his little girl in.

Lacey followed him and found him leaning with his hands and head against the wall. He looked over at her. "What kind of animals does the senator get to do things like this to a young girl? I could kill him with my bare hands!" He hissed out the words of the last sentence.

"That's what we are investigating."

Lacey and Richard both jumped since they didn't hear Sheriff Pierson and Ken approach.

Richard began sobbing, "It's entirely my fault!" He hit his fist against the wall. "The senator warned me if I printed anything in the paper about his gambling debt, I'd be sorry. I thought maybe I'd get a rock through my car window, but I never expected he would kidnap my little girl."

Ken and Luke exchanged looks: kidnapping, drugs, underage, sexual and physical abuse.

The sheriff put his hand on Richard's shoulder, "Come over here and have a chair. I know you have been driving a long time, but we need to talk a little more. According to the police report, it said a possible runaway."

Richard shook his head, "No, no running away. She got off the school bus two blocks from our home. The goons picked her up. We got the call they had her and we should get some big money ready to cough up, they would call us later where to leave it and if we didn't, we wouldn't see her again." He looked at them all, "My God, I'm a reporter; I don't pull down big money. They called twenty-four hours later asking for $50,000.00. I asked for more time so I could get to the bank and borrow some money using our house for collateral. They put Charlene on the phone and her voice was all slurry. She was crying 'Daddy, they keep giving me drugs; I want to come home, Daddy! Daddy!' They gave me another day's reprieve to get the money. I didn't hear anything from them and then I got your call she saying she needed surgery and would I give consent for it."

The sheriff spoke, "We have him in custody, and there is no way he is getting out on bail. After you spend some time with your daughter and are settled into a motel room, would you come down to the courthouse where our jail is and give a deposition and sign it? I do have one more question: why didn't you call the police?"

Richard had this lost look on his face, "They said they would kill her and I had no idea where she was. I thought if I could get them the money." He looked at the sheriff, "I know it was stupid to think a crook would keep his word." Richard straightened up; the tone of his voice was like cold steel, "I'll do anything you need to get his hide nailed to the wall. I don't suppose this state hangs scumbags like this?"

Mona came up to them, "Is everything okay, Richard?"

"Yes dear, just filling the sheriff in with what we know." He put his arm around his wife, pulling her close to him, trying to shield her from more irritation.

Lacey pointed at Luke, "Mrs. Hartel, this is Sheriff Piersen the man who led the arrest team, and the other gentleman is Ranger Ken Dickinson, the man who found Charlene and assisted with the investigation."

Both men shook her hand and expressed their sympathy.

"Thank you." Embarrassed and upset, she looked over at her husband, "Richard, I'm going back by our girl." Without saying another word, Mona turned and retraced her steps to Charlene's room.

"Lacey, are you ready to go back to Sam's?" Ken looked down at her with tenderness in his eyes.

Lacey nodded. "Yes, I need to pick up my things back in the room and say good-bye to Charlene and her mother.

The two slowly walked down the hall while Richard stayed back and conversed some more with the sheriff.

Lacey went to the bedside and touching Charlene's hand, "I'm going home now, Charlene. Your mom and dad are here."

Mona grateful to this young woman and her compassion, "I'm sorry; I don't remember your name."

"I'm Lacey McCann." She pointed at the cast on her leg. "I recently had an accident and had a stranger stay with me which I appreciated. I just didn't want Charlene to be alone until you could get here."

Lacey gave Mona a hug, "I'll come back tomorrow if it is okay with you."

"Yes, please do and thank you." Tears came to Mona's eyes.

Ken picked up Lacey's things and they left for home. It had been a long day for everyone.

CHAPTER TWENTY-TWO

QUIET

One Ear licked his tongue once more around his mouth making sure it was clean from his meal. If mountain lions could smile, he was smiling. He had gorged his empty stomach on the deer he took down and now he was ready to doze.

The sun was warm on his body as he looked over the area where the huge monsters remained quiet. He felt a surge of power as he remembered leaping out at the small noisy contraption that the two-legged animal narrowly escaped on. Maybe now they understand that this is his mountain and to stay away.

Perched on the tree limb, his world peaceful, slowly he closed his eyes in slumber, letting his large meal digest.

***

His chair tipped back against the wall, Gunner looked at the five men in the room. He still couldn't believe his luck. Of all the men arrested, the six of them were the only ones who didn't test positive for drugs or have their DNA on that poor kid. He shook his head. He had done things in his life he wasn't proud of, but abusing a young girl that was drugged wasn't for him.

The judge put them on house arrest until the trial is held, they were witnesses, but not dangerous. If they left the ranch for any reason, they will sit out the rest of the time in the crowded cells. They were all wearing those GPS ankle bracelets as they called them. The only reason Gunner wasn't sent back for drinking and violating his parole was because he would be a witness.

Now he was sweating it out. The senator gave him orders to cut trees. The trees were on the national forest and they didn't have a permit. Cut trees and get arrested, federal charges. Don't cut trees and he doesn't get paid and the senator would make his life miserable or have it snuffed out. That man had his ways and Gunner wasn't sure how he would accomplish it but he had seen too much of how the senator worked that he didn't doubt for a minute Gunner would end up like that little blond girl, in the hospital or the morgue.

Turning his head, he looked out the window and wondered if that ranger fellow was watching them. He had to admit, the guy might wear a badge, but he was fair.

Letting the chair fall down on all four legs with a thud, Gunner spoke up. "I need to talk with you boys."

They put down their cards and looked over at him. It was obvious Gunner had been very quiet and upset ever since their release.

Gunner's voice was gruff. "We have a problem. How many of you want paid for being here?"

Buster a loner whose real name was Jackson, spoke up. "Why yah asking a dumb question like that. I don't know about the rest of the guys but I didn't come out here for the fresh air and scenery."

Gunner splayed his huge hands on the table and slowly looked at each one of them. "Well, if you want paid you might want to think about your choices. First, let me tell you the senator doesn't have a permit to cut trees on this area of the mountain. Second, if we do cut any, we will be arrested and fined, as it is a federal offense. Third, if we don't, we won't get paid and the senator told me in no uncertain terms, if I don't get wood cut and delivered, my body parts are going to be rearranged." He wiped his hand across his mouth and wondered if it was safe to sneak a drink or not.

"We'd have to cut them down and get them out at night so we wouldn't get caught and call in another driver to haul them out," he shook his head, "I don't know if we could do it."

"Shoot," Buster laughed, "We can get a driver out here on the sly, there is always someone who will work for cash under the table. We can fill one truck and then lalagag around here all innocent and all." He looked at the rest of the men around the table, "You guys in?"

"There's one more thing I didn't tell you." Gunner licked his lips, "The mountain is haunted by spirits, sometime they come in the shape of a mountain lion."

His face got red as the men hooted and hollered at his expense.

Gunner waited in silence while the men enjoyed teasing about him being a sissy. "You can laugh all you want. Even the Indians say it's dangerous if logs are taken off the mountain for the wrong reason."

Buster still thought it was funny that Gunner was scared, he could see it in his face and hear it in his voice. Gunner? The meanest fighter of them all? He snickered.

Ignoring Buster, Gunner continued, "I was there late one day checking to make sure all the machines were good to go, oiled up and all. Some of you might remember you left early. When I went to leave, it was getting dark and for some reason my four-wheeler didn't start. I fiddled with it a bit and just as it took off; something jumped and just missed me. I didn't look back, just gave that machine all the gas I could. But I felt the hot breath on my neck and it had a stinky smell."

The men sobered up and were silent, each in their own thoughts. They knew Gunner wasn't one to exaggerate or lie. To work in the dark was asking for injuries, even with some battery-operated lights. Was there a spirit of the mountain, one that would kill?

Would greed win out or the fear of arrest?

CHAPTER TWENTY-THREE

THE STRUGGLE

Quickly Jean rose from the beige couch and moved away from her husband and stood stiff by the window. "I can't do it, Phil! I can't! Don't ask me!"

Slowly, Phil followed and put his arm around her shoulders.

Shrugging off his arm, Jean moved away. "I told you Phil to leave me alone. I'm no good anymore. Go back home."

The nurse stood watching from the doorway of Jean's bedroom. Alice, Jean's sister listened from the dining room.

"Jean, don't you understand if you testify what that evil man and his body guards did to you, we can have him locked up for the rest of his life, never able to harm anyone again. Please, Jean. That girl is only sixteen. Sixteen." Exasperated Phil rubbed his hand through his hair.

Whirling around to face her husband, Jean had a shocked look on her face. "You, you," she spit the words out, "You actually want me to sit in a court room full of people with cameras and tell the world what they did to me! The humiliation, I could never look anyone in the face again. It would ruin our magazine. Think about the bad publicity."

Leaving her unobserved spot in the dining room, Alice slowly approached her sister. Gripping her hands on Jean's shoulders in a firm hold, "I've watched you lay around eating tranquilizers like candy, talking with your shrink; acting like the world has come to an end. Well, my dear, I'm sorry this happened to you, but you are alive, you have a husband who loves you dearly and it is time to stop this pity party and do something. You or no one else can undo what happened to you. This is your time for some legal revenge. Not just for you, but that young girl who is lying unconscious in the hospital. I love you dearly, and having you here to help you get through your traumatic time was what sister's do."

Alice loosened her hold on Jean's shoulders, her voice softer, "Now, Jean, it's your time to step up to the plate for someone else." She pulled Jean into her arms and held her tight. "You can do it, Jean. Phil and I will be there with you."

The nurse approached them, "Mrs. Wilson, you mustn't talk to Mrs. Conway that way. It's upsetting. I'm going to call the doctor."

"Well, she did and she's right." Phil joined them. "I have been calling a couple of times a day, sending you flowers and cards declaring my love for you, coming here and you refused to see me, and even now you have turn away from me. Jean, darn it, we grew up on the same block, dated in high school, we went college together and took over the magazine when dad died. I love you so much, you are my Jean and nothing and nobody can take that away from me. Now, go look in that mirror, see that Jean I fell in love with twenty years ago, and tell me that she still has that grit and spunk to change things in the world. You will be that girl's hero!" He held out his arms to her.

Jean walked into them and began to sob. She cried out all the anger, fear, being ashamed of her assault, and feeling so alone and empty inside.

Phil held her tight and looked over at Alice who smiled and the nurse who knew this assignment was over.

Exhausted from crying having let all the emotions out, Jean leaned back and straightened up her shoulders, "Okay, Phil, now what do I do?"

"Come home. We need to call the sheriff and see if we can help that girl. We can also see Lacey. Oh my God how I've missed you." Phil hugged her tight, feeling her soft hair against his check, the warmth of her body against his.

Joining them in a group hug, Alice added, "I'll help you pack. We need to call your doctor and cancel the nurses." She looked over at Phil, "How many days will we be gone so I know how much I need to pack? Oh, and do they have any decent places to stay?"

"First I think we should give the sheriff a call, I have his number, and then I'll call Lacey and ask her those other questions. We may only have to give your testimony to the sheriff and we press charges and go back later for the trial if you are called as a witness." Phil gave a warm smile to Jean, "And I think a visit to that young lady from you would be so beneficial for her recovery, if she survives."

Arm and arm Phil and Jean walked over to the phone. She felt so safe and secure with him here by her side. Why did it take a young woman being treated worse than she was to make her want to fight and put that man away behind bars for the rest of his life.

CHAPTER TWENTY-FOUR

SOME POSITIVES

Charlene could hear her mother's voice coming through a long tunnel. "Honey, dad and I are here, you will be fine."

Where was here? Her body hurt. She was cold. Was she dead and her mom and dad were at the funeral home?

Charlene tried to open her eyes, but it was too much work. Then she felt that gentle touch on her hand and arm and the voice that had been with her when she was so alone.

Lacey spoke with a soft but cheerful voice, "You are looking so much better today, Charlene. I told you praying and imagining your recovery would work."

That was the voice and touch of her angel. Charlene wondered if her angel wore white soft wings. Oh, she needed to open her eyes to see her.

"Richard, Richard, look! Her eyelids fluttered! Charlene honey, open your eyes." Mona was so excited to see some signs of life from her only child.

Slowly Charlene blinked a few times and finally her still swollen, blood shot eyes opened. She tried to focus and slowly the blurred faces cleared and she could see her smiling parents. She tried to raise the one arm that wasn't wrapped but it was too much work.

"Angel," was the only word her hoarse barely audible voice uttered, and then she closed her eyes and drifted off into the first restful sleep in days. *Everything was okay. Mom, dad and her special angel were here and she was safe.*

***

Ken's cell phone rang and he pulled Winner to a stop. Glancing down he saw it was from Sheriff Pierson. "Hi Luke, what's up?"

"You aren't going to believe the phone call I just received from the Conway's. Mrs. Conway has agreed to give us an affidavit about her sexual assault from the senator and his thugs, plus they have pictures. Hopefully we can have her testimony done with a closed court room, the same as for Charlene if she makes it. Mr. Conway said they will be arriving tomorrow. He will let us know where they will be staying."

Ken smiled, "Great news. Can I share that with Lacey and the Swenson's?"

Winner turned his head and looked at his rider. He could feel the good vibes.

Luke chuckled, "Considering it was Lacey that got Mr. Conway to open up to us, and he mentioned they were calling her next, I don't think that is going to be a problem. Oh by the way, are you keeping an eye on the Senator's ranch to see if any of the men wanted to take a walk?"

Turning Winner to go back toward the ranch, Ken replied,

"Matter of fact, I was just checking out the area where all the big machinery is. No sign of anything here. But, I think you ought to know that some of Bob Running Horse's tribe are keeping an eye on the place. They are out of sight, but no one is going in or out of that ranch without them knowing it. By the way, are any of them deputized?"

Luke chuckled. "Well you know, they would be watching the ranch if they were deputized or not. We have an agreement, they watch and if they see anything unusual or anyone trying to sneak off, they give you or me a call. They aren't to do anything else nor try to stop them. They charge nothing for this and the county provides the steer and hog for their fall celebration. So, no, they aren't deputized." Luke sighed, "I wish more people felt this type of respect for Mother Nature. Well, gotta go." The phone went silent.

Ken placed his phone back in his shirt pocket. He was anxious to see if Lacey was back and how Charlene was doing. He wondered if Mr. Conway had called her.

As Ken rode away, One Ear relaxed. He had remained hidden and watched from his place on the large tree limb. The wind had blown the man's scent toward him. It was the smell of the one who shot at him when he was ready to pounce on that two legged near the fire that smelled of blood. That night he had been so hungry and with a wounded paw, it was hard to hunt. Well, he wasn't hungry now, there was still a little bit of that deer left.

Unbeknown to Ken that One Ear had been observing him, Ken enjoyed the ride back to the ranch. Back in the barn, he gave Winner a through brushing and let him out with the rest of the horses. He was just closing the barn door when Sam's old Jeep left a trail of dust as he drove up the lane to stop at the house.

Taking long strides, Ken reached the Jeep as it stopped and opened the door for Lacey.

"Oh Ken, you'll never believe what I have to tell you. Mr. Conway called me; he and Jean will be arriving tomorrow! She is going to press charges placed against the senator too!"

CHAPTER TWENTY-FIVE

THE DARK NIGHT

Mona had dozed off in the chair next to Charlene's bed. Richard had gone to the waiting room to rest. They had agreed to take turns staying with Charlene so she wouldn't be alone. After her one moment of opening her eyes and asking for the angel, she had fallen into a more natural sleep.

It was a little past midnight when Mona was jarred from her nap from the hoarse scream of Charlene.

"Stop, get away from me! Ouch! No, don't!" Charlene was turning her head side to side. She moaned and grimaced off and on, as she must have been reliving her life threatening abuse. Her face had fear on it but her eyes remained tightly closed.

The nurse quickly entered the room and went to the head of the bed where she began to sooth Charlene's forehead as she assessed her.

Mona stood on the other side of the bed, bewildered and feeling helpless.

Hearing his daughter's voice, Richard quickly joined them.

"Charlene, it's alright. You are safe here." The nurse continued to talk quietly and calmly to her. "Open your eyes. You are at the hospital and your mom and dad are here."

The trembling quit and once again Charlene struggled to open her eyes.

"Good, Charlene. Keep them open. I'm Nurse Smith. Can you tell me what you are feeling right now?" The nurse was watching Charlene and the different machines she was attached too.

The blood shot eyes slowly moved from the nurse to the other side of the bed. "Momma, Dad?" The words came out hoarsely. A tear escaped from her eye and slowly moved down the still swollen battered face.

"Yes, Honey, we're here." Mona touched her daughter's hair as Richard took a hold of her hand.

The lump in Richard's throat was so huge he couldn't speak; he just held Charlene's hand. Then he raised it to his lips and kissed it. Taking a deep breath, "Charlene, we were so worried about you and came as soon as we knew where you were. I'm so sorry, baby."

Charlene looked around the room with a look of panic in her eyes. "Where are they? I'm afraid. Momma I hurt all over."

The nurse answered seeing how touched Mona was. "You are in the hospital and those bad men are locked up at the jail. You are safe here. I'm going to press the button on this machine and give you some medication to ease your discomfort so you can rest again. Would you like a sip of water?"

Charlene shook her head and gripped her dad's hand. Then feeling safe that her parents were here with her, she closed her eyes and went back to the world of sleep, her hand slowly relaxing her hold on her dad's hand.

Nurse Smith swiped her ID card and adjusted the amount of pain medication needed to keep Charlene comfortable and indicated it on the computer. She also made a note of the other vital information. Checking the dressings, she was pleased with the healing progress in the short time since the surgery. Being a healthy teenager before the assault was a plus in Charlene's healing.

Nurse Smith beckoned the parents to follow her out of the room. She could see how deeply touched they were by their daughter recognizing them. Standing by the nurse's station, she looked at their tired faces. "Charlene maybe in and out of consciousness, not remembering where she is or what has happened, just afraid. However, she may also wake and sleep normally like people do recovering from injuries and surgery. I want you both to be prepared for either one and don't expect too much either way and don't question her or cause her any distress at this time. Our job is to let her heal as much as possible. I know the sheriff will want to speak with her, but not until the doctor says so."

She put her arm around Mona. "I know this has been hard on you both. The fact is, barring any unforeseen circumstances she will physically heal. I strongly suggest you have her get some sessions with a psychiatrist when she is released from the hospital, it would be better yet, when she is fully conscious, to have her been seen by someone here."

Glancing into Charlene's room to make sure everything was okay she continued, "In cases where someone is raped and beaten, so many negative thoughts will go through their mind and can have devastating results and actions that can last a life time without the intervention of one who deals with this type of situation. Above all, Charlene needs to know it wasn't her fault."

Richard reached out his hand to the nurse and shook it. "Thank you. I think her mother and I will need to talk with someone too." Tears welled up in his eyes. "It pains me to see my little girl used so cruelly and the anger I have inside for those animals." He reached for the box of tissues on the counter and blew his nose.

"What if I leave a note for the morning charge nurse to call one of the doctors on staff and see if they can come up and visit with you? Would that be alright?" Nurse Smith looked at both of them.

They nodded in agreement and returned to their daughter's room, glad that she had responded to them but sick at heart of the trauma she still had to go through.

Richard sat down with his laptop and began to type out everything from his first contact with the senator. He had to do something and still stay close to his family. Also, he could do the reporting for his newspaper…at least he would have all the facts and not guess work and he could protect his daughter.

CHAPTER TWENTY-SIX

FEAR OR STUPIDITY

Once the police officers had finished with their investigation and had taken any evidence they needed, they told the loggers they could clean up the main house. The six men did and moved their few belongings up there and made themselves at home. There was plenty of food and booze. So far, none of them had touched the booze because they weren't sure if someone would come out every day and check on them or just go by the electronic leg bands they had on.

The six men dressed for work had finished a hardy supper and were sitting on the porch waiting for it to get dark enough so they could head for the mountain.

Gunner slowly stood up. "I was just thinking that maybe we should go about three AM instead of now and at least have some early morning light so we could see better. Then go back tomorrow night and finish getting the logs all loaded and driven out." He looked at each man.

"You getting cold feet thinking of that little imaginary lion of the mountain waiting up there to get yah? Roar." Buster's eyes smiled but his voice was sarcastic.

Grizzly, a logger who always wore a bushy beard laughed, "Why, you ain't gonna let that little kitty ghost scare you off the mountain?" The rest of the men hooted and hollered at Gunner's expense.

Gunner didn't comment. *They will be laughing out the other side of their face if they meet up with any of the spirits that are up there. One thing he knew for sure, when they got there, he would be keeping the key to the four-wheeler he rode on in his pocket. No way was he wasn't being left out there alone.*

Luckily, Gunner didn't flush with the teasing or his fear, but his heart began to beat faster. "No, I'm just afraid someone is going to get hurt up there working in the dark. It's dangerous enough in the daylight much less having to keep track of where everyone's at in the dark and where the equipment is."

Teach whose real name was Arnie, who got his nickname because he was always reading when not working, stepped closer to Gunner. "Think man. We work in daylight someone is going to see us. We all have cut enough trees by now to know when to stay safe and we can fill a truck in no time."

"Yeah?" Gunner looked over at him, "If you recall, we didn't get the path cleared so we can't use the stripper to clean off the branches. That means we will have to fell the trees in the dark, use a chain saw to take off the branches then loop a chain somehow around the tree to snake it out and load it on the truck All this done in the dark. We ain't even got a full moon." Gunner glanced at the other men hoping someone would agree they shouldn't go. "It's like waiting for an accident to happen."

No one said a thing and Gunner watched as the others assembled their few things to take with them to the mountain. He was surprised to see all of them had their hard hats on. It was regulation but half of them usually ignored it. It would dangerous trying to do their work in the dark; they needed to take all the safety precautions they could. Not going at all would be better. He did an internal shake.

Gunner was getting nervous. He left the group and went to the bathroom. He always got the runs when afraid or nervous. His stomach was upset too; he was ready to throw up. He wouldn't go up in the mountains at all if he knew for sure none of the guys here would get word to the senator that he refused to cut down the trees as he was told.

He had thought about going to the ranger and cutting a deal to see if he could get a new identity like they do on those TV shows, but was afraid the ranger would laugh in his face. Plus, he wanted paid for the work that he'd already done, he had places for that money and getting enough trees down and to the mill was the only way.

Pulling up his heavy-duty work pants, Gunner slid the suspenders over his shoulder and flushed the toilet.

As Gunner stepped out onto the dark porch, Grizzly went, "Boo!"

The men stood around him laughing.

"We ain't gonna get any wood cut standing around here and it won't get any darker." Buster spoke out thinking he was funny.

Gunner nodded. "Make sure you all have water with. I hope the batteries have enough juice in them to last the night. If we can get enough trees felled and trimmed, we can load them tomorrow night and be on their way. Oh, we need a rifle on each four-wheeler too. Never know if we will need it or not. Snakes travel at night and lions." Gunner tried speaking in a matter of fact tone, but he differently wasn't in any hurry to go up to the haunted mountain.

He continued, "And remember, whoever you ride with, make sure to come back with the same one after we are done working. And I don't know about you guys, but I'm not risking my life for the senator, so we have to make sure we know where each other is when we are moving any of the big rigs, cutting off tree limbs, notching and felling the trees. It's gonna be hard working in the dark. Work slow, double check before you make any moves. Hopefully we can to get enough cut for one full load to night; we might not be able to get out there for anymore."

The sun had gone behind the mountain a few minutes ago. It didn't take long to get dark here.

Gunner looked at the men. "Okay guys, time to go. Don't rev the engines and follow me at the speed I go." He took one of the rifles off the table and led the way to the four-wheelers showing way more confidence than he felt.

CHAPTER TWENTY-SEVEN

THE WATCHMEN

Bob Running Horse rose from his place near the small campfire. He touched his ear and pointed toward the field. His three other friends nodded. Soon they saw two of the Indians that had been watching the senator's ranch from the Swenson side come riding in on their horses.

"Maiku, Bob. The men are on their way to the forest. Time to let the ranger and sheriff know."

Bob nodded, "Maiku, to you. We thought we heard the sound of four wheelers not too long ago."

Bob's cousin shook his head. "They were moving slowly trying not to make a lot of noise. Those crazy white men should know Mother Earth and the Spirit of the mountain are not happy with their actions. They haven't prayed and asked for her bounty. She would have said no if they did. She needs the trees and their roots on that side."

The men banked the small fire they had in the ring of stones while Bob called Ken instead of the sheriff since he was close by and this was ranger work.

Ken removed the phone from his shirt pocket on the second ring and saw that it was Bob. "Evening, Bob. Anyone trying to get away over there?"

"No, not toward the road, but all six men are headed for the mountain on the four-wheelers. My cousin said they were watching by the grove of trees on Sam's ranch, not far from the joining fence and said the loggers have rifles on the four wheelers. Do you want us to ride our horses from Sam's side and follow the fence line up there?"

"How many men are with you?" Ken asked.

Bob quickly answered, "Six of us here. There are six more hidden up by the mountain."

Ken thought for a minute, "Have two stay behind in case any of the loggers double back. Also the rangers coming in trucks may have their horse trailers or SUV's and will appreciate them being there. I'll tell them to come up on Sam's ranch, better traveling with their trucks or horses. I'll give Sheriff Pierson a jingle so he knows we are going up to the mountain. He can call your cell phone with what he plans to do. I'll wait here until your four men get here. We have to give the loggers enough time to start cutting on the trees. We only need two trees down for evidence. They can't claim they were just getting fire wood that way. They don't have a permit for firewood either."

"Okay, see you shortly." Bob shut off his phone. He related his conversation with Ken to the men. "Two of you need to stay here and watch the gate."

The two older men volunteered to stay. As much as they wanted to be there for the arrest, they also knew they weren't in condition to race around the mountain or get into physical contact with heavy set loggers armed with axes and guns.

Bob nodded at the men, "Thanks for electing to stay. Call if anything comes up. One of us will inform you of the arrest as soon as possible. Be safe and don't take any chances if any of the loggers would show up."

"We have Dog back by the horses and our guns just in case. Not to worry." Jesse commented. "If I was younger, I'd go and show you how to capture six men in no time."

The men laughed and Bob mindful of giving the elders respect replied, "I bet you could and still can."

With that, the Ute Indian men mounted their horses and melted into the night as they headed for the Swenson Ranch.

***

"But, Ken, I'm a journalist, I really should be there." Lacey's eyes were full of excitement.

Ken looked over at Sam and Martha, "I think she has printer's ink in her veins instead of blood." Then he glanced back at Lacey. "I know you want to be there, but you aren't going and that is final."

The tone of his voice let her know, 'final' meant just that, she wasn't going. Not being one to pout, "Okay, but can you leave your phone on or call me with anything I can write up for the paper?"

Ken put his hands on her shoulders, "Oh Lacey, I'll do what I can, no promises, okay?" His face got very serious, "I do hope they surrender peacefully, and no one gets injured up there. I can't imagine anyone trying to cut trees in the dark. I sure hope they have lights of some kinds and don't try having a fire. It's too dry up there."

They were interrupted by a knock on the door and Bob and Gus entered. The others stayed with the horses.

Gus spoke up, "Bob here filled me in on what's happening. I told my men to be prepared for anything. You want me to stay here at the house or go with them."

Sam went over to Gus, "You can suit yourself. I'm staying here with the ladies and we have Molly here. I'll call you if Molly acts up. You will also be able to see if any lights come back this way from the mountain, and the boys in the bunk house can observe if anyone goes flying by over at the McCann ranch. What do you think, Gus?"

"Sounds okay to me. You gonna close the shades?" Gus looked from Sam to the ladies.

"Nah, I don't think so. There is going to be plenty of men up there. If anyone does get away, Molly will let us know first. We just won't stand in front of the window with the lights on. Thanks for asking and you and the boys be careful." Sam walked out to the porch with Gus, "I'll have Lacey keep her phone on vibrate in case you need to make a call to us. Leave the TV on at the bunkhouse and if I need to get a hold of you, the phone will sound like part of the program."

Gus nodded and went back out to the porch and talked with the four men waiting for Bob.

Bob spoke in a quiet voice. "Ken, when do we start out for the mountain? Are you going on horseback or taking the truck?"

"I'll go on horseback with the rest of you. Frank and the boys are coming with the SUV's and one horse trailer. I don't think we will be racing with the trucks. If two of your men or the ones waiting for us up at the mountain keep the four-wheelers watched so no one can use them to get away, we should be okay. Have you had any conversation with the men up them?"

They were interrupted by Lacey's cell phone ringing. "Hello." She listened for a bit then, "Wait a moment, I need to speak with Ken."

Putting the phone away from her mouth, "It's Mr. and Mrs. Conway. They are in town. Can we give him the scoop on the arrest and put out the information we had on the condition of the mountain and all?" Lacey was so excited, she was practically bouncing.

Smiling at her Ken answered, "Why not have him go by the jail. He can talk with Luke and see about being there when/if we bring the men in. The loggers may change their mind and wise up and not play with sharp objects on the mountain. The only thing we can get them on then is leaving the ranch. In the mean time you can fill him in on what we are doing, BUT, he can't say anything to anyone about it until we bring the men in."

Lacey nodded and repeated what Ken had said to Mr. Conway.

Bob's cell phone went off. "Un ha. Okay. We are on our way." Looking at those in the room, "The loggers have battery operated lights rigged up and the men heard a chain saw whine. They have started cutting."

"We are leaving as soon as I get Winner saddled." Ken grabbed his canteen with water in it, his saddle bag containing a few bandages, flashlight and things that might be needed and a rolled up blanket to tie on the back of the saddle. He stepped out on the porch surprised to see Winner ready for him.

Gus stood there smiling and patting Winner on the neck.

"Figured if you took the truck or not, you'd want Winner."

Going down the steps, Ken shook his hand. "Thanks, Gus, you're a good man. I really appreciate this."

Turning to the men Bob brought with him Ken asked, "Do any of you need anything before we go?"

The all shook their heads no.

"Then I guess it's time to ride." Ken reached for the reins.

"Ken, I think you forgot something." Lacey's soft voice stopped him.

Ken dropped the reins and taking the steps two at a time, wrapped his arms around Lacey, tipping her back and gave her a warm kiss in front of everyone. He straightened her up, gave her a quick peck on the cheek and started down the steps when he turned to face her, "You don't have to wait up for me this time."

The men waiting smiled and turned toward the mountain. They knew she would be waiting up.

CHAPTER TWENTY-EIGHT

THE MOUNTAIN

One Ear was sated having finished his meal from the deer he had taken down two days ago. What was left of the carcass, the rest of the small forest animals would finish off.

Quietly One Ear padded over his familiar territory in the dark night. There was enough of a breeze to ruffle the leaves. It was a peaceful sound as he slowly ambled back to the cave to let his stomach digest his food.

No more had he gotten comfortable in the cave when his rest was disturbed by those noisy monsters. The sound was getting closer. One Ear stood up and switched his tail nervously back and forth. He pondered on what to do. He had left his message of urine soaked leaves by those iron smelling things and almost got that two legged one. Leaving the cave, he thought he might have to attack one of them to defend his territory. Enough was enough.

***

Gunner parked his four-wheeler to one side and shut it off, slipping the key into his pocket. Nobody would be leaving him up here alone. How he wished he had a miner's hat with the light on it. The night air was cool, but he was sweating. Never in his life had he felt fear like he was experiencing now. He stood there struggling with himself of wanting to get on the four-wheeler and head back to the safety of the ranch house where he would experience the wrath of the senator or dealing with the danger of logging at night. Between the supposed Spirit of the mountain not being happy or a wild lion, Gunner didn't know how he could possibly work in the dark constantly fearful of being attacked by something in the night.

The men set out the huge battery run lights about twenty feet apart. The start of the trail had some smaller trees that they couldn't use, but could knock down with the equipment needed to grab the downed trees and bring them back to the truck. Further up the trail they couldn't take that machine and would be forced to use a huge chain that they could hook into the tree and drag it back out. It was going to be a very long night.

Looking around, Gunner saw everyone was accounted for and motioned for Will to knock over the smaller trees with the bulldozer. When that was done, Will pushed them to one side out of the way. Then the men grabbed an axe or the chain saw and headed for the huge trees close to the narrow small rock strewn path. They had agreed only one man at a time would use the chain saw on a tree. Then they would clean off the limbs, clamp onto the tree and drag it out to the clearing. When they had enough there, they would load them on the long truck bed. That would make sure everyone knew where they all were. Freak accidents happened all the time when people weren't cautious.

The Indians from the Ute tribe watched as the mountain was violated by the non believers in the Spirit of the mountain. Should they call the ranger or wait and see if the Spirit would stop things.

Their eyes weren't the only ones observing the men, so was One Ear who was intently watching his enemies.

The steady chop, chop sound of the axe making the first groove in the tree sounded out of place in the cool night air. This was done so when they used the chain saw, the tree would fall where the logger wanted it to. The whine of the chain saw ripping through the tree followed by the loud crack of the tree separating and then the muffled thud as it landed on the forest floor.

This action was repeated two more times unbeknown to the loggers that it was being filmed by the rangers, Bob and the men with him.

The rangers circled the area ready to proceed with their plan to grab the men when the sound of the chain saw once again disturbed the quiet night. The tree fell followed by the scream of an injured man that pierced the night sending shivers up the men's back as they closed the space to reach him not knowing what they would find.

One Ear heard the cry of pain, his ears straightened up and he nervously kept turning around. The smell of blood reached his nostrils. He was in high alert. He wanted to get closer, but there was the odor of men, the monsters and guns. Climbing up a tree, he waited.

When Teach's anguishing screams filled the air, everyone dropped whatever they were holding and ran slipping and sliding over the loose rocks toward him.

Gunner hollered, "Swede, flip that light beam over here"

Teach had tripped as he turned to get out of the path of the falling tree. His legs were caught under it and blood was darkening the rocky soil.

Suddenly the forest was alive with rangers and Ute Indians converging on the accident scene.

Gunner took charge. "Get chains, hooks and wedges over here. Hurry up! We need to get that tree off him! More light! Grizzly, bring the bulldozer up here!"

The screams of the injured man were reduced to groans.

Ken leaned over to access the injured man as he punched in the 911 number on the phone requesting a helicopter and gave the location.

The men worked together as a unit getting the hooks and chains into place on the tree so they could lift it off Teach. Sliding the wedges in many places was crucial or when they tried to lift the tree off him, they would either mangle him more or crush him. They didn't have any margin for error. If the chain or any of the hooks slipped, Teach was a dead man.

Ken kept watch over everything going on. He was concerned once the weight was off the legs that Teach might bleed out. Pulling bandage wrapping and the blanket out of his saddle bag he prayed silently the medic helicopter would get here soon.

He turned toward the rangers who had driven their SUV's here. "Get those vehicles in a circle with the lights on for the helicopter to see and shoot up a couple of flares so they can find our location!"

Ken bent down next to the injured man and observed he was getting pale and no longer making any sounds. He looked up at Gunner.

Gunner nodded, turned to the men and shouted, "Everyone ready? When I drop my arm, slowly back the bulldozer up while you men lean on those wedges we slid under the tree allowing the other men to slide Teach out. Careful, we only have one try." Gunner felt sick, if the hooks didn't hold or the chains were placed wrong, they would crush him and injure those putting pressure on the wedges. He glanced once more at the men assuring himself they were all in place and slowly lowered his arm.

Those not involved in the procedure held their breath knowing one wrong move or the bulldozer backing up to fast lifting up the tree and Teach was a goner.

Sweat poured down Grizzly's face wetting his beard as he put the big machine into gear and slowly released the clutch allowing the tension to tighten up the chain. The creaking and cracking sound was neither threatening nor comforting to the men as they kept their eyes riveted to the space opening up so they could pull the injured man out.

What seemed like an eternity, Gunner signaled with his arms for Grizzly to stop. The men quickly took Teach by the arms and dragged him free from the weight of the tree.

Blood gushed from the legs and the men quickly wrapped tourniquets on them and put bandage pads on the legs to applied pressure. Teach never said a thing. Mercifully he had passed out.

Grizzly shut off the bulldozer, weak with relief, put his head down on his folded arms he had resting on the steering wheel. He had seen a lot in his days as a logger, but one never got use to it.

The whirling of the helicopter filled the air and landed inside the circle of lights provided by the ranger's vehicles. All the men gave a sigh of relief, help was here.

CHAPTER TWENTY-NINE

NOW WHAT

Frank, Captain of the Rangers showed up just as the helicopter lifted off.

The men all gathered by him. The five remaining loggers stood in the middle with the rangers and Ute Indians around them.

The five men were once more read their rights by Frank. "I talked with the judge on my way out here knowing you were in contempt of court for leaving the ranch buildings and for logging on the national forest without a permit. Because of the crowed jail, we would have to send you to the next city. The other alternative is to keep you under guard at the ranch. The judge has given permission to do that." Frank slowly looked at the faces of each man and saw sickness and despair in them and knew that none of them were going to run.

"The electronic ankle bracelets evidently were just a game to you. This time you will be under constant armed guard and if you put one foot off the perimeter around the house, you will be shot, no questions asked. Do you understand? We will arrange for lawyers tomorrow for you."

Frank saw the faces on the men were like whipped dogs. "You don't have to answer my question without legal representation, but I don't understand why you would take this chance. You were being held more as witnesses, not that you had done anything illegal. Now, you have done an illegal action and almost killed one of your friends. Why?" He shook his head.

None of the men raised their heads nor offered an explanation. The ranger didn't realize how much power the senator could weld behind bars. They did.

"If you change your minds, you can have one of the guards contact me or Ken." Frank then turned to Bob.

I want to deputized about twelve of your men and have them work along with the rangers at the ranch. Which men would you suggest or should I let them volunteer?"

Bob nodded. "Some of us have town jobs; let me talk with the men that are here that have been watching over the mountain and there are others on the res that will be glad to assist. We still have some taking turns watching the gate to the ranch who will continue to do so."

Bob scanned the faces of his people. "Men? Any questions? If not, those interested in working and being deputized by Captain Collins, step forward." One by one, those who could and wanted to help came closer to Bob. There were some words exchanged in their language. Satisfied, Bob turned to the Captain. "Your men."

Captain Collins looked over at the volunteers. "Step over here and I'll deputize you. I will have you sign your names to that effect. That will also get you on the payroll. I'll be over at the ranch and we will decide who works what shift. Are you all able to leave here and meet me there?"

There was a silent nod of heads.

"Good."

Shifting his gaze back to the five prisoners, "Are the keys in the four-wheelers, I need I need them driven back to the ranch."

"All but mine, sir." Gunner fished the key out of his pocket and handed it to the captain.

The captain in turn gave it to one of the men who would be deputized.

Ken leaned over to the captain. "Ah, Frank. Can I speak to you in private for a minute?"

Frank nodded and they walked over to Frank's truck. "What's up?"

Looking around to make sure they were alone, Ken spoke. "I think there is more than one reason these men risked coming up here at night. They are all professional loggers, not some rookies. They know the dangers under perfect conditions. Why would they leave the comfort of the ranch house to illegally cut down trees? I think if I could talk with each of the alone, especially Gunner, I might get some more information about the senator."

Frank shook his head. "Legal rights, Ken, you know that. They need a lawyer in the room if you are going to question them."

"Of course I do. I just want to plant a seed of thought that if they cooperate with us, things will go better for them. I will also say they will be given a public defender that has no ties to the senator. I feel they are afraid of him for some reason. Plus, I could also record our conversation stating that they were under no way be threatened or forced but giving a statement of their own free will. I think if we tell the men that by keeping them on the ranch, they will also be protected from any intruders."

Frank was silent for a minute mulling this over. "Alright, but, contact the city attorney before you say or do anything." He looked at his watch and smiled, "I'd wait until at least eight AM if I was you. Talk with the men individually so whoever would give you pertinent info, the others won't know which one it was."

They walked back to the group of men.

The captain addressed the five upset loggers. "Before we take you back to the ranch, I want you to know how serious this invasion of the forest was and the fact that a man may die of his injuries. You all could be charged with his death. Was it worth it?"

Pointing at two of his rangers, "Divide the loggers up to ride back in your vehicles and take them back to the old McCann ranch. The men being deputized will meet you there. I'll be there shortly. Anyone have any questions? If not, let's get moving."

Soon the roar of the four wheelers, the SUV's moving out and the creaking of the saddles as the riders mounted their horses filled the air as they all left the area.

One Ear waited until it was all quiet, and then leaped out of the tree to survey the area. He sniffed the blood on the ground from the injured man and wondered where he was. He checked out the big equipment, satisfied that finally, he was alone; One Ear went back to the comfort of his cave.

CHAPTER THIRTY

THE LONG HALLWAY

The nurse's shoes squeaked on the polished floor as she pushed the wheel chair Charlene was sitting in to her new room. Charlene had progressed so quickly that she could leave the intensive care and go to a regular private room. Charlene was still receiving pain medication through her IV but she could now sit up and eat with some assistance. Having her parents with her gave her a peace of mind letting her heal faster. The first visit with the psychologist had gone very well.

Nurse Smith slowed down and turned into the room. "Here we are, your new abode for awhile. I think you will like your view from the window." She positioned the wheelchair close to the bed then touched the buttons to bring the bed down as low as possible. Folding the sheet and light blanket down, she turned to Charlene.

"Do you think we can get you into bed by ourselves?"

The young girl gave Nurse Smith a small smile and nodded her head. Her face was still a little swollen. "I need to move and get strong."

"You're correct with that statement. I'm going to help you stand up. I want you to get your bearings just like you did when I got you out of bed. Then you will turn and sit down on the bed. If you aren't too exhausted, you can sit there for a minute or two, otherwise, I will help you bring your legs over and get you comfortable. Ready?"

Charlene nodded. She would do anything to get well enough to go into court and make all those men pay. Daddy said she could give her testimony in the judge's chambers, but she wanted those evil men to squirm and be just as embarrassed as she was when they hurt her so.

Nurse Smith had just finished pulling the covers up to Charlene's waist when there was a knock on the door.

"Its mom and dad, can we come in?"

Nurse Smith opened the door. "Our young lady is all settled in. I think she may need a little nap. She did real well with the trip to her new room. How about you two, did you get rooms at the bed and breakfast?"

Richard spoke, "Yes we did and thank you for suggesting it. Can we still take turns staying with Charlene?"

"Of course. That chair over there makes into a bed if one of you would like to stay all night or part of it." She moved closer to Richard and whispered, "Sheriff Pierson is still keeping a plain clothes officer outside. He will be checking ID's of everyone who comes in here. Make sure you do too. If anyone looks or acts unprofessional, call out."

Richard nodded. "Thanks." He looked over at his daughter who was exhausted from the small move lay very still holding onto her mother's hand.

He walked over to the bed, leaned down and kissed her on the forehead. "Rest my dear."

Looking over at his wife, "Mona, do you want to stay tonight or should I? I think we should both need to take care of ourselves and get some rest."

He didn't hear her answer as he was distracted by the helicopter landing on the pad near the Emergency Entrance.

Turning to face his wife, "What? I'm sorry. What did you say?"

Mona left the side of the bed and put her arms around her husband. "I said Sweetheart, that I will stay here tonight and you go get some rest. Tomorrow, they want her to walk a few steps and I think you should be here for that. I'll come back in time for our meeting with the doctor. How does that sound?"

Richard kissed his wife. "I don't know if I can sleep or not, but we both need to try. Are you sure you will be okay? Do you need anything?"

"No. Wasn't it a lucky thing to find a Bread and Breakfast just a block away?" She looked over at Charlene, "I'm so relieved she is getting better, I was so scared we'd lose our baby." Tear welled up in her eyes.

Richard hugged her. "Me too." He took her hand, "Let's pray."

***

Gunner looked over at the ranger as he brought the SUV to a stop in front of the ranch house. "Do you think I could talk with Ranger Dickinson?"

"Sure." He clicked the speed dial for Ken's number.

"Hello?"

"Hey Ken. We just got here at the old McCann ranch and," he turned to the logger, "What's your name again?"

"Gunner."

"The man Gunner wants to talk with you." He handed the phone to Gunner.

"Ranger, I was wondering if I could go to the hospital and be with Teach. He doesn't have any family here, I don't know if he even has a family, and I, well, I hate for him to be alone. He looked pretty bad and if he doesn't make it," Gunner's voice was real low but full of emotion, " no one should pass away alone."

"Yeah, I think I can arrange it. I'm almost at the Swenson Ranch, I need to get my vehicle and I'll be right over."

The phone went silent and Gunner handed it back. No one spoke and no one got out of that SUV.

Gunner felt like a whipped dog. If he only had enough guts to go to the ranger or sheriff and tell them about the senator's conversation and threat…he hung his head in remorse. He wished he could change the way things went. Sick with grief he couldn't get rid of the screams Teach had made. He wished he had been the one to get hurt. Then maybe all his troubles would be over with.

***

Ken and those riding horseback were surprised when they rode into the yard that everyone was out on the porch to greet them.

Sam waved at them all. "Tie up the horses and come on in. Martha's got a big kettle of beef stew simmering away."

"And a fresh batch of cookies." Martha added.

The smell wafting out the door caused stomachs to start growling. It didn't take long for the men to dismount and clamor into the house, after carefully wiping their boots off on the rug.

Lacey moved closer to Ken and reaching up hugged him. "How did everything go?"

"Bad accident, the guys can tell you about it. I need to get my truck and pick up Gunner. He wants to be with Teach, the one who got injured. The 'copter took Teach in. I don't know if he is going to make it." Ken shook his head, "What would make men take such dangerous action to cut trees in the dark?"

Lacey gripped his arm. "Let me go with you. Give me my camera and I'll get my notepad. Please?"

Ken looked at those big blue eyes; he knew she was a good journalist and he felt bad refusing to let her be part of the bust. "Okay. You get what you need and give me time to unsaddle Winner, brush him down and feed him."

Gus had overheard their conversation. "No need for that Ken. You fix a plate while Lacey is getting her things and I'll take care of Winner."

"Thanks, Gus. It seems lately you've been taking care of my horse for me a lot. You're a good man."

"Well, he's a good one, reminds me of one I had years ago." With that, Gus grabbed an apple out of the dish and went out the door.

Ken smiled; he bet Winner would be getting the apple, not

Gus.

Ken had just taken one bite of the stew when Lacey came down the hallway with her backpack and a light weight sweater draped over her arm. Using her cane didn't seem to slow her down.

"I'm ready when you are." She flashed him a big smile. He would never know how happy she was to be going with him to the hospital.

Ken quickly finished up the stew, grabbed a handful of cookies and took the cup to go of coffee Martha handed him. "Thanks, Martha. It was delicious as usual." He gave her a kiss on the cheek.

As the two young people drove the short distance to the old McCann Ranch, Ken gave her a quick overview of what had transpired on the mountain.

Pulling up next to the ranger's SUV, Ken could see the forlorn Gunner sitting in the back of it.

"Ready?" He looked at Gunner.

"Yes, sir." The words came out in the tone of an exhausted man as he slowly got out of the vehicle.

Ken looked over at Gunner. "You realize that you are still under arrest and I should put you in leg chains. I want your word you won't make any attempt to run or cause any problems or you will be down in the local jail so fast you won't know what happened. Understand?"

Gunner nodded but his eyes registered fear. "You have my word; I just want to be there until Teach wakes up so he knows he isn't alone. I don't want to be in that jail. You have my word. I won't do anything stupid. I, I, wanted to call and make a deal to keep us safe from the senator but…" Gunner groaned and turned his head. "I was too much of a coward and Teach paid the price for it." Gunner looked up to face Ken, "I mean it."

"Remember, anything you say could be used in the court of law, so don't go answering any questions unless we have a lawyer here for you." Ken looked over at Lacey, "Do you *understand* that too? No questions that might incriminate him. If Teach dies, it may no longer be a logging matter, but a murder charge. You don't want to jeopardize his rights."

Lacey was surprised with the word murder. "I am a journalist and will comply."

"Gunner, when we get to the hospital, I'll see about you having a sandwich or something."

"Thanks. I'm not really hungry, just worried about Teach. Thanks though."

Ken slid the window separating them from the extended back seat and locked it along with the back doors.

Ken looked over at Lacey and gave her a smile as he put the Sierra into gear. Even though this was business, he was glad she was with him.

CHAPTER THIRTY-ONE

INTENSIVE CARE

Teach was still in surgery when the three arrived at the hospital. Ken kept his word and took Gunner down to the vending machines to him get a sandwich since the cafeteria was closed. They found a table to sit at. Lacey and Ken each had coffee.

"Ranger, I've been thinking." Gunner looked around to assure no one could hear him. "I need to tell you why we were out there and I need to see the senator."

"Whoa, don't say anything to me here. I think we need to go over to the jail, make sure you are represented legally and I also arrange for you to see Senator Donaby. Finish your sandwich and we will leave."

Ken flipped open his phone and called the sheriff and related the latest to him. Then he checked on Teach. He was still in surgery, alive and getting more blood. Ken left word where he could be reached and gave them his cell phone number if anything changed.

At the jail they took Gunner into the interrogation room and once again read him his rights.

"Gunner," the sheriff leaned back into his chair, "You really need to wait for a lawyer."

"No! Just put one of those recorder things on and ask me anything you want and I'll tell you anything and everything I know. I don't care about me, I'm worried about Teach. None of this would have happened if I wasn't so afraid I let common sense go out the window."

Sheriff Pierson stood up. "Okay, I'm going to video tape you and also have a tape recorder on. When you are done speaking I'll have this transcribed and you can sign it. He got everything ready and they began the session. Gunner told them everything about the logging agreement and what he knew about the party.

Gunner looked at them and nervously licked his lips. "Before I left for a place to sleep, them gals the senator brought with them were taking some pictures on their phones. I don't know of who or why."

Ken and the sheriff exchanged glances...more evidence. "Thanks, Gunner, I do have all of those phones available to check out."

"Sheriff?" Gunner spoke the word quietly. "Can I see the senator for a minute?"

"Why?"

"He's a mean one. Like I told you, we failed and he will order someone to make us sorry. I'm scared. But, I just want him to know what happened to Teach, see what he says. I want to know if he has any decency left in his black heart." Gunner looked down, then back up at the two, "I'd really like to beat him to a pulp for everything he has done to that poor girl, Teach, everyone! He makes me sick!" He spit those last words out like venom. His large hands were closed in a tight fist, his face red with emotion.

Ken put his hand on Gunner's shoulder, "Take it easy man. We can't have you getting into a fight."

Sitting on the edge of the table, Sheriff Pierson looked intently at Gunner. "What if we brought Senator Donaby in here? You can tell him what happened on the mountain. We will video it just as we did with you. You promise not to touch a hair on his head?"

Gunner nodded.

The sheriff picked up the phone, "Bring the senator up to the interrogation room. Shackle and cuff him."

Coming down the corridor, the senator angrily addressed the sheriff. "What is the reason for these chains and handcuffs?"

Opening the door, "Step inside and take a chair, you have a visitor. And remember, anything you say can and will be held against you."

The senator stopped when he saw Gunner. "What are you doing here? I thought you had some work to take care of."

"Well, your idea of working in the dark…"

"Shut up, Gunner!" The senator's face had a menacing look on it.

Gunner continued, "Like I was saying, your idea of working in the dark has Teach in surgery right now and he may not make it. I just thought you ought to know that and no trucks went out either."

"You fool. I don't care about whatever his name is, you can always get someone to work, but I need that money now to pay my attorney!" Donaby hit the table with his fists. A string of swear words ripped out of his mouth. He stood up, leaning close to Gunner and hissed out at him. "You know what I told you to do you big oaf and you failed. I have my ways. You just got a big bulls eye on your chest. Nobody messes with me and gets away with it!"

Sheriff Pierson pointed at the chair, "Sit down, Donaby. What you just said to Gunner sounded like a threat to me. You're in big trouble as it is; you might want to watch your mouth unless you have something you would like to tell us about the party.

Donaby scowled at the sheriff, "Don't tell me how I can talk to my employees. I have friends in high places that can put an elected nobody like you in your place. Take me back. I don't have anything more to say."

The sheriff picked up the phone, "You can take Donaby back."

At the same time, Ken's phone rang, "Yes. Thanks, we'll be there shortly." He snapped his phone shut. "Teach is in ICU, he's still unconscious."

Donaby never turned his head but kept walking, "I'm not paying his hospital bill."

***

The three were taken to Teach's room in intensive care. A security guard was sitting outside the room.

Lacey glanced at Ken, "This was Charlene's room. She must be doing much better."

They all used the cleaner on their hands before entering the room.

Nurse Smith was on duty. "Arnie has had a lot of repair done and will need physical therapy. He has lost a lot of blood, and the next couple of days are going to be challenging, but I think he will make it. They will put a cast on later; right now they have his leg wrapped since they did some grafting."

"Teach."

The nurse turned around, "What did you say?"

Gunner stood looking down at his friend. "Teach. We call him Teach because he reads a lot."

"Will he respond to that before his given name?" She questioned.

"Yeah. He will. Nurse, I don't know what type blood Teach has, but I'm willing to give some of mine to help him." Gunner had to do something. If he would have had enough guts to refuse cutting trees in the dark, this never would have happened.

She made a notation on the chart. "I'll check with the lab on this. We don't normally do one at a time, but wait for a blood drive. Do you happen to know your blood type?"

"O positive is what they told me when I was in the service. Can I stay here awhile with him?"

"That's up to the ranger. As long as you are quiet and don't touch him. He doesn't need any germs." She smiled at him and looked over at Ken.

Lacey walked out with the nurse. "Where's Charlene?"

"She was moved out of ICU, she is still on this floor though. It was amazing how she has recovered once her folks got here. I think you being with her really helped. She has a long way to go and is lucky she is young." Leaning toward Lacey, "She still has a guard twenty-four seven and now they tell me this man will too."

Lacey smiled, "Both are for their safety...Teach isn't going anywhere on his own for awhile." Her smile evaporated, "I feel so sorry for him."

Lacey stopped outside of the door, Gunner was talking to Teach.

"I told him Teach. We don't need none of his bull crap anymore. The senator is rotten to the core. I've told the sheriff everything I know. Sorry I didn't have enough guts not to do what he said. I was plain scared of him and his thugs. That's what landed you here and that piece of dirt doesn't care. When you're up to it, you tell the ranger and all everything you know. I can't stay, but I'll try to get back again. It's up to the ranger. Heal fast." Gunner wiped his eyes with the sleeve of his shirt. He felt sick inside.

He turned to the ranger, "Thanks for letting me come and talk to him. I appreciate it. You can take me back now."

As they left the building and took a deep breath of fresh air, the sun was just coming over the mountain. A new day was dawning.

CHAPTER THIRTY-TWO

SHARING

Back at the Swenson Ranch, Martha was busy making breakfast for the tired couple.

Gus and Sam joined them for a second cup of coffee and to get caught up on last night's event on the mountain and Gunner's request to visit Teach at the hospital.

Sam related his conversation with Bob. "I still can't figure out what would influence men to take such dangerous actions to try logging out there at night. Anyone can see it was an accident waiting to happen." He shook his head, a sad expression on his face.

Martha turned from flipping a pancake over and pointed the spatula at Ken. "Did that injured man make it?"

"Yes, but he's not out of the woods yet." Slowly Ken brushed his hair off his brow with the back of his hand. "One thing we know, with all the injuries to his leg, he won't ever be working in the woods again. Matter of fact, he will be lucky if he can even walk."

Lacey, although tired was still excited over what she had been privy to during Gunner's revealing about the senator and the interchange between him and Senator Donaby. "I think with

Gunner talking, the other men might too, even the ones that are incarcerated and charged with the rape of Charlene."

Sam stood up and took the filled plate of pancakes, eggs and bacon from Martha and placed it in front of Ken.

"Martha, only one pancake and egg on my plate," Lacey smiled at her, "You're going to make me fat with all your wonderful cooking."

Martha slid some eggs and two pancakes back into the pan. "Dearie, you're just fine, isn't she, Ken."

Ken looked over at Lacey and with a smile on his face replied, "Yes, she's perfect."

Lacey blushed and felt her heart give a few extra beats. She ran her hand over her hair to smooth it down. She must look like a mess.

The attention was off them as Martha asked Sam and Gus, "You men have room for a little more breakfast?"

Gus nodded and Sam put his arm around his wife's shoulder. "We always got room for your great cookin'."

Martha beamed but enjoyed her husband's compliment.

Finished eating, Ken pushed his plate away. "Thanks once more for a wonderful meal, Martha. I need to get some sleep, I'm bushed." He pushed his chair back.

"Ken, wait a minute." Lacey put her hand on his arm. "Remember what the senator said last night about needing money?"

Ken put his hand over his mouth to cover a yawn. "Yes."

"What if we buy it from him...not the price he paid mom and dad, but enough so we can get him out of this area. He'll end up in jail anyway with all the charges and more to come. What do you think?" Lacey's eyes were sparkling with excitement.

That woke Ken up. "We? I thought you wanted to free lance with reporting and photography. What would you do with the ranch?"

Lacey slid off her chair and brazenly sat on his lap, putting her arms around him, looked deep into his eyes. She spoke quietly and slowly, "We both know there is something special between us. We aren't a couple of teenagers having a summer romance. We've both been married before for love. As for my work, I can still write feature articles and take pictures, but on my schedule. You have always wanted a ranch to run enough cattle to pay the taxes and raise some horses like Winner. You could still be a ranger. What do you *say*?"

"I'd *say* that sounded like a marriage proposal to me." He gave her a hug.

"And?"

"I *say* yes to marriage, you mean the world to me but..."

She stopped him from saying anything more with a very loving kiss.

Gus, Sam and Martha clapped their hands, happy with the thought of a marriage with the young couple and circled them with hugs.

When the merriment settled down, Ken spoke. "Lacey, I want

to marry you, but I can't swing the price of the ranch. I'm renting a five acre place we can live on."

"Ken, I received money when Shane died and from my grandparents when they passed away. I've invested most of the money I've made. I live in a small efficiency apartment because I'm always gone on assignments and don't need a bigger place. I'm sure you received some money from the unfortunate death of your wife and unborn child. If we need more to cover the purchase, my folks will loan it to us or maybe give it to us as a wedding present." Lacey paused, "I think we can make it financially."

Sam quietly entered the conversation. "I happen to know that Mrs. Donaby's name isn't on the deed to the ranch, and I'm sure she won't want anything to do with it. No one has even seen her visit here. I imagine after that last debacle her husband has done, she will divorce him. The attorneys will no doubt get most of the money from the sale or if you wanted to gamble, you could pick it up for back taxes in a couple of years since he won't be making any money to pay the taxes while he is in jail."

Ken and Lacey stood up. "As much as we need to talk, I need to sleep, it's been over thirty-six hours and my brain is getting fuzzy. One thing I know for sure, Lacey you and I have a wedding to plan." He kissed her warmly.

"Night, or I guess I should say morning, folks." The exhausted man slowly walked down the hall to his room.

The last thing he would remember hearing the next day was Lacey saying to Martha, "Oh my gosh, I can't believe I actually proposed. I'd do it again, I love him."

CHAPTER THIRTY-THREE

GUNNER AND THE MEN

Gunner woke up to a sense of not being a patsy when he stood up to Donaby. He sighed.

The men were sleeping when he got in last night and today, he looked at his watch, it was noon already, he needed to talk to the men to tell the authorities anything they knew.

Swinging his feet over the side of the bed, he sat up and got his bearings.

Grizzly stepped into the room. "Thought I'd check on you to see if you were alive or not. How's Teach doing?"

"Let me get dressed and I'll tell you all what I know." Gunner reached for his jeans lying on the floor by his boots.

"Okay, dinner's ready too by the way. Oh I guess you know we have Indians, Rangers and deputies taking turns watching over us. I never felt so safe." Grizzly laughed and left the room.

Gunner's stomach growled from the smell of the food as he entered the huge dining room. Fried potatoes with onions, beans and ham smell filled the room. They all greeted him.

Swede sat the last bowl on the table as Buster filled the mugs with strong coffee. They all sat down and filled their plates giving Gunner time for a few bites of food.

Gunner put his fork down and glanced around the table. "I know you are all wondering about Teach. He's in intensive care with a guard posted at his door. He didn't look good." Gunner paused, "Don't know how he will be. He was in surgery quite a while and they didn't put his leg in a cast. Something about grafting and steel pins. I, I." He looked slowly and fully at each one. "I asked to see the Sheriff and told him everything I know."

He was interrupted by Will, "Did you get some brownie points for that?"

"Will, I didn't ask for anything, I just want to get the senator's butt in jail for the rest of his life and it isn't going to happen unless everyone here tells the authorities what they know. And," Gunner leaned on the table, "I talked with the senator, with the Sheriff and Ranger Dickenson present. You aren't going to believe this. The senator said I had a bull's eye on my chest! He said that in front of them. Who does he think he is? They reminded him that was a threat and he responded by saying he had friends in high places and he would see the Sheriff lose his job! Can you believe he threaten the Sheriff?"

The men chuckled and exchanged glances.

Grizzly reached for a biscuit, "Doesn't that moron realize that with all the charges against him, he doesn't have any friends or henchmen to do anything? No one works for nothing. And right now, he's got plenty of that."

Taking a swallow of coffee, Gunner pointed his mug at them,

"And I want you to know, that Ranger Dickinson is one okay guy. He could have been a jerk, but he wasn't. I think he will go to bat for us with that logging bit if we tell them everything we know about the senator. I have a feeling there is more against the senator than what we know. Oh, and I found out that the little gal those men raped and beat survived, but she is still pretty weak."

Will passed the bean dish, "How do you know that?"

"Cause the lady the ranger is sweet on, mentioned that Teach was in the same Intensive Care room Charlene had been in. That's what they called her, the girl, her name is Charlene."

Gunner laughed, "When those two look at each other, you can hear the love birds cooing over their head.

Buster had been silent throughout the discussion. "Yah think he was just being nice so you would talk?"

"No. He's not stupid either. He knows more and figured the senator was putting the screws on us. Remember, the guards out there aren't just to keep us here; it's to keep anyone the senator might have something on that would try to shut us up. I just figured I'm not taking anything more off him, so I told what I knew. I'm a man, not a coward anymore.

Grizzly stroked his beard thoughtfully. "I'm up here working off money owed to the senator because I didn't want my nephew to end up like that little girl. The kid is going to college and was working with the senator's campaign. The senator invited him and a couple of others for a friendly card game. Something was put in the kid's drink and when he woke up, the senator said my nephew owed him ten thousand dollars and waved an IOU in front of him. The kid said he had no recollection of signing anything or even playing cards. They sat at the table had a drink and that was it until he woke up with the worse headache he'd ever had. They worked him over and threatened to do more and that's when he told me about it. Of course he was told if he went to the authorities, his mom would get a little taste of what they gave him." Grizzly shook his head, "I'm ready to talk to the ranger or Sheriff." He straightened up and took a deep breath, "I'm a man too." He looked around the table. "You got a similar story, or just wanted a job? How about the rest of you? Gonna go with me and nail the senator's ears to the floor?"

Buster, Will and Swede looked at each other and nodded in agreement. "We're with you."

They smiled, free of the burden of keeping secrets and taking blame.

Gunner walked to the door and stepped out on the porch. He waved at one of the deputies, "Can you have Ranger Dickinson give us a call or come over here. We need to talk with him."

"Everything okay in there?"

"Yeah, just fine." Gunner went back inside, no matter what happened they were good men. It was a relief not to be afraid anymore.

CHAPTER THIRTY-FOUR

TODAY'S NEWS

THE WEEKLY SENTINAL

Guest Reporter: Phil Conway

Photos by: Lacey McCann

"Two days ago, Senator Donaby was arrested along with his guests and some employees.

From information released by Sheriff Pierson, charges levied against the senator are state and Federal. They include kidnapping, sexual assault, extortion and illegal logging done in the National Forest. As of now, discussion is on arrangements to move the accused and the trial to the county seat for larger jail accommodations and jury selection.

Due to seriousness of the crimes, the accused are being held without bail.

Sheriff Pierson and Captain Frank Collins gave thanks to all of those involved with the detection and capture of the arrested men.

Quoting Sheriff Pierson, "I don't remember anything as depraved, immoral, and flagrantly disrespectful of the people and the laws ever being committed in our small community. These were all perpetrated by the senator and his so called friends and employees. Our own Lacey McCann was injured and one of the loggers due to the force and threat of the accused, Senator Donaby.

I also want to give credit and thanks for everyone who assisted us in the collection of evidence and the arrest of those involved in the unsavory actions."

There were pictures of those arrested and some from the activity on the mountain.

Richard, Phil and his wife Jean were sitting at a round table in the waiting room reading the paper.

Richard put down his copy. "You condensed that well, Phil. I didn't realize Lacey was a photographer. She was with our daughter when we came and we are grateful that Charlene wasn't alone."

"Lacey actually works for my magazine as a journalist and photographer, usually on special assignments. That's why she was here, I had a hunch due to some private info I got that the senator might do some illegal logging here. She only knew she was to check on the health of the forest and ended up fracturing her leg. Her assistant won't go near any woods since that. He is a hundred percent city boy." Phil paused, "Her folks sold the senator their ranch. Lacey was raised there."

Jean spoke up. "Don't forget there was my mistreatment in Reno by him…I hope he rots in jail."

Phil put his arm around her shoulders and gave her a hug. "He will Honey, he will."

Leaning forward, Richard rested his arms on the table, "I'm a reporter in Reno, I've got some info on his negative dealings with gambling and I've been keeping a journal of everything especially concerning the kidnapping and ransom for her release. I contacted my paper and I'm getting paid to send reports to them too. With all of the documented material we have, there is no lawyer that will get him off!"

He look around and with a hushed voice, "Charlene, my wife and I are all getting some counseling to deal with Charlene's attack. We needed professional help so we wouldn't say the wrong thing, to let her know it wasn't her fault. She was an innocent that paid the price for my reporting a non flattering article on that creep." Tears welled up in his eyes. "I don't know which is worse for Charlene, the physical or mental pain."

Jean left her chair and went behind Richard wrapping her arms around his shoulders. "I went through some of what she experienced. Stay with the doctors, they are a tremendous wealth of help. Love her, listen to her, the physical will heal, it will take longer for the mind to let go of it. The fear of going to sleep, remembering it." Jean looked over at her husband, "And sometimes you need to have some tough love to get rid of the fear and embarrassment. I know."

Richard reached up and squeezed Jean's hands. "Thanks."

The three were silent, each in their own thoughts when Phil picked up the page with the photos. "Look." He pointed at a small spot on one of the pictures. "What does that look like to you? Right there, up in the corner on the limb of the tree. I wonder if that's the mysterious lion everyone says lives on the mountain." He had a puzzled look on his face, "I can't recall what Lacey called him."

Jean went back to her seat. "Why does it matter Phil? A mountain lion is a mountain lion."

Phil was hitting Lacey's number. "Hi, it's me, Phil. Say; did you see all of the film taken on the mountain?"

"No, why?"

"I think you may have a side story to the logging. Look at the top left corner of today's picture. I think that is a mountain lion. What do you call him?" Phil had stood up and was excitedly walking back and forth.

Lacey's voice was pensive. "One Ear. He got that from some rancher who saw two lion's fighting. His other ear was pretty chewed up. He's pretty elusive. The Indians say he is one of the spirits that protects the mountain."

Phil was getting more enthused. "See if you can find any more pictures of him. Get that one in the paper enlarged and tell your story of the night you almost became his dinner. The fear, the camp visited by him and the loss of your food. And I think you mentioned something about one of the loggers being paranoid about it. If the local paper won't print it as a side to the senator's story, no problem since I also want it in mine along with the articles on taking care of our national forests. Oh yes, Charlene's dad writes for a paper in Reno, he might be able with your permission to use all or part of it for that. Could be some big money in it for you, if I recall most of the picture rights are yours."

Lacey was feeling the excitement Phil was expressing. "I've got a lot written on the logging expose that we were originally sent up there to do and plenty of pictures."

"Good, good. I'll go over and see the local editor and if

doesn't want the human interest stories, I'll print some and Richard can work with his editor. I'll call you back, in the meantime, check out your photos and start writing. I want something to send in tonight." Phil shut off his phone, a huge smile on his face.

He looked over at Richard. "Have you talked to the sheriff about what you have on Donaby with the gambling? Can you use that without compromising anything to do with the abduction and torture of your daughter?"

Richard nodded. "I mentioned it briefly, but I'll go over and visit with him. I can still do another write up on the dangers of gambling, the addiction, and the terrible consequences of the non winners. Then when the charges to do with Charlene come up, I will report from the courthouse."

As Richard stood up, "I think we better book some rooms at a hotel close to the courthouse at the county seat. I'm keeping the one here so we can be close for Charlene too."

"Yeah, you're right. They will be hard to get if we wait." Phil looked over at his wife, "What if we rent something with three bedrooms, a sitting room and kitchen? Richard, you and your wife could take two of the bedrooms, with the second one for Charlene when she is ready to leave the hospital. I don't know about you but I'm sick of eating out all the time. We can fix a few meals."

Jean nodded yes.

Richard stood still for a moment, mulling it over. "I think it is a great idea. Let me talk with my wife." He glanced at his watch, "I'll call you after I fill her in on our conversation. I'm sure she will agree. We'll be spending most of our time at the courthouse and it will be a relief to come back to something more homelike, especially when Charlene needs to be there." He waved and left the room.

Phil reached out his hand to Jean. "You want to go with me to see the editor? You've had a little experience of dealing with a hard nose editor."

She grinned as she put her arm around his waist. "Yeah, I sure have. In a way it seems like old times doesn't it, before we owned the business."

As they walked toward the elevator Phil realized he truly had his wife back.

CHAPTER THIRTY-FIVE

THE SALE

Senator Donaby paused before entering the room and one by one looked over the people sitting at the old round table. *Um, that ranger person, the cute photographer whose pictures can nail my hide to the floor; I'd like to nail her to a bed. Two suits who smell like money hungry lawyers and one of my attorneys. I wonder what's up?* He stepped into the room and took a seat, placing his handcuffed hands on the table.

The man sitting next to the woman stood up and addressed those in the room. "My name is Timothy Bartle, Miss McCann's attorney." He gestured toward the other man, "And seated with Mr. Dickinson is his attorney, James Woodman.

We are here today with an offer to purchase the McCann ranch. Under the circumstances we know your finances are badly strained. Due to the damages to the ranch buildings, fences and equipment, plus the fact that you have sold off all of the livestock, they are offering you a cashier's check today for $300,000." Handing the senator the document, he sat down.

Throwing it down on the table, the senator laughed. "You must think I'm crazy to take that chicken feed. I paid three times that much. Forget it." He stood up and looked over at his attorney, "Did you know about this joke?"

"Yes. Perhaps you should sit back down Mr. Donaby."

Donaby threw him a withering look, but sat down.

His attorney leaned close to him as he slid a folder with the name of his firm on the front over to the senator and spoke very low. "In there are papers showing your financial obligations. You need money now to cover the legal expenses of this situation you find yourself in. Considering everything that has transpired, I suggest you accept their offer."

The senator's face turned red with his anger. "Are you nuts? This offer is unacceptable. You and your gang will no doubt bill for the total amount!"

Mr. Vernon Malone, his elderly attorney once more bent close and whispered. "With all the charges that have been filed in just this suit against you, I see nothing but life in prison at the end of the trial. No one is going to want that piece of property because it will be tainted by what transpired out there. And I don't know of any lawyer in our firm that can get you off. As you yourself know, other attorney's have turned you down. Even your wife refuses to be here for your trial. You better think this over and not be too hasty in refusing their offer." He sat back in his chair and folded his hands in the steeple fashion.

Donaby ignored the lawyer's packet and picked up the offer for the ranch. Quickly skimming through it, he looked up. "It says here, Lacey McCann and you." He pointed his finger at Ken. "Is this what dumb rangers do to get a ranch dirt cheap, cheat people?"

Ken and Lacey remained silent.

Mr. Bartle spoke as he picked up the check. "Take it or leave it, Mr. Donaby. Your decision." He stood up as did Lacey and Ken along with Ken's attorney, James Woodman. Removing a card from his brief case, Mr. Bartle laid it on the table next to the offer to sell contract. "Call me if you change your mind."

The four turned to leave when they were stopped by the senator's voice. "Wait. Make it $400,000 and we have a deal."

They turned back to face him, but only Attorney Bartle responded. "Senator Donaby, you haven't paid taxes on the property since you purchased it. All the live stock was sold off, they need to replace that along with all the repairs. Sorry, the offer for $300,000 is firm. They are being generous with that. Perhaps you should consult more with your attorney." He nodded as a goodbye and the four left the room.

Donaby sat there seething. He took his hand and swept the documents on the floor. "Is that all you're good for is to sit there and tell me to sell the ranch for peanuts? And you call yourself a top notch lawyer. I'd say you are a top notch loser!"

Malone stood up, snapped his briefcase shut and looked down at Donaby. "For your information, no one else from our firm would come to represent you once we heard what all the charges are. You are a despicable person. We have gotten you out of scrapes before and we were paid very well. My daughters are grown up and married. My beloved wife has passed away and I still miss her terribly. So they sent me, no family at home so I could stay for a long drawn out trial. Trust me; trying to come up with any type of defense for you as a good attorney is impossible. You need to find someone with the same lack of moral fiber as you. You can work with me or you can fire me from this case." Picking up his briefcase he nodded at the police officer to open the door.

"Come back, now, I have your firm on a retainer." Donaby motioned to Mr. Malone.

Moving just enough to face Donaby, "My name is MR. MALONE to you and that is how you shall address me from now on and you will be civil. No more cursing, ordering, threatening or trying to think you are in control or I walk off this case for good. Understand?"

Donaby nodded his head but remained mute. It was like he finally realized he had come to the end of his rope and he couldn't bully, threaten or buy his way out of this fiasco.

CHAPTER THIRTY-SIX

HAPPY

Ken entered the quiet house. "Hello, anyone home?"

"In here, Ken. I'm working on the lion piece for the paper." Lacey's voice came from her room.

Ken walked down the hallway stopping at the door. He leaned against the frame. "Hey Pretty Lady, how about you take a break and we go for a short ride on the horses? We haven't had any time together lately." Pushing away from the door he walked over to her, leaned down and gently kissed her.

Her eyes lit up with happiness. "I'd like that. Give me five minutes to close this up and send it off to Phil."

"Okay. I'll go saddle the horses after…" He kissed her, "Another kiss."

They both laughed.

"Where is everyone anyway? It's so quiet here, Martha is usually baking or something." Ken glanced down the hallway.

"They went over to visit one of neighbors. They will be back in time for supper." Lacey laughed. "You won't miss any meals."

Ken waved at her and left to saddle up the horses.

As he led the animals to the house he saw Lacey waiting on the porch. His thought she was so beautiful in the sunlight. He brought Gracie close to the porch so Lacey could slide on her.

"Comfy?" Ken asked after he adjusted the stirrups.

"Yes, thank you. Where are we riding, anywhere in particular?" She pulled her hat down over her head so it wouldn't blow away.

Ken swung into the saddle, "I thought it might be nice to ride over the ranch and see how many repairs need to be done. I really don't know the whole layout of it. Was there a favorite place you liked to go to when you were young?"

The young couple headed for the old McCann ranch. When they got to the gate, they didn't see any of the Indians but knew they were there and kept going. Turning to the right to follow that fenced area, they cantered the horses, enjoying the day.

Lacey stopped on a knoll where a lone big old tree stood. "How about we take a rest in the shade?

"Sounds good to me." Ken dismounted and letting the reins drop. Then he reached his arms out for Lacey to assist her down. He held her in a warm hug for a moment, then taking her hand led the way to the shade of the tree. They sat down, their backs against the huge old tree, comfortable with each other.

Lacey took off her hat. "I use to bring my sketch pad out here when I was younger."

"You can again. Right before I left town, Mr. Woodman called and said the senator agreed to our offer. We can sign papers tomorrow. Still want to buy back the ranch?"

"Yes. He did? You waited all this time to tell me? You still want to be a partner with me?" Her blue eyes scanned his face wondering why he didn't tell her this earlier.

Taking off his hat, Ken reached into his vest pocket and pulled out a small dark blue velvet box. "I want to be your husband first and then your business partner." He opened the box and took out the engagement ring, his voice husky with emotion, "Lacey, will you marry me? You mean the world to me. Be my wife." He slid the antique ring on her finger.

Tears filled her eyes and she nodded yes and then flung her arms around him holding him tightly. There were so many thoughts running through her mind. A new love, something she never thought she would have again and to be back home. She leaned back to look at him. "I love you, but I think I actually proposed first." And they both laughed.

Lacey sat back and lifted her hand admiring her new ring. "It is very beautiful."

"I'm glad you like it. It was my mother's ring. We can pick out a different one when we buy the wedding bands if you would rather have a new one."

"No, no. I love this. I'm surprised it fits perfectly." She smiled at him.

Ken took a hold of her hand. "Mom had slim fingers like you do." He looked up at her. "She would have loved you as much as I do and given you the ring as her new daughter."

Lacey's spoke softly. "I'll treasure it always and wear it only on special occasions. When we are married, I will only wear the wedding band. With everything I do, I'd be afraid of losing this beautiful diamond."

They were interrupted by the both horses whinnying and they heard the sound of a galloping horse. Soon Bob Running Horse came into view. He slowed his mount coming to a stop by the couple. "Hi, looks like you two are really working hard. Can I get hired on?" He grinned at them as he slid off his horse.

Ken helped Lacey to her feet and she took the few steps to Bob. With a huge smile on her face, she raised up her left hand. "Ken just proposed to me."

"Did you say yes?" Bob asked in a teasing voice.

Lacey gave him a slight punch on his arm. "Of course, Dufus."

Bob gave her a hug and then shook Ken's hand. "You take good care of her. She's like a sister to me."

Putting his arm around Lacey's shoulder's Ken response was quiet but filled with emotion. "Never fear, I never thought I'd be so fortunate to find someone as special as she is."

"Okay, okay, don't go getting all teary eyed on me. What are you guys doing out here anyway besides holding up that tree?" Bob rubbed his horse's neck.

Lacey gave Ken a look of 'should we tell him'? Ken nodded.

"Well, Bob. Yesterday we gave Senator Donaby an offer on this ranch. The lawyer called Ken today and said he accepted it. We sign papers tomorrow. Isn't that great!" She clapped her hands.

"Hey, that's wonderful news. Does that mean I can continue to cut across your property to get home?" Bob gave them a big grin.

They both said together, "Anytime."

With that, Bob took a hold of the reins and swung onto his horse and with a wave, galloped across the field.

Lacey looked at her watch, "I guess we better head back too. We didn't leave a note for Sam and Martha and they will wonder where we are or if something happened."

Ken picked up her hat and handed it to her.

Lacey put her good foot into the stirrup and Ken gave her a boost up and she settled into the saddle.

Ken swung up on Winner and the happy couple walked the horses and talked about signing the papers for the ranch until they got back to Sam and Martha's home.

CHAPTER THIRTY-SEVEN

THE MEETING

Frank, Luke, and Ken sat in the comfortable chairs Judge Robert had in his private chambers.

"I've made arrangements for the case to be moved to Pine Tree County Court House. Their jail is large enough to handle all those involved. The judge there will set up the date for picking the jury. They have a larger pool to chose from than we do and many of the good people around here are ready to hang them all." The judge leaned over and picked up a folder.

Pulling a sheet of paper from the pack, he looked at Ken. "It says here that you suggest bringing the loggers from the ranch to our jail instead of going with the rest of the men to the county seat to wait for the trial to start. Why? They have already tried my patience by leaving the ranch and the drama that happened in the mountains."

The sheriff spoke up instead. "Charles, it's not safe for them to be in cells with the rest of those characters. Everyone one of those men are scared of the senator and his henchmen. Yesterday they contacted Ken asking to come in and tell why they violated the court order. Each man has a member of their family that the senator has used in one way or another to extort money from them. If those men didn't do as they were told," he shook his head, "they or their family member would have received a similar assault as did Charlene. They felt they had no choice. We have their signed copies here." He picked up the file on his lap. "I thought you might want to see them. We are getting more and more stories of the senator's misdealing."

Ken spoke up. "They are ready for their day in court to testify against Donaby. They aren't trying to get any special treatment. This is our suggestion," he gestured over at Frank, "that we dismiss the federal charge of logging on the mountain in exchange for their cooperation and testimonies. You can have them sit in jail racking up expenses for our town or perhaps, we could have them work off some of their energy by doing chores on the ranch. The fences are in bad shape. It would be cheaper for the town."

He continued since no one objected. "They were out there because they didn't rape Charlene or have drugs in their system. They all were drunk from drinking too much. We need their testimonies. The men are use to hard work in the outdoors, not lying around in a crowded cell. The fences around the ranch need repaired and they can be paid for that."

Judge Roberts gave Ken a questioning look. "And who is going to pay them or watch so they don't take off?"

"Well, we can start with repairing the fence bordering the Swenson ranch. Sam would pay half and…well, Lacey and I gave an offer to purchase the McCann place from the senator which he accepted and Lacey and I sign papers today. We would pay the other half. We could still keep the electronic bracelets on them but technically, they wouldn't be under arrest any longer but only needed as witnesses against the senator. There is no way any of the Indians aren't going to keep watch over the place as long as the men are there, no

THE MEETING

matter what we say. In their mind, the sacred mountain was violated and they don't want it happening again. Plus, you know the Indians have Dog who is more wolf than dog. When they have him on guard duty, no one is leaving that house or ranch."

The judge looked over at the other men. "What say you?"

Frank spoke up. "Well Charles, until this trial is over, Ken is basically at the beck and call of those involved. His work with the rangers is going to be sporadic. Therefore he would be available to keep a watch on the men too. I also listened to their stories, and I don't think any of them will run. They want to see justice done. They are victims of the senator as are others that are coming forth. I vote to let them stay on the ranch."

"And you, Luke?" The judge nodded at the sheriff.

"I concur with them. All the guns have been removed from the place. The loggers are no longer afraid for themselves and their families with the senator and his men locked up. I've contacted the authorities where the families live to keep an eye out. But the bottom line is the senator has lost his power over them. The bad boys will have no allegiance to him once the money dries up, and according to all my sources, the senator is strapped for money."

The judge tapped his pencil against his notepad. Everyone kept quiet knowing that this was an unusual request.

"So Frank, you will drop the Federal charges so that only leaves the men to be on the list to give evidence against the senator, correct?"

"Yes."

"Okay, bring them in, I want to talk with them."

Luke stood up. "Well, Charles, they just happen to be over at the jail yet from giving their testimonies to me." He smiled, "I could have them over here in minutes."

Charles smiled. "You got me on that one. Make the call."

***

The four men were uneasy being in the judges' room. The silence in the room was deafening.

Grizzly was nervously stroking his beard; Swede and Buster kept putting their hats from one knee to the other. Gunner sat quietly, not fidgeting. For some reason, he felt safe from the senator here; even though he still wasn't sure all policemen were good.

Judge Roberts picked up a folder. "In here are the federal charges against you for cutting down trees on the mountain. A federal judge could fine you and or send you all to jail. Because of the situation presented by Senator Donaby, and your testimonies of the senator's actions and behaviors, Ranger Captain Frank Collins, Ranger Ken Dickinson and Sheriff Luke Pierson have recommended we drop those charges. Because we want you here or I should say close to the Pine Tree County Court house to testify, we have a proposition for you all."

I can hold you in the local jail, I can have you pay for your own room in the city, or, I can let you stay back at the ranch and work fixing fences or anything else that Lacey or Ken want taken care of. For that Mr. Swenson and Ms McCann or Ranger Dickinson, the new owners, will pay you. The wages will be between you and them. What do you men have to say

THE MEETING

about this arrangement?" The judge looked each man in the face.

Gunner also looked at each man and gave a slight nod of his head. The men in return also gave a slight motion with their head. They agreed. Jail or ranch, food and wages. Like that was even a question that needed answered.

Gunner stood up. "The men and I will work the ranch. None of us will cause any problems. I have one question, Sir."

"Yes?" Judge Roberts replied.

"Can we only be in court to testify but we would like to be there when the verdict is given?"

"Gunner, we will notify you the day before you need to be in court. We will try to have you all there at the same time. You will be in a room off the court room or you can be seated in the court room. Your choice. As to when the verdict comes down will depend on the jurors. We never know when that is. If it happens to late to get everyone back into the room, we will have it the next day. Is there a reason you don't want to be there for all of the trial?" The judge looked intently at Gunner.

Gunner stood up and nervously kept turning the brim of his hat around in his hand. "The senator has his ways to take action against anyone who crosses him. I, we don't want to be there every day wondering if when we walk out of the building, it might be our last day on earth or we would wish it was, if you get my drift."

The sheriff stood up. "Judge Roberts, when Gunner met with the senator at the jail, the senator told Gunner because of his failure to deliver the lumber and money from the sale, he had a bull's eye on his chest. From some of the past dealings of the senator, Gunner knows what the senator is capable of doing." The sheriff sat back down.

The judge nodded his head. "I understand. You will be there for your testimony and you want to be there for the verdict. In the meantime, you will be at the McCann Ranch working for Mr. Swenson and Ranger Dickinson. If for any reason you want to talk with me or aren't satisfied, call me." He handed Gunnar his card.

Judge Roberts looked at each one of the men. "I take it he speaks for each of you too."

The men all stood up as one and nodded their heads.

The judge spoke. "I've been curious as to why of everyone out there at the party, none of you took drugs nor violated any of the women."

Grizzly took one step forward. "It's like this Your Honor. We work in dangerous places. One small step and...well something bad happens like it did for Teach. We've seen how those drugs mess with men. Yeah, we drink too much once in awhile, but none of have ever had a woman that was paid for or forced. We are men."

The look on the other men's faces showed they agreed with Grizzly's reason.

"You men can go and for your peace of mind, our Indian friends will still be watching over you so no one will visit you that shouldn't be. They also have a dog they call Wolf, because he is part wolf. He is trained beautifully. The sheriff will contact you when you are needed in court. Good day, gentlemen."

Once the five men got outside, they slapped each other on the back as they breathed a sigh of relief. No jail. They got to stay on the ranch and make some honest money. And the judge called them, 'gentlemen'. There must be a God looking out for them.

For some rare reason, none of them wanted to celebrate with a drink.

CHAPTER THIRTY-EIGHT

NEW PLANS

Ken, Lacey and Gus had just let the horses out into the corral when they observed a cloud of dust trailing behind Sam's old Jeep as he drove up the lane. The three continued walking to the porch to wait for the couple.

Gus leaned against the porch support and Ken stood next to Lacey with his arm draped loosely around her shoulders as they watch the vehicle approach.

When the Jeep stopped, Ken went over to open the door for Martha.

As she stepped out, she looked first at Ken and then at Lacey. By the smiles lighting up their faces, Martha knew something was up.

Sam came around to their side and opened the back door. "If you all aren't too busy I could use a hand with these bags. Martha made a side trip to town after the visit."

"Sam honey, wait a minute. Those smiles beaming on Ken and Lacey's faces makes me I think they have something more important on their minds that some grocery bags. Am I right?" She had an idea as to why they were so happy.

Lacey caught Martha up in a hug. "You're right! Ken asked me to marry him today!"

Sam grabbed Ken's hand and began pumping it up and down. "Congratulations, son, you sure know how to pick a winner."

Then he turned as Gus joined them, grinning ear to ear.

"Aren't you going to join with the congratulations, Gus?" Sam asked him.

"I done that back in the barn when they told me the good news. I wasn't a bit surprised though." Gus had a smug look on his face because he was the first to know.

Martha spoke up, "Well, we can go up to the house and finish celebrating if you men can bring up the groceries. Hand me the cake box, Sam, don't want you men dropping that. Oh my. Lacey I got you a store bought birthday cake because we were so late visiting, but I guess we can use it as an engagement cake too."

"What?" Ken looked over at Lacey, "Why didn't you tell me it's your birthday?"

She laughed at him, "I guess I had other things on my mind." She waved her hand with the ring on it.

The women headed for the house leaving the men to carry in the groceries.

"Have you called your folks yet?" Martha looked over at Lacey as she placed the cake on the counter.

"No, it just happened this afternoon when we went for a ride. Oh Martha, I'm so happy. Look." Lacey held out her hand showing the antique ring on it. "Ken said this was his mother's. It must have special memories for him. He said I could get a different one when we pick out the wedding bands, but I told him no, this is perfect." Filled with emotion, she reached out to hug Martha again. "I never thought I would be in love again."

"Sam and I think he is a good man too. And young lady, you better quit jumping around with that cast on your foot."

"Oh, you don't know, they called and said I should come in and I can have it removed. I'm going to do it tomorrow."

The men trooped in with the bags.

"Do what tomorrow, Lacey?" Ken sat his bag on the counter.

"Oh, in all the excitement, I forgot to tell you. After you left this morning they called and said I can get the cast off tomorrow. Then I want to visit with Charlene too, and I think we need to sign some papers."

Sam put his hands on his hips and looked back and forth between them. "Sign what papers? You two aren't doing that fancy dancy thing with signing those pre numps or whatever they call them. If you love and trust one another, you don't need those things."

Gus nodded in agreement as he pulled items from the bag and handed them to Martha.

"Oh, Sam." Lacey put her arm around his waist. "Ken informed me today that Donaby is ready to sign off the ranch. He's accepted our offer. That's the papers we need to sign."

"That's what I wanted to hear. Yes, siree." Sam rubbed his

NEW PLANS

hands together. "So, when's the wedding, when do we start looking for cattle, is there any feed at all over there."

"Hold your horses, Sam." Martha plugged in the coffee pot, "Give the kids a moment to fill us in."

Ken pulled out a chair for Lacey and then sat down next to her. "We don't want to set a wedding date until the trial is over with. We need to talk with her folks. As for the ranch, we can't stay there anyway for the time being. I should be asking if it is okay for Lacey and me to stay here until the five men vacate the ranch after the trial. I can go to my place but Frank would like me to oversee the men there without being too obvious."

"Well, of course we say yes." Martha had turned around to face them pointing the knife she was slicing tomatoes with. "You start the marriage out AFTER the vows are said."

Standing up, Ken walked over to the counter and turned around so he could face them all. "I should tell you what else transpired today. Frank, Luke, myself and Judge Roberts met with the five loggers. Because of their testimonies as to why they violated their release, the judge has agreed to let them stay there until it's time to go to the county seat for the trial. In the meantime, they are going to work repairing the fences and anything else that needs done since the senator purchased the place and he has let some of it run down. I said you might be willing to kick in some when they work on the line fence." Ken looked over at Gus, "I know your men can do it, but these guys need to be kept busy and make some money."

Sam, Martha and Gus exchanged looks. Sam went over and shook Ken's hand. "Well, neighbor, looks like we have a deal."

They all laughed.

Martha set the tray with sandwich makings on the table and some beans she had warmed up as they were talking.

They all sat down and filled their plates.

"Sam, Gus. Lacey and I were able to get enough money to buy the ranch and we will be able to purchase about twenty head of beef and feed for this year. I have two horses at the place I'm renting that need a little more training in order to sell that I can use to buy cattle. I'm going to have to rely on you two to help me pick out the right stock. It will take awhile to build up a herd. We figure if we keep the calves we can do it."

Lacey nodded her head and slid over the plate with the sandwich she had made for Ken while he was talking. "I agree. You two are the best ranchers around here."

Gus actually blushed, but he felt proud not only to be included in everything but appreciated for his knowledge on animals.

Squirting some mustard over his piece of ham, Sam asked, "When did you want us to start looking for the cattle?"

"I'm not sure. We need to check out the fences, buildings, see if there is any hay to cut and how the fields are. I was wondering if we would be better to buy in the spring instead of wintering some yearlings especially if we need to buy hay. What do you think?" Ken looked at both men.

Sam spoke up. "Why not let Gus and I mosey around the ranch tomorrow and check it out and then we can talk about it, unless of course you want to ride with."

"Actually, Lacey and I need to sign papers and I also have to go over to my place and check on my horses and I need to go to the office and do some reports there for Frank. The government you know. Lacey is getting her cast off and I want to be with her for that. And she can pick out a different engagement ring if she wants to."

"I told you, I don't want to. I love this one, and you." She leaned over and kissed him.

Sam waited. "I don't understand why the federal charges were dropped."

"Because when Frank heard their testimonies, he figured being hard nose wasn't the thing to do. Then we took everything to the judge and he concurred. What good would it have done? Two trees for a heavy fine and or prison? The four of us figured what had been done to the loggers and Teach was punishment enough. Of course, this info isn't to be broadcast. I came up with the idea of having them work for pay while they were on the ranch waiting for the trial to begin. Hopefully it won't be too long. They are in the process of bringing in people now to select for the jury." Ken took a bite of his sandwich and smiled at Lacey.

Martha left the table and went into the other room. She came back carrying a couple of boxes which she placed next to Lacey. "You can open these now, and then we will have your birthday cake."

First Lacey unwrapped the one from Martha. It was a recipe book. Lacey flipped through it. "These are ones mom made." She smiled at Martha.

"Yes, I took all those hand written ones and typed them out. Your mom was a great cook. If you look in the back, I have some of mine too that are for bigger groups of people, like when you have the cattle round ups." She grinned at Lacey.

The next package was wrapped in brown paper and tied with twine. On the front it said, 'To Lacey from Gus'. Opening it up, she found her best riding boots. They had been resoled and polished so she could almost see her reflection. "Oh, Gus. What a wonderful thing to do. Thank you. Every time I wear them I will think of you."

Once again, Gus blushed. "A good pair of boots taken care of last a long time."

Martha slid an envelope over to Lacey. It was an overnight delivery from her parents. "Cliff from the post office called us and said it was there, so Sam and I picked it up for you today."

Lacey opened the card and a folded check fell out with a note attached. "Happy birthday Sweetie. After our conversation about you and Ken offering the senator to buy back the ranch, Dad and I figured you might need some money. We will call you. Love mom and dad."

Lacey unfolded the check and gasped. "Ken." She handed him the check. $50,000. "This can go for getting some cattle!"

Just then the phone rang. "I'll get it; I bet that is the folks." Excited Lacey went to the phone.

"Hello." She listened for a minute. "Yes, I just opened it. Thank you so much." She paused listening to her mom and her dad who was on the extension.

"Yes, that will be great! Daddy are you sure you feel up to it?" Lacey twisted the phone cord around her finger. "Well, there are five loggers staying there now and the place needs cleaned up."

Martha tapped her on the shoulder. "They can stay here."

"Mom, Dad, Martha just said you can stay here. Oh, and I want you to know that Ken asked me to marry him today! I'm so excited."

Her folks were both talking at the same time.

"Of course I said yes, and what do you mean you weren't surprised?" Lacey laughed.

They talked some more and then Lacey nodded. "Okay, are you driving in or flying?"

After some more discussion, "We will look for you then in a few days. Take your time and don't push it. Dad, you know you need to take it easy. Love you both and thank you so very, very much for the money and everything." Lacey hung up the phone.

Turning to face everyone, "As soon as the loggers get off the ranch, they want to help get the main house back into shape and be part of our wedding plans. Our wedding, money for the cattle, oh my." She went back to Ken, hugging him hard.

He pulled her down on his lap and kissed her tenderly. "Happy Birthday."

Martha, Sam and Gus, clapped their hands and off keyed sang, "Happy Birthday."

CHAPTER THIRTY-NINE

HOSPITAL VISITS

"Boy that feels good." Lacey rubbed her leg where the cast had been. "I didn't realize how heavy it was."

"You healed very quickly. Take care." The doctor gave her a pat on the shoulder and with a wave, left the room.

Ken glanced at his watch, "Well, I think we have time to see Charlene before we sign the papers for the ranch." He patted his shirt pocket that held the check for the sale, "Unless you wanted to see her by yourself."

Lacey looped her arm through Ken's as they strolled down the hallway. "Of course I want you with me. This isn't a 'girl' talk time, but a visit."

Reaching Charlene's room, they discovered she was in Physical Therapy, so they went to visit with Teach who had been transferred to a regular room.

"Knock, knock." Lacey and Ken stood at the doorway of Teach's room. "Feel up to visitors?"

Teach was sitting up in a recliner by the window. A pair of crutches leaned against the wall close to him. He gave them both a questioning look.

Ken stepped forward extending his hand. "I'm Ranger Dickinson, remember, and this is Lacey McCann. We brought Gunner in to see you the night you were brought to the hospital. I was there in the mountain that night. You're looking good, at the time we weren't sure if you were going to make it from loosing so much blood."

Teach gave them a disgusted look. "You should have let me die. I'm a logger and not having a leg…" His voice trailed off as he looked away.

Lacey knelt by his chair. "You have a lot going for you. I just had my cast removed today from my leg, also injured up in the mountain, so I know the difficulty getting around."

"Ha!" The word spat out. "You still have a leg!" He patted his hand in the empty space where his leg would have been. "It hurts and there is nothing there, I've no insurance, a big hospital bill, probably have a warrant out for my arrest for cutting down a stupid tree on Federal land, and no job. So you tell me what I have going for me."

Ken slid a chair over by Lacey. She took his offered hand to stand up and then sat in the chair.

"The workman's comp will cover your hospital bill. Your loss of the leg and pain you have will be part of your life. They do have so many prosthetic legs that will make you mobile and allow you to do whatever you want to."

Lacey reached for his hand. "What have you always wanted to do?" She was glad he didn't jerk her hand away.

"It sure wasn't sitting in jail with one leg."

"Did you always enjoy being in the outdoors working in the

woods as a logger?"

Teach never raised his head, just mumbled, "I didn't choose this job, it was chosen for me." He sighed.

Lacey glanced over at Ken then back at Teach. "If you were to go back to that time, what would have been your preference?"

"I, ah." He looked up at her, "You'll laugh."

She shook her head, "I'd never laugh at anything someone wants to do that they have a passion or aptitude for."

He felt he could tell her, she wasn't making fun of him. "Teach. I've always wanted to teach the little ones, like first graders." His voice had changed from angry and empty to being interested in the subject. "Have you ever watched how they are like little sponges and enjoy learning? Their enthusiasm for new ideas is wonderful."

Ken stepped closer, "Gunner said you were always reading, what type of books were they?"

"Everything, I like to stay abreast on things."

"Have you taken any college courses on elementary education?" Lacey asked.

"Yeah," His momentary positive attitude faded, "but then I had to drop out, money and family, and now this." Teach sighed.

Ken spoke, "I guess you haven't heard then. The judge is dropping the charges against you because of the senator's actions. I also know there are programs out there for people with disabilities. Let's get your physical therapy out of the way, and then plan on getting you enrolled in some classes very soon."

Teach had a shocked look on his face. "What? I'm not going to prison? But I have a guard outside my door!"

Ken smiled, "The guard is to protect you from any repercussions the senator might try. I think his power is gone now and once you are released from here, I think you will be safe."

Lacey offered. "I have many friends in different areas and I'll help you with a lot of the paper work if you would like me to? By the way, what is your given name?"

"Arnie. Arnold Thompson."

"Well, Arnold Thompson, we think you need to rest now, but we will be back." Reaching into her purse, she removed her business card. "You can call me at that number. In the meantime, they do have a computer in the waiting room and you could start checking on schools. I'm sure the doctors have plenty of information on artificial limbs."

Lacey stood up.

"Thanks. Thank to you both. You have given me hope today." Arnie's eyes got teary.

Lacey reached down and put her arms around his shoulders and gave him a hug. "Where there is life, there is always hope. I'll see you in a few days and we'll compare notes." She smiled at him.

Taking Ken's hand, the two left the room and went to see Charlene.

They will never know how much their visit meant to him. They left him with hope and a reason to live.

***

They found Charlene, her parents, and Jean and Phil Conway in the waiting room. They were laughing about something which was a good sign.

"Hey, if we knew the party was here, we'd come earlier." Lacey commented as they entered the room. "What's so humorous?"

Charlene picked up some cards, "My friends have sent some of the funniest get well cards."

"That's great, can we see them too?" Lacey stopped by her.

"Sure." Charlene handed them to her as Ken got two extra chairs for them.

Charlene glanced at Lacey's leg, "You're cast is off. Yeah for you."

"I know and it feels great, I feel like I could leap through the air."

They all laughed.

"Hey, what's that?" Phil pointed at Lacey's hand.

She waved it in the air. "Oh, you mean this beautiful ring I received yesterday from this handsome man." She leaned against Ken.

The women oohed and ahed.

Phil left his chair and shook Ken's hand. "I assume our gal said yes." He laughed. "You are getting one sweet, intelligent women. I won't give you a lecture on how to take care of her because with her intuitive nature, she would only pick a man who would love, cherish and treat her with respect."

Smiling, Jean joined them putting her arm around her husband's. "Now Phil, that sounded more like the father of the bride instead of her employer."

He turned to face Ken and in a serious voice, "In the time she has worked for us, she has become like part of the family. And you young man, when Lacey told me how you went to the hospital with her after the accident and what it meant to her, I knew you were a good person. She was a stranger and you gave her comfort."

"It was more like he saved my life." The tone in Lacey's voice conveyed her emotion.

"What! He saved your life too!" Charlene eyes opened wide with surprise. "Tell me about it."

"She doesn't have to," Phil chuckled, "The local paper will be publishing in tomorrow's edition. Lacey has a series of articles concerning the mountain and the mountain lion that the Indians feel is a spirit protecting the mountain."

Richard joined the conversation. "And my dear, they are also going to run that series in the paper I work for, along with articles on the arrest of Senator Donaby and the upcoming trial."

Charlene's face lost the happiness. "Oh, the trial." Her glance took in them all. "I have such mixed emotions about the trial. Part of me wants it started right away so that evil man and his sick friends get locked away forever, and the other part of me is afraid. I'm afraid to be alone. I want my mom or dad with me all the time." She teared up, "And part of me would like to pummel him with a big stick."

Jean knelt down by Charlene's chair. "I know how you feel, honey. But we are winners remember. We won't let him take our lives away from us. We will stand up in court and have our day. He will never walk free again! When you are healed up, we need to take a self defense class."

Ken spoke up. "I heard that they are selecting jurors now at the county seat and the prisoners are going to be transferred in the next few days. As a matter of fact, Lacey, we need to go and sign the papers."

"What papers?" Phil asked.

Jean laughed, "It's none of your business Phil." She rolled her eyes, "Once a reporter always asking questions."

Lacey stood up, "No problem. Ken and I are buying back the ranch I grew up on from the senator."

"You want to live in that place after that dirty man was there?" Charlene's face was pale. "I could never go back, never." Her voice ended with a hiss.

Lacey responded, "Oh, Charlene, it isn't the house, it was the man. We will have it totally remodeled and cleaned up and then we will go through the house with sage to purify it and say a prayer that the house will once again be a home. The Indians do that too. Have a blessing put on their abodes. The ranch will once more be a place where people are healthy, happy and feel safe like it was when I was growing up."

Ken touched Lacey's elbow, "We better go, the sheriff was going to bring the senator to the visiting room to sign papers before their lunch because then the officers get busy. Oh," he patted his shirt pocket, "I'm out of lemon drops, I need to pick some up."

Lacey laughed, "I think we better make you a dental appointment with all that sugar you consume."

They all said their good-byes. It had been an interesting morning.

CHAPTER FORTY

THE SIGNING

Drumming his fingers in frustration on the table, Senator Donaby was already seated in the room with his lawyer when Lacey and Ken arrived.

"Well, I see the cheating land grubbers are finally here." Donaby sarcastically blurted out as he sprawled out in the chair.

Lacey gritted her teeth at the sound of his voice. She felt Ken's reassuring touch on her elbow as he led her to the chair next to their attorneys. She observed Mr. Malone, Donaby's attorney gave him a look of disgust that said, "Shut up."

Ken's attorney, James Woodman addressed Attorney Vernon Malone. "Have you and Senator Donaby read the sale contract? Are you ready to sign over the deed?"

Donaby opened his mouth to reply but Malone shot him another glare.

Mr. Malone removed the deed from his briefcase. The other attorneys had their papers ready and the check of course. The necessary papers were signed by Donaby and witnessed by the attorneys.

As Mr. Woodman slid the check toward Mr. Malone, Donaby grabbed it off the table.

Waving the check in the air, he harshly remarked, "I suppose you two will be laughing up a storm now for taking me for a ride."

Mr. Malone reached out and grasped Donaby's arm forcibly taking the check from him.

"What are you doing?" Donaby snarled.

"All of your income has been frozen per orders of the court until your finances can be sorted out. We have a folder on claims sent to us on your business and personal transactions. You are being sued from so many states." Mr. Malone put the check and the signed copies into his briefcase. Pulling out another envelope addressed to the senator, he handed it to him.

"What's this?"

"From what I understand, they are papers from your wife. She filed for divorce, and she wants the house in Reno. She said that was a wedding gift from her folks. I'm not handling this, just the charges levied on you from this state. I'll be back tomorrow if you want to discuss anything." Malone stood up and motioned to the jailer to let him out.

Walking down the hall he could hear the loud swearing coming from the room. Guess his client wasn't a happy camper. Tough.

CHAPTER FORTY-ONE

ANOTHER CHALLENGE

Ken and Lacey, Attorneys Woodman, Bartle and Malone stood in front of the jail discussing the changes to be made to the ranch once the loggers were gone. Ken's phone rang. "Excuse me I have to take this call."

"Hello."

"Frank here. I want you to see about getting all that equipment off the mountain. As long as the loggers are at the ranch, I see no reason why they can't load them onto the flat bed trailers and take them back to the ranch."

Ken groaned. "Those men aren't going to be happy about doing that. What if they don't want to go back up there because of Teach's injury?"

"If they don't go, then hire someone from town. I want those rigs off the mountain this week.

Ken knew Frank was irritated with the equipment on the mountain because he could hear him tapping the eraser end of the pencil on the desk pad.

"No, I think they will. They were relieved not to be facing a prison sentence plus able to make a few bucks. Look, I need to

ANOTHER CHALLENGE

talk with Donaby's lawyer about this; he is here now. Ken motioned to Mr. Malone not to leave. "Lacey and I just bought the ranch back from Donaby."

"Wow, you must be moonlighting to afford the ranch. We sure don't pay that kind of money." Frank laughed.

Ken wasn't smiling and his voice was low when he responded. "No, it was the combined insurance money from the loss of our loved ones."

Frank was embarrassed he had teased Ken. "Sorry, Ken, the reason for your money slipped my mind. I'll let you go. Keep me apprised on the equipment removal." The phone went dead.

Timothy Bartle and James Woodman, their attorneys, shook hands with Ken and Lacy. "We'll get the deed recorded at the court house and mail you both a copy, and of course, our bill. Have a good day." With a wave, they walked toward the courthouse.

Ken turned to Attorney Vernon Malone. "Mr. Malone thanks for staying." Pointing with his arm, Ken indicated a local coffee shop. "Would you like to step into the café for coffee? I need to talk with you about something else."

"That would be fine. I don't know about you, but I could use a sandwich too. I never like to eat before talking with my client." Mr. Malone gave a slight smile.

Ken nodded but didn't say anything. He figured being around the senator for any length of time was enough to give anyone an upset stomach.

Lacey, Ken and Mr. Malone walked the few steps to the café.

Once seated and they had placed their orders with the waitress, Ken looked around, seeing no one close enough to overhear began to speak. "My Captain called and wants the logging equipment off the mountain, pronto. He suggested I have the loggers load the equipment up and bring it down by the ranch house. I don't know if they will. The mountain doesn't hold fond memories for any of them. If they won't, I'm to hire someone from town to do it and charge Donaby. Frank could be a jerk and legally confiscate it for being illegally on the mountain and sell it all with the money going to the park service. He prefers not to deal with that."

Mr. Malone leaned back in his chair and waited to speak while the waitress to set down their coffee and left. "Some of the equipment still has some payments due. I appreciate the fact Mr...," He paused, not recalling Frank's name.

"Frank Collins," Ken said.

"I thank you and Mr. Collins for the consideration on this matter. I will have to call the corporate office and see what the status is on the equipment. Then it can be determined if they are to be sold or not." He shook his head, the tone of his voice showing his exasperation with the whole mess.

After the waitress brought their sandwiches she congratulated Lacy. "Lacey, I see you got your cast off. I bet that feels good."

"It sure does, Ginny." Lacey laughed, "I never realized how heavy a cast could be and having to use crutches really slowed me down."

"Enjoy your meal everyone, let me know if you need anything." Ginny left knowing the from the looks on their faces and lack of conversation as she approached the table, this was private business.

"I have a question to ask." Mr. Malone directed his query to Ken. "You may not be at liberty to tell me the answer. I find it completely contrary to the law that the loggers remain free at the ranch instead of in jail with the rest of the men. They were gathered up with everyone at the time of the arrest and I believe caught illegally logging on Federal land."

Ken placed his sandwich on his plate as he weighed his answer as this was Donaby's attorney and he didn't want any problems. "Let me just say that those men were the only ones whose DNA wasn't found on the young lady. The criminal charges have been dropped on that crime. Let's leave it at that."

Mr. Malone nodded in agreement. "It's good those men won't have to pay the curse of working for Donaby."

Lacey whispered in a quiet voice, "Arnie paid a huge price."

"Arnie?" Malone's eyebrow arched.

"He's the man they call Teach who lost his leg during the logging accident that night on the mountain." She sighed, "You must have a very hard time representing Donaby."

Nodding, he sighed. "You're correct Ms. McCann, I do. But even the devil gets his day in court."

***

As they drove toward the ranch, Lacey opened the bag of lemon drops offering one to Ken. "Can I go you with tomorrow when the equipment gets moved? Maybe we should take Sam and Gus also."

"Sure, that sounds like a good idea. Give Sam a call and see if he can meet us shortly at our ranch. I have no idea what condition we will find the house today, so don't be upset if it's messy." He popped the round candy into his mouth. He had no doubt both men would be there about the same time as they were. He knew Sam's calmness would be an asset.

Lacey made the call, the men agreed to meet them at the McCann ranch.

Ken tapped his hand on the steering wheel. "Remind me to take the Sierra in this week for an oil change. Gosh, I like this truck."

"Yeah, she sure rides smooth over the rough terrain. Maybe I need one, too." Lacey grinned over at him.

"What's with calling my truck a 'she'? This is a man's truck, rough, and able to handle anything."

Lacey slapped Ken's arm playfully, giggling she said, "Oh, like you, rough, able to handle anything…even me?"

"Yeap." Squeezing her hand gently, he drove through the gate entering the McCann Ranch. "That sign comes down soon. I'd like to have the boys put up the wood one we designed. What brand will we call our ranch?"

"Let's think about it. If you want to just raise and train horses, it would be different than if our main product is beef, or both. It has to be something that feels right for us both."

He looked over at her. "It's always been known as the McCann ranch since the beginning. I bet God pointed his finger at that plot of land and said, 'This is the McCann Ranch'. Lacey, I have no problem with leaving it that way. Everyone knows and calls it by that name. Even after three years of Donaby of owning it, no one refers to it as the Donaby ranch."

Lacey laughed, "I have a feeling that perhaps God didn't take into consideration the Indians weren't too thrilled with that heavenly announcement."

As Ken pulled around the circular drive, he wasn't surprised to see Sam's Jeep there. Sam and Gus were sitting on the porch talking with the men.

Before getting out of the Sierra, he pinned on his badge. This was official work. Walking around the truck, he opened the door for Lacey, giving her a wink as he lifted her down.

As they approached the porch, they could see the loggers were uneasy about the visit.

"Hi, how are you all today?" Ken asked as they climbed the steps.

Ken heard the quiet replies of "Okay."

Gunner stood up, offering his chair to Lacey.

To ease the tension Ken smiled and then slowly spoke. "Men, I'm here today because I have a job offer for you. My boss, Captain Collins, wants the logging equipment off the mountain as soon as possible." Ken saw the apprehension in their eyes. "Since you all know how they work and how to secure them on the flat beds, we figured you would rather make the money to bring them down from the mountain than for us to hire others in to do it. Once the loaded trucks are back here by the ranch, the attorney for Donaby will hire drivers to take them wherever they are to go."

The men again exchanged glances. No one wanted to go back up to the mountains for various reasons. But they would get paid for it and they did know how to operate the equipment. That made sense.

There was silence, than Gunner nervously spoke up, "You would be there with us, with a gun? We would only work during the daylight hours?"

Ken gave an internal sigh of relief that they weren't going to say no. "Yes to both questions. It should only take one day to load everything up and bring it here and clean up the area. The couple of trees that are down, I want you to saw them up and bring the wood here to be used."

Gunner's eyes were wary, "The rifle, you're sure you will be there the whole time and have a rifle in case any wild animals show up."

Ken knew he had to put him and the rest of the men at ease so they didn't make any mistakes because of being fearful. "I will have a rifle, Sam and Gus will have their weapons too. And I wouldn't be surprised if our Indian friends wouldn't be there as watchers. Now," he looked at each one, "Would tomorrow be okay to bring the equipment down and then the next day we could work on the fences? At the rate they are picking jury members, the trial may be starting soon and then our time won't be our own for awhile."

Grizzly stood up, gave each logger a look then addressed Ken. "I say we should be ready an hour after sunrise. That gives me time to fix a good breakfast for the men. Since we are to buck up the wood, I better pack us a lunch. We can bring that wood back on one of the trucks and have no need to ever go up there again."

"That sounds like a plan to me. Is everyone in agreement?"

All the men nodded yes.

Lacey stood up and turned so she could face them all. "Gentlemen, I will be there tomorrow, taking pictures and writing up a final article on the mountain for the paper. I won't use any pictures showing your faces unless you say it is okay...like the reason for using safety equipment and procedures. I will also pay for a steak dinner for you all if I use anything in reference to your expertise in the logging occupation and get paid for it. That steak dinner can be when it's convenient for you."

That free steak dinner brought smiles to the men's faces and released some of the tension that was hovering in the air.

"Tomorrow morning then." Ken waved and he took Lacey's arm as they stepped down from the porch and headed for their vehicle. Tomorrow would be a long day.

CHAPTER FORTY-TWO

MOUNTAIN SOUNDS

Ole One Ear had returned to his den sated from his night's hunt as the sun was peeking its rays over the mountain. Tired, he got his aging body in a comfortable position to allow his gorged stomach time to digest the contents. He sniffed the air and all seemed right with his world. He let his eyes close for a much needed nap.

It seemed as if he had just shut his eyes when he heard a disturbing noise. He moved slowly, stretching his aching body. He became alert as the sound of the metal monsters came closer. Leaving the shelter of his cave he made his way to a safe view point. There they were, three of them coming nearer. From the other side came horsemen. This wasn't good. He snarled, lashing his tail back and forth in anger.

***

All the men except Gunner, felt good to be doing what they knew, working with lumber and huge equipment. They divided up to ride in Sam's Jeep and Ken's Sierra truck. Gunner, Grizzly and Will rode with Ken and Lacey.

While the rest conversed, Gunner was quiet in his own thoughts. Beads of sweat were on his brow and yet the morning was cool. As far as he was concerned, the Federal

Park Service could blow the equipment up along with that elusive lion hiding up there. He patted his right hip, assuring himself that he still had his knife buckled on.

He raised up his head when he heard what Lacey laugh about what she saw as they reached the area.

There waiting next to the equipment were five Ute men on their horses. Gunner was very pleased to see rifles in their saddle gun holder. So more than the ranger would be armed, that was good. He looked around and took a deep breath; he was feeling a little safer.

As they exited the vehicles, Ken asked Bob Running Horse, "Hey man, how did you know we were coming up here today?"

"Ah Ken, you have to ask? The Spirit of the mountain wafted over to our homes." Then grinning he added. "Well, that and Gus told the men by the gate yesterday and they called us. We thought you could use some help putting the area back to nature."

The men organized themselves getting the wood sawed up and placed on the trucks. Then they loaded all the equipment and secured it tight for the ride down to the ranch. Taking rakes, they smoothed the ground repairing the damage done by the equipment.

One Ear watched the activity from his secure place high in the tree, the leaves blending in with his tawny color. He didn't know what to make of it. The noise, the smell of machines and men were troublesome to him. It all made him upset. He kept his eye on the one two legged animal who kept looking around all the time. One Ear could smell and feel his fear. He swished his tail and snarled. Could he get him in three leaps?

Finished with everything, the men were congregating by the loaded flat bed trucks. Gunner was the last one coming down the path when Grizzly hollered at him. "Gunner, one of the axes got left by that larger rock, better pick it up, we don't want to lose it."

Ken stopped to wait while Gunner turned back to retrieve it. It was then that Ken noticed the mountain lion crouched low on the limb of the tree. Sliding the strap holding the rifle off his shoulder, Ken slide the safety off and quickly raised the gun holding it tight against his shoulder as he zeroed in on the lion, his finger ready on the trigger. "Gunner, don't move!"

Gunner froze, the hairs stood up on the back of his neck and he didn't need to be told why or see why, he could smell it. He screamed silently, "Shoot it!" But he didn't say a thing or move a muscle, just kept his eye on the snarling lion that was now standing up.

In an instant moment, Bob seemed too appeared out of nowhere next to Ken. "Wait man, don't shoot." Bob slowly walked toward Gunner murmuring something in his native language.

Gunner didn't want to hear anything but the sound of the rifle going off and the thud as that creature hit the ground. He stood as still as that large rock keeping his eyes on the huge mountain lion.

Bob began chanting louder as he got in front of Gunner and they slowly began to back down the path. The other Indians had crept up on each side of the trail and were also singing out in their language asking the Spirit of the mountain to protect man and beast as they returned the mountain to her keeping.

One Ear was confused. Part of him wanted to leap on that two legged enemy but something in the tones were telling him to go back to the higher mountain, back to Mother Earth, back to safety. He slowly eased his taunt body down onto the limb and watched as the beings lengthen the distance between them.

Ken put the safety back on his rifle and everyone breathed a sigh of relief with the danger over.

Lacey had been clicking away catching this moment of Indian faith on her camera. Many would never believe this, but those who witnessed it would never doubt the power of the Spirit of the mountain. Could she convey this in print? It would be the final installment of her series.

Gunner sat down on the running board of a truck and waited for his blood pressure to return to normal. When he looked back up the trail, he blinked twice; the lion was no longer there. Standing up he grabbed Bob's shirt sleeve. "Where did it go? I never saw it get down!" He whirled around looking behind him.

"Relax man. That is the way of the spirits. You should thank your God too. This has been a good day. "

Ken got everyone attention when he called out, "Time to move these rigs down to the ranch. Leave them in the field by the barn. I'll be the last one to leave and follow you all down."

Ken and Lacey watched as the trucks roared into life and slowly make their descent down the steep hill. Sam and Gus headed toward their ranch; and the Indians mounted their horses and spread out each to their place.

Hand and hand Lacey and Ken turned around and looked at the mountain. Lacey touched the camera, "I got many impressive pictures today. Soon, the scars will be gone, more seeds will take root and she will be once more dressed in her green finery. Let's go, I've got some articles to write."

"Not until you give your wonderful driver a kiss for your safe travel up and down the mountain." Wrapping his arms around her, he leaned down his head and was rewarded by her very loving kiss.

One Ear never observed that, he was back in his den, sound asleep.

CHAPTER FORTY-THREE

DONABY

The cell door clanged shut behind Donaby. He had finished another unsuccessful discussion with his attorney and was extremely upset. Things weren't looking good for him. Money was tight and that mouse of a wife was leaving him and taking everything she legally could. His so called friends that had enjoyed his money, wining and dining were turning their backs on him, disappearing like cockroaches when the lights came on. Those ratfinks had been at his beck and call when the money was rolling in, but now, when he needed some help, they were hiding in their well feathered nests.

Exhausted, he wearily plopped down on his bunk. He held his throbbing head in his hands. His wife, ha! That cold ugly fish. He only married her for her ole man's money. I always wondered why she never got some plastic surgery done, some bigger boobs, become a blond and show it off. She could wear something sexy instead of those clothes that reminded him of a board meeting. Maybe she doesn't look in the mirror. Well at least they didn't have a bunch of brats running around for him to act like a doting parent for the media. He smiled, well none that he knew of, some of the babes he's been with…nah, they all knew how to take care of those types of mishaps.

Something surfaced from the back of his mind about money.

Her dad's will, there was suppose to be another release of funds, when and why the delay? He laughed, ah yes, the delay...to prove to the attorney he could handle money and be responsible as in ethical. There was some clause in there for his wife too, what was it?

He got up and paced the small cell. He rubbed his chest, it felt tight, must be that rotgut coffee they served here. Divorce. That was it. If his wife got divorced and wasn't in contact with him, the attorney could turn over some of the finances sooner to her. The ole tightwad didn't want his hard earned money wasted and wanted to make sure his only daughter was taken care of.

With a smug look on Donaby's face, he knew if he could get his wife here to see him, he could sweet talk her into giving him some money. He knew how to play her strings. He had done it enough times. She was so desperate for attention and easy to sway his way.

He needed more cash so he to hire some money hungry attorneys who would get him off by any means possible. Old Malone didn't like him in the first place and Donaby doubted if he would really put on a good case for him. Matter of fact, he bet Malone would go to the other side in a heartbeat if he could.

When they bring me my meal, I'll have the jailer call Malone and tell him to come back and see me tonight. I can convince him to use a little leverage to get wifie poo to come visit me. Just because she filed for divorce doesn't mean a thing. I'll put my arms around her and tell her all the things she wants to hear and she'll melt. It always works.

In the meantime, he didn't like the way his men and so called friends were giving him the cold shoulder. Who in the heck did they think they were? Not of them were choir boys and they all had fun that night.

He took a couple of deep breaths, it sure was warm in here, probably didn't have a good air exchange. Figures, hick of a town, lucky they have indoor toilets.

Man his men had scored some strong drugs, good liquor and hot women for the party. Everyone was bombed or drunk and having fun. So he broke in that newspaper reporter's daughter. Big deal. Someone was bound to sooner or later. Besides if her jerk of a dad hadn't put my picture and name in the paper about that gambling fiasco, he'd never had his boys pick her up. Too bad the cheapskate didn't get the money together fast enough to prevent that. I don't know who roughed her up, but it wasn't me.

So far he told his men and so called friends not to say a word about the party, don't offer anything, and just remain mute. Let the burden of proof fall on the police. Don't admit to anything. Plus they were po'ed because they needed some top notch attorneys and they weren't getting them. Those with wives were putting up with the crying and 'how could you do this to the family' bit.

His thoughts were interrupted by one of the deputies.

"Tomorrow we are moving you all to the county seat. The jury has been chosen and the trial will start on Monday. You might want to contact family for clothes unless you don't mind wearing the jail jump suits. We will assist each of you in your calls after the meal which will be served soon."

"Call my attorney, Malone now. I need to talk with him."

"I will as soon as I get all the meals served." With that, the deputy left the area.

The words going through Donaby's mind at that time were R rated. He needed more time, what to do, what to do? Think. He wiped the sweat from his brow.

Malone, he needed Malone. He hated waiting. He tried before by making obscene noises to get the guards attention and respond to him. Instead they ignored his actions, telling him to mind his manners. Jumping up he started pacing his small cell again, he was ready to explode he was so angry.

Donaby kept pacing back and forth irritated that Malone didn't get here right away. It wasn't like the town was this big he couldn't be here in minutes. And his excuse of a wife, she wouldn't accept his phone call. He rubbed his left shoulder that had been aching off and on. He felt nauseated, must have been that poor excuse of a meal they brought him. He only took a bite or two. The jailer didn't know how close he came to throwing it in his face.

Sweating, Donaby dropped down on his bunk to get his breath. He was so mad at Malone making him wait; visions of different things came to his mind that he'd like to do to him, or have his men do to him. He didn't like to get his hand bloody, but he didn't mind watching them make people do his bidding. Too bad the cops made them visit in that interrogation room. If they met here, slamming Malone against the bars a few times changing the contour of his nose might convince him to quickly produce some positive results.

Um, that heartburn was getting worse. He perked up as the jailer came to his cell.

"Mr. Malone is here to see you." The jailer spoke into the mike on his shoulder, "Open cell door five." There was a click and the door opened.

"About time that old geezer got his…" Donaby went to stand up but felt dizzy. He used both hands on the mattress for leverage.

"You okay, Donaby?"

"Yeah, it's just the crummy food you jerks serve here." Holding on to the bunk pole and taking a deep breath, he slowly stood up. The few steps to the door seemed a long way off.

Offering Donaby his arm, the deputy spoke. "You don't look good, need some help?"

Shrugging off the offer, Donaby leaned against the wall to support himself and swore, "I just need some fresh air. Keep your crummy hands off me."

Watching the slow progress that wasn't like Donaby, the jailer was wondering if he was trying to pull something on him by acting sick or was he ill. "I'm going to get you a wheel chair. It won't take a minute."

"You can put that wheelchair where the sun doesn't sh shinne…" Grabbing his chest, he collapsed.

From the control booth, "Is he faking or he is really down?"

Trying to find a pulse, "He's down, better call 911 and get some oxygen down here." And he began CPR on Donaby. He sure was glad he didn't have to do the mouth to mouth resuscitation; he didn't want to be that close to that sorry excuse of a man. Now the medics say just keep up the chest compressions. He'd do that since the EMTs would shortly arrive.

CHAPTER FORTY-FOUR

NEWS FLASH

THE WEEKLY SENTINAL

Special Edition

"Senator Donaby, the key figure in the arrests that took place at his ranch, passed away last evening in the city jail. He was declared dead from a massage heart attack by the Emergency Department physician.

In a conversation with Mr. Donaby's attorney, Mr. Malone, he stated there was no evidence of heart problems and the senator wasn't taking prescribed medication of any kind, but it was also noted Senator Donaby hadn't had a physical in many years. The senator's life style wasn't a healthy one.

Per the attorney, the body is being flown to his home state where a private immediate family burial will be held.

Senator Donaby has been in the senate for ten years.

The rest of the prisoners are still being moved to the county seat for the trial that begins on Monday.

Our city isn't use to this type of notoriety. Hopefully we will remain aware of what excessive alcohol and drugs do to people and the community."

Phil quit reading out loud and let the paper fall down on the table. No one said a thing, each in their own thought. He, Jean and the Hartel family were having breakfast together at the hospital as they had been doing daily.

Charlene was the first one to speak. "Do they have pain when they have a heart attack? I hope he did, that he had lots and lots of pain and suffered and begged for help and everyone just stood around and laughed at him like they did to me! I'm glad he's dead, he was a mean, mean man!" She burst into tears.

Her parents put their arms around her; they didn't say anything just held her tight and let her cry out her emotions. Perhaps all the anguish of what she experienced would be lessened.

Phil took Jean's hand and squeezed it, they didn't need to speak either, after all the years together, each one knew what the other was thinking.

Teach, or Arnie as everyone was calling him, came rolling down the hallway as fast as he could roll it and entered the hospital cafeteria. He knew they ate together for breakfast. "They just had the news on the TV. Donaby is dead of a heart attack; no one did him in for all his cruelty." He stopped his wheelchair next to their table and saw The Weekly Sentinal lying there. "Oh, it's in the paper too!"

He took in the tears on Charlene's face. "Are you okay?"

"Yeah. He's dead." She tapped the paper with her finger. "There is a God! That mean old man will never hurt anyone again like he did us! Who knows how many others are out there that suffered because of him!"

NEWS FLASH

Looking at her parents, Charlene asked, "Does this mean I don't have to go to the court house now, we can go home?"

Mona handed her a tissue. "No, Honey. There are still the other men who need to be tried for their actions. Remember, the judge said you can remain in a different room."

Arnie wheeled closer to her. "Yeah, this sure has been a crazy ordeal. I don't know what is going to happen either. Did you folks know that the federal man dropped the charges for cutting wood in the National Forest? We were still to be in court, but now I don't know what is going to happen. The doc said I could be released from here and come in for therapy, but where am I going to go? I don't have any money. How am I to get around?" He shook his head.

Phil spoke up. "Where is home Arnie? Do you have family there?"

"Yeah, I have family and friends who could drive me for PT and I want to enroll in school but I could do online classes. My home is in California."

Nodding, Phil continued, "I think until the court deals with the senator's death and how this all translates to his illegal actions, we all need to stay put. You will be getting some compensation from the logging job for your injury. I would suggest you hire an attorney. I assume you would be eligible for some government assistance with your injury too. Let me get in touch with Lacey. She will know if and what there is available here in town and then see about your home town. By the way, have you eaten breakfast yet?"

Arnie nodded. "But another cup of coffee would be nice. It gets rather boring eating alone all the time."

Richard pushed his chair back, "I'll get it. Cream or sugar?"

"Black is fine, Sir."

Wiping her eyes on her sleeve, "Daddy, get him one of those blueberry muffins too." Charlene looked over at Arnie, "Mine was really yummy."

"Aye, aye, captain." Richard saluted his daughter and made his way over to the food.

Phil's phone rang. He looked down at it than answered. "Good morning, Lacey."

"Phil, did you see the news on TV? Donaby is dead."

"Not the TV, but the paper put out a special edition with that and a rundown of the arrest. I'm glad you called. Arnie, or Teach as you call him, is here with us. I was wondering if you would know who to see here in town for some assistance for him that would also connect with those in his home town in California. The doctor could release him if he had someplace to go and get his pt as scheduled. With Donaby dead, I don't know how the workmen's comp claim will work. Was Donaby sole owner?"

"Gee, I don't know, Phil. Is this an assignment for me?" She laughed. "Just wondering if I was getting paid for this from you or doing because of the wonderful charitable person I am."

"Um." Phil rubbed his chin. "You know, I think this would be a good assignment, the human interest part of the difficulties people who have this type of injury run into. You could also tie this into the trial and the type of extortion Donaby had over his men causing them to do dangerous things."

NEWS FLASH

"Tell Arnie, I'll be in to see him this morning and then go to a few places in town for some info and also check out his hometown options. Until we know what the court decides, he can't leave town. Mom and Dad should be arriving today or tomorrow, and then we will start making some wedding plans. As soon as the men are gone from our ranch, we are going to get the house spruced up too."

Chuckling, Phil commented. "Well my dear, you can never say you are bored. We'll be looking forward to seeing you. Oh, do you have that installment about the lion ready?"

"Well, I have it written, but I wanted to go up and see if I could get another picture, a close up one. You know, make it more personal."

"Lacey, no. No more injuries. The pictures you have are enough and that's an order. Oh, have you turned in your time to the office so they can cut you a check?" Taking his pocket calendar from his jacket, Phil looked at current month. "Because of Donaby's dying, I doubt if the court proceedings will take even two weeks. Jean and I will be leaving when that is done, unless you plan on a quickie wedding."

Phil listened as a laughing Lacey turned to tell those in the kitchen what Phil had just said about a quickie wedding.

"Phil, Ken said that might not be a bad idea. See you in about an hour. Bye."

Hearing the phone click, he relayed to the rest at the table what Lacey had said. Then he rubbed his hands together, looking at Arnie. "Once that little lady sinks her teeth into a subject, she will get all the info you need."

Richard set the tray with the coffee and muffin in front of

Arnie. "Enjoy."

Looking at everyone around the table, Charlene smiled; this was the best day since she had been here. Donaby was dead.

CHAPTER FORTY-FIVE

THE DAY BEFORE

Ken felt a sense of pride as he drove under the large wooden sign of the ranch with the burned in letters *THE M&D RANCH*. A new beginning as Lacey McCann and Ken Dickinson make a new home and life together on the ranch. He had the rest of his belonging except for his wedding clothes in the back of his red Sierra to put in the closet. His three horses were already on the ranch along with the small herd of cattle they had purchased.

He smiled at how Sam and Gus enjoyed checking out the sale barns for the cattle and the new bull. Thanks to the healthy check from Lacey's folks, the herd they purchased was of good stock.

Tomorrow. The big day, he was marrying the most wonderful woman. He never thought he could love anyone again after he lost his wife. They were two different women, but both loving, caring, intelligent ladies. He was a very fortunate man.

As he pulled to a stop by the house, Lacey came out on the porch to greet him.

"Hi beautiful." Getting out of the truck Ken greeted her by taking her in his arms and kissing her warmly. Holding her close he looked around, "Where's your folks?"

"Over at the Swenson's. They are having the time of their lives with our wedding. I think they have enough food ready for the whole state." She snuggled closer to him. "Hum, you smell good."

Ken laughed. "Good ole soap and water." Reaching into the back of the Sierra, he pulled out a garment bag which Lacey took and two large suitcases. "I left just my wedding duds at the rental place. It sure seems quiet and lonesome over there since I brought the horses over here." They carried the clothes to the master bedroom.

"It's only one more night, Honey." Lacey smiled up at him.

"I know. Sam and Martha said I could stay there with them, but it has been so busy with all the preparations going on and I do have my job it was easier to stay at my place. Hey, good news, I do have next week off after all. Are you sure you don't want to go on a honeymoon somewhere? People will think I'm too tight to take you on one." He laughed.

Hanging up the last shirt, Lacy shook her head. "Nope. I've spent too many weeks in motels with my job. After remodeling the house, I can't wait for us to start our life here together. Here, on the M and D Ranch, our ranch, our home." She turned giving him a warm hug. "Oh, mom and dad are staying with Sam and Martha tomorrow night so we can have the house to ourselves. Then they are leaving the next day… Dad has another medical appointment to go too. He has been pretty good as long as he doesn't over do it."

Ken looked out the window at the buildings, "I want to check on the horses and then what would you like to do or is there something I need to do?"

"Well my dear soon to be husband, the horses have been fed, watered and brushed. If it's all right with you, what I would really like to do is look in on the decorating of the tent where the lunch and dance will be held. We could take the horses; I think they could use a little exercise."

Ken was surprised by her answer. "Okay, let's saddle up." Taking her hand as they walked toward the horse barn he asked. "How are the two workers doing?"

"Fine. You realize letting Gus and Sam hire them and pick out the herd was the smartest thing we could do. I'm afraid though, the horses might be getting spoiled with all the attention they are getting." Lacey laughed. "And for some reason, Sam and Gus just happen to mosey over just about every day checking on the men. Of course with the folks here and everything we were doing, it just seems normal."

Adjusting her worn western hat to keep the sun out of her eyes, Lacey smiled over at Ken. "I'm so glad the trial was quickly over with. I was afraid it would take forever and put Jean and Charlene mentally through the whole ordeal over and over with the questioning. Oh guess what, I received an email from Charlene this morning saying she is back in school and caught up with her homework. She is such a good kid."

Nodding his head in agreement Ken said, "She sure is. I think the counseling she received right away was instrumental and the fact that she could share with Jean was a plus. Letting all that anger, fear and stress out helped the mental healing begin. Physically she will be okay too."

Working together, Ken saddled up Winner and Lacey chose Gracie. She would be riding her tomorrow for the wedding. The horses Ken was training were not ready for the excitement of all the other horses and people that would be there tomorrow.

Once in the saddle, they walked the horses for a short way when Lacey looked mischievously at Ken, "Race you to the tree."

"You're on!"

Both riders urged their horses on but Ken won. Winner was a younger, faster horse, but the two didn't really care who won, they were just enjoying life together.

Laughing, they got off their horses, embraced, and then secured the animals to the rope corral set up for tomorrow.

Stepping into the quiet tent, the two were amazed with the decorating. "Oh Ken; look at the card box on the gift table." The two walked over to examine it closer. Someone had made a replica of the ranch house and even had dolls in the rocking chairs on the porch. On top of the porch roof was a miniature copy of the M&D sign at the entrance to the ranch. The tables were decorated in white and turquoise as were the bows attached to the chairs. The side of the tent would be rolled up so their guests could see the happy couple take their vows next to the special tree.

The refrigerated truck would be there two hours before the wedding with food and beverages needing to be kept cold along with the wedding cake. "Mom and Martha have a lot of bars and cookies to go on the table with the cake. The men from Sam's place will have the steer roasting over a pit starting this evening. I'm getting so excited." Lacey's eyes were sparkling as she threw herself into Ken's arms smothering him in kisses.

Pulling back slightly Lacey asked, "Have you written down what you want to say at the ceremony tomorrow?"

"Don't need too. I'm marrying the prettiest, smartest lady in the world; I'll just be speaking from my heart." He kissed the tip of her nose. "I hope considering your way with words you won't have a small book to read." He laughed.

"No, not that long, I just want to make sure you promise to honor and obey me or I'll never help muck out the barn." She broke out laughing.

Picking her up and twirling around he responded, "Oh, that's what I was going to say."

"Funny. Put me down. I think we better get back to the house so you can think of something very unique to say." Laughing as they walked to their horses, both were thinking, "Life will be good."

CHAPTER FORTY-SIX

MORNING OF THE BIG DAY

Lacey woke up to a beautiful, perfect day for their wedding. The large tent had been put up yesterday with the plywood floors for dancing after the meal. The refrigerated truck was coming this morning with ice, food and beverages. The porta potties were in place and a rope corral was put up for the horses. A stock tank with water was next to it. All other vehicles would be left at the field by the house. The ceremony would take place by the huge old tree where Lacey spent a lot of time as a young girl.

In the silence of the early morning, she laid there comfortable in her bed which would soon be their bed. Ken's clothes were already in the closet. She got up, opened the door, taking the sleeve of his favorite jacket, lifted it up to her nose and took a deep breath. She loved his clean smell.

Twirling around, she started singing, "I'm getting married this noon to a wonderful man."

She was interrupted by her mom knocking on the door. "Love the singing my dear, but we have things to get done, soon to be Mrs. Ken Dickinson."

Opening the bedroom door, Lacey gave her mom a big hug. "I'm so happy mom, I feel like I could float around in the air.

I'm in heaven."

Hugging her back, her mom said, "Well, let your feet touch earth and take a look at the list to make sure everything is okay."

The two were looking over the note pad and checking off everything that was done when there was a knocking on the door. "I wonder who that is." Lacey asked as she reached for her robe.

Opening the door she found Bob Running Horse. "Is everything okay, Bob?"

"Yes. I have something from our people for you." He turned and pointed to the most beautiful all white mare complete with an expensive new saddle and woven saddle blanket.

Lacey was completely overcome with emotion. "For me?" Barefoot she slowly went down the steps to the almost mystical horse that turned her head toward Lacey as if she knew Lacey would now be her new mistress.

Putting her arms around the horse's neck, she leaned against her. "Oh, you beautiful, beautiful lady." Lacey rubbed her hand along the horse.

Turning to Bob, "I thought you were training her for your princess to ride in the parade. Are you sure she is mine?"

"My people have done this. You will ride her instead of Sam's, Gracie. A white horse for a new beginning. She is young, and be with you for a long time."

With tears in her eyes, Lacey threw her arms around Bob hugging him tightly. She knew the value of a well trained horse and this one also had good formation. Not to mention the specially made saddle to fit the animal. They aren't cheap. "I will be so honored to ride her to my wedding ceremony. I am extremely humbled by this amazing gift. I can't thank you and your kin enough."

"You already have in more ways than you will ever know, Lacey McCann. You and your family have always been there for us." Bob put her at arm's length, "Now, I know you have a lot to do, I'll put her in the horse barn. What are you going to name her?"

"What have you called her as she was being trained?"

"White Beauty."

"Then White Beauty she remains." Lacey touched the muzzle, "Yes, you are a beauty." The horse nickered and nuzzled her head against Lacey as if to say, 'we will make a good pair'.

Taking the reins, Bob lead both horses toward the barn, "See yah in a couple of hours."

Lacey watched her amazing gift until Bob and White Beauty entered the barn. She turned to go in the house. "Mom, can you believe that?"

Her mother smiled, "What a wonderful way to start the day. Now, off to the shower, time to get busy, we have a wedding today." She was interrupted by the phone ringing, "I bet that is Martha. Scoot."

CHAPTER FORTY-SEVEN

THE WEDDING

Ken drove into the yard already full of trucks pulling horse trailers and SUV's. For those not riding their own horses, two wagons with hay bales for guests to sit on were hitched to large work horses. The harnesses were polished and someone had braided the tails of the horses and woven turquoise and white ribbons in them.

Pulling into the garage, he shut the Sierra off. Hopefully no one would look in here to decorate it. Lacey might change her mind about staying here tonight.

Patting his shirt pocket to make sure her wedding band was there; he picked up his black western hat, slid out of the truck and locked it. He closed the garage doors and went in the back door to the house to bypass all the well wishers out front that hadn't headed toward the wedding ceremony area.

He opened the door to see Martha, Sam, and Gus and Lacey's mom conversing.

"Well, son, you finally made it. We thought maybe you were getting cold feet and skedaddled out of town." Sam laughed as he shook Ken's hand.

"Never fear, I've been looking forward to this day. My bride to be hasn't flown the coop has she?"

"No way!" Came the laughing voice of Lacey from what would be their bedroom. "I know a good man when I see him and I'm gonna put my ring on his finger."

Then as she walked into the kitchen, Ken took in a deep breath and removed his hat. "You are so beautiful."

There was total silence for a moment as the message of love traveled across the room to each other.

"Ain't there suppose to be something about bad luck seeing each other before the ceremony?" Gus was looking at the parents.

Lacey came over and put her arm around Gus. "We don't believe in that old wives' tale." Raising her skirt a bit, she gave a kick with her foot. "Did you notice I have on my boots you gussied up for me?" She gave him a kiss on the cheek.

Gus blushed and shook his head.

Then Lacey twirled around and with sparkling eyes, "Do I look okay, Ken?"

"Stunning."

Lacey had on a white gathered peasant blouse with a turquoise Concho belt. Her white full skirt rested on the top of her boots. She was wearing her mother's turquoise necklace and a very happy smile.

Ken stepped forward and she met him for a hug. "I think this will go with your outfit." Removing a box from his black trousers, he handed it to her.

Lacey opened it to find a pair of earrings of turquoise and silver that had the initials of their ranch sign. M&D. The M&D were small and blended in the silver around them. "Oh Ken, how perfect!" She immediately put them on.

Martha interrupted, "The last wagon with guests just left, I think it's time we head out too."

"Thanks, I'll hurry and get the horses saddled." Ken gave Lacey a quick kiss on the cheek and grabbed his hat from the table.

Sam chuckled, "Just mosey out you two, Bob has the horses ready. Gus is going to drive us folks in the buggy. Don't forget the license and wedding rings."

"I got them." Lacey's dad called out. He had been resting until the last minute.

When Lacey and Ken stepped out on the porch, Ken gave a whistle. "Wow, where did you get that horse? What a beauty."

Bob holding the reins didn't say a word, just smiled, but Lacey answered, "It's a wedding gift from Bob and the families on the res. Her name is White Beauty."

Ken whistled. "And that she is. We will take very good care of her."

Lacey's mom came quickly out the door. "Lacey, you forgot the shawl." She put the white sheer lacy shawl on her head, placing a round turquoise band to hold it in place. "Okay, now you are ready."

Ken bent giving Lacey a leg up on the horse and then got on Winner. Gus climbed into the driver's seat of the open surrey as the men assisted the ladies in it. Bob jumped on his horse and went ahead of the wedding party to let the guests know the family was coming.

As the group approached the waiting guests, they could hear the strains of music from the guitar players. Bob hitched the horses to the corral and then stood at the back of the full tent.

Lacey and Ken had walked hand and hand to the front with Lacey's parents, Martha, Sam and Gus following behind and then taking the seats left for them in the front.

Judge Charles Roberts was officiating. He smiled at the couple, "I'm happy to see neither one of you got cold feet."

There was a ripple of laughter from the guests.

When it was quiet, he began, "We are gathered here to witness these two young people take the vows of marriage. If there is anyone to object, let them make it known now."

There was a twitter of laugher when Gus stood up and looked over the assembly of wedding guests.

"Sit down, Gus," hissed Martha tugging on his sleeve.

"Well I just wanted to make sure no one said anything 'cause those two are meant for each other."

There was another round of laughter as everyone there knew Gus was an honorary member of the family.

The judge continued, "Our gal Lacey met her man in an unusual way, being saved from being supper for a hungry, injured mountain lion. And her hero, Ken is now being saved from being single."

That brought out appreciative smiles.

"Lacey told me this place right here by this tree is her favorite place on the ranch where she has spent many hours and it is fitting that it will now hold the memory of becoming Ken's wife."

He went on with interesting facts about Lacey as a child, barrel racing at the county fair when the horse rounded the barrel and she didn't, to how she grew up to being involved with the different charities and organizations in town and her thirst of knowledge leading to a career as a journalist and photographer.

"We are a small community and protective of our own so when Lacey and Ken asked me to marry them, I thought I better learn more about this man." He looked over his glasses at the gathered friends. "We all know if you weren't born and raised here, you're a new comer."

Someone from the back of the tent called out, "You got that right judge."

Ken was getting embarrassed and moved slightly. Lacey squeezed his hand.

The judge waited for the crowd to quit laughing.

"I went back to the city he came from and talked with his co-workers at the police department and some of his friends. I couldn't even find a parking ticket."

That comment brought out some more quaffs from the guests.

"What I did find was a man of good morals, one who pays his bills, goes the extra mile, is a good friend and keeps his word.

In the short time that Ken has lived here working as a Ranger, he has shown that he is a man of ethics, good with people and animals and respects Mother Nature. You can't ask any more of that in a man."

Looking at the assembled people, Judge Roberts saw only affirmative head nods. "Now I'll have them say all the proper words to make it legal and then they can share what they have to say to each other." After Lacey and Ken said their vows and exchanged the gold wedding bands, and declared their love for each other, he had them turn and face their family and friends. "Let me introduce, Mr. and Mrs. Ken Dickinson."

There was clapping of hands and some whistles from the younger ones and those on the drums gave drum rolls as the couple hand and hand went down the aisle followed by the family.

A meal, a dance and lots of fun and then the day was over. Everyone had left, even the caters had cleaned up and were gone with their truck. The men would deal with the tent and make shift corral the next day. Lacey and Ken rode their horses home in the moonlight. Home. Their home. They sat in the rocking chairs on porch and went over the whole day and how special it was.

"I bet you never thought saving my life would result in marrying me did you?" Lacey laughed.

"No, and I think maybe I should go check on that old lion and leave him a hunk of beef as a thank you." Ken chuckled as he rose from his chair. Taking her hand he gentle pulled her up from the chair.

"Mrs. Dickinson, I hope you didn't eat too much wedding

cake so I don't wrench my back when I carry you over the threshold." He swooped her up in his arms, holding her tight, smothered her face with kisses.

"If you do, I'll play nurse." She laughed as they entered the house and Ken shut the door with his foot.

CHAPTER FORTY-EIGHT

THE RIDE

The newlyweds were having breakfast. "I can't explain it, Ken." Her face was serious. "I woke up with this pull towards the mountain, like I was meant to be there. I know it doesn't make any sense. Maybe because it was where I first met you and you saved my life and now we have joined our lives together." She shook her head slightly looking to see his expression. "Oh, I don't know. Maybe I have lived too long around here and believe in the spirit of the mountain and perhaps I'm supposed to give her thanks for giving you to me." She gave him a half grin. "You didn't know you married a slightly crazy woman did you?"

Ken was quiet for a minute. In the short time he had lived in the area, this request of hers wasn't to be taken lightly. Taking her hands in his, "If you want to go up to the mountain today, we will. I can see and feel this is very important to you."

Lacey jumped up from the chair, throwing her arms around Ken hugged him tightly. "Thank you. This means a lot to me."

They saddled up the horses and Ken grabbed the bag from the Sierra that was equipped with the usual necessities a ranger always carried, tied it on the back of his saddle and slid the rifle in the boot. Mounting up, the happy couple turned their horses toward the mountain.

THE RIDE

They rode for a short while in a comfortable silence in the sunny day enjoying the beauty of the land.

Patting Winner on his neck, Ken looked over at Lacey. "I still find it unusual that you would want to go back up in the mountain to the area where you were injured. I would think it would bring back the fear."

Any comment from Ken was cut off as Bob and the elderly medicine man from his Ute tribe came into view. They waved and waited for Ken and Lacey to join them.

"Good Morning. What brings you two here this fine morning?" Ken inquired.

"Grandfather woke me saying the mountain was calling." Bob spoke for them both.

Ken nodded. "Do you have any area in mind? We," he smiled at Lacey, "are riding up to the area where we first met."

"Grandfather said, 'the path'. I hope you don't mind." Bob felt uncomfortable between letting his friends have time alone this first day of their married life. Yet, there was no way he couldn't follow the wishes of his elderly Spiritual Leader. He couldn't deny his upbringing and faith.

Lacey looked at the wise old gentleman with respect, "I too was awaken about 1:00 this morning with a silent call from the mountain. I could not discern the message." She gave a slight bow with her head. "I am honored to have you with us. Would you please lead the way?"

"It is good you listened to the wind." The elderly man lightly touching his horse led the way.

The four riders rode in a comfortable silence, each had their thoughts but also appreciating the majesty of the mountain. Conversation wasn't necessary. They passed by the spot where the small camp had been and continued up the path. The soft thud of the shoed horses and the songs of the birds were the only sounds as they rode under the leafy canopy, until the ears of the horses perked up and they got restless. The riders stopped. Then they heard it too, the snarl of a wounded animal. White Beauty was well trained for even with the smell of the mountain lion and blood; she didn't rear or try to bolt like most young horses would.

Ken moving his horse to the front of the small group took the lead. He was glad he rode Winner who didn't get upset easily. He pulled out his rifle as they got closer to the sound. No animal should suffer.

There in the same area where he first saw Lacey laid the injured lion, his leg red with blood. He raised his gun to shoot but was halted by the medicine man putting his hand on the barrel of the gun.

Shaking his head no, the medicine man released his hold of the gun. "It's not his time; the Mother Spirit of the mountain says to help him."

Old One Ear recognized the scent of the two-legged animals. He snarled but didn't try to get up and run, with the injury it was something he had tried and couldn't do. For some odd reason he didn't feel fear like he usually did when humans were around.

Looking at the elderly shaman, Ken quietly spoke. "Let me get a tranquilizer dart out of my pack and see what we can do." He didn't totally comprehend this mystical pull of the mountain and the Indian's belief, but he would go along with them providing the old lion didn't suffer.

Removing the live ammo from the rifle, Ken inserted the tranquilizer shell, taking careful aim, pulled the trigger. The lion gave a grunt and fell back.

"We have fifteen minutes before he wakes." Ken informed them as they all dismounted from their horses.

Lacey looked closer at the animal. "Ken, that's One Ear! Darn, this close to him and I don't have my camera."

Accessing the injured leg they could see it was infected, from what, no one knew. The old man began chanting as he opened the worn leather bag that had been slung over his shoulder and removing items, proceeded to clean the leg. He shook ground up herb power into the wound and then poured some smelly thick goo over that to seal it in. Removing from a plastic bag a piece of blue material that looked like an old bandana and stunk to high heaven, he wrapped that area of the leg and secured it all with a few small strips of plain old duct tape that would allow the bandage to come off as the swelling went down.

Looking up at them he said, "The bandage One Ear will leave alone since it tastes terrible, allowing the medicine to work." Leaning back on his legs, he looked up at Bob, "Bring me the two packages from my saddle bag."

When the old spiritual leader opened them up, Ken and Lacey were astonished to see that in the first one, the medicine man removed a wooden bowl in which he poured water from his canteen. The second one held a raw, plucked, but not gutted chicken. He placed them next to the injured animal so he didn't have to struggle to reach them.

Picking up the remains from cleaning the wound, the medicine man put them into a plastic bag and back in the leather pouch. "We wait until he opens his eyes and moves, then we leave."

The four remained quiet as they waited for the tranquilizer to wear off so the lion wouldn't be killed by any young male wanting to take over the territory which is no doubt how that injury happened in the first place.

As the lion began to stir, they mounted their horses and reversed their ride with no one saying a thing, the only sound being the creaking of the leather saddles. Once they arrived where the forest ended and meadow began, they halted.

"You are a good man with respect for the mountain and her wishes." With that the medicine man nodded at Ken and touching his horse with his heel, left.

Coming closer, Bob commented, "It is good you listened to the spirit of the mountain, Lacey. And Ken, thank you for letting us do what we had to." Then he smiled, "It was a good wedding yesterday. Everyone had a great time. You make a good couple." With that he went to catch up with his grandfather.

Ken and Lacey watched as the two Indian friends rode away.

Lacey broke the silence. "This wasn't exactly what I had in mind for today."

"Oh, and what did you expect to happen on our trip down memory lane?"

"I guess it was to finalize that we turned what originally was a bad thing into a positive. I don't know, maybe just a woman thing. I might never have met you if not for the accident and One Ear." She leaned toward him, "I love you so much it scares me."

Moving closer he put his arm around her. "I know what you mean. This second chance for life with someone special…"

He was interrupted by the warmth of her lips on his. He didn't need the spirit of the mountain to tell him he was one blessed man.

***

Hours later, Old One Ear feeling stronger having the medication on his leg taking away the pain and after eating the raw chicken had slowly made it back to his cave. He stood still, looking around his domain. For now there was peace on the mountain, no two legged enemies, stinky iron animals or loud noise. Hearing nothing but the usual night sounds, he got comfortable and soon was sound asleep.

The End

ABOUT THE AUTHOR

Donna Bryan was born and raised in La Crosse, Wisconsin. She has also lived in Minnesota and Missouri with her family. Throughout these moves, she has always enjoyed writing articles, worship services, children's stories, and programs.

It wasn't until Donna retired, that her children insisted she publish her stories. Her first book, *Truck Drivin' Man: Warrior of the Road*, was followed by *The Mansion*.

While visiting her three sons and grandchildren in Colorado, a lion was seen dragging a deer across the road just yards from the home she was staying at. The story of the lion meant to be a two page story for her grandchildren kept growing and became *Spirit of the Mountain: The Lion - The Ranger - The Journalist*.

Donna hopes you enjoy reading her books as much as she did writing them. More about Donna and her latest writing projects can be found at: www.DonnaMBryan.com.

Made in the USA
Lexington, KY
11 December 2016